Praise for *Leonard*

Irish Book of the Ye

British Book of the Year Award finalist

Selected for One Dublin One Book 2021

"This beautiful, heartfelt book is fed on wit and
purpose . . . it challenges us to take happiness seriously.
The result is that its readers may be nourished by it and in turn
nourish others. Hession practices the gentleness he preaches,
and gives readers a restorative glimpse of what a world
based on embracing our best human quirks could look like.
This is a novel to hearten us for whatever lies ahead."
—*The Believer*

"This quietly brilliant book is as funny as it is wise,
as tender as it is groundbreaking. Rónán Hession mines for
gold in the modest lives and ordinary friendships
that might appear unpromising to another writer, and
my goodness, he finds it."
—Diane Setterfield, author of *The Thirteenth Tale*

"A charming, warm-hearted celebration of all that is
treasurable about everyday life."
—*The Guardian*

"Radiant ... A charming, luminous debut."
—*Kirkus Reviews* STARRED Review

"Charming without being twee,
this funny, warm book will bring you sunshine."
—*The Irish Times*

LEONARD AND HUNGRY PAUL

LEONARD
AND
HUNGRY
PAUL

A
N
O
V
E
L

RÓNÁN
HESSION

MELVILLE HOUSE
BROOKLYN · LONDON

LEONARD AND HUNGRY PAUL
First published in 2020 by Melville House
Copyright © Rónán Hession 2019
Originally published in the UK by Bluemoose Books

First Melville House Printing: April 2020

SCRABBLE® & © 2019. Hasbro, Inc., United States and Canada.
Used with permission.

Melville House Publishing
46 John Street
Brooklyn, NY 11201

mhpbooks.com
@melvillehouse

ISBN: 978-1-61219-908-5
ISBN: 978-1-61219-849-1 (eBook)

Library of Congress Control Number: 2020930975

Printed in the United States of America
10 9 8 7 6 5 4 3 2

A catalog record for this book is available from the Library of Congress

This book is dedicated to Kathleen Smyth,
for your brave and beautiful heart.

Chapter 1: LEONARD

Leonard was raised by his mother alone with cheerfully concealed difficulty, his father having died tragically during childbirth. Though she was not by nature the soldiering type, she taught him to look at life as a daisy chain of small events, each of which could be made manageable in its own way. She was a person for whom kindness was a very ordinary thing, who believed that the only acceptable excuse for not having a bird feeder in the back garden was that you had one in the front garden.

As sometimes happens with boys who prefer games to sports, Leonard had few friends but lots of ideas. His mother understood with intuitive good sense that children like Leonard just need someone to listen to them. They would set off to the shops discussing conger eels and have a deep conversation about Saturn's moons on the way back; they would talk about tidal waves at bath time, and say goodnight with a quick chat about the man with the longest fingernails in the *Guinness Book of World Records*. But Leonard grew up at a time when quiet, imaginative children did not yet enjoy the presumption of innocence. His mother often found herself having to take his side against ornery teachers who complained that they found it impossible to get through to him. With patient maternal endurance she would sit by herself at parent-teacher meetings explaining that, like his late father, he 'just lacked a Eureka face.'

Even into his thirties, Leonard's mother still liked to fuss over him, buying his favourite ham for lunch—the one with fewer veins running through it—leaving tea by the bedside for when he woke up, and ironing well-meaning creases into his jeans, which Leonard would quietly iron out later. He repaid her thoughtfulness by keeping her company through her later years and generally including her in the uncrowded bandwidth of his life.

Leonard was not exactly sure, but there must have come a point when their relationship grew from a purely filial one into one of partnership. Though an adult son living with his widowed mother is a situation about which society has yet to adopt a formal position, it is clearly seen in second-best terms. In so far as anyone noticed, they might have assumed that she was overbearing or that he lacked initiative and possibly a sex drive. In reality, neither sought to limit or interfere with the other, both being independent people who liked their own space and who, quite simply, got along. Leonard did recall some awkwardness around the suggestion that they go on holidays together, though he was not entirely certain which of them had first proposed it. Mother/daughter holidays are normal of course, and father/son trips are famously storied as a way to come of age. Mother/son holidays, though, have the connotation that one of them must be a burden on the other. But truth be told, they were well suited as travelling companions. She was a keen walker and had good gallery feet, being able to wander around any reasonable exhibition in its entirety without being distracted by the gift shop honey-pot that drew in tired women half her age. They both liked churches and even though Leonard was not religious himself, much of the world's art is. He would enjoy visiting famous paintings and sculptures in European cathedrals, while his mother would busy herself lighting a candle in the side chapel for her fragile, long-departed husband.

She had never really asked Leonard about girls, knowing the delicacy of the subject for him, and also because of her own doubts about whether his apparently celibate life was due to a lack of interest or opportunity. For Leonard, the fact that he still lived at home with his mother led to a certain self-restraint on practical grounds. He had wondered what would have happened had he brought a girl home only for them to wake up to two cups of tea at the bedside the next morning.

His mother passed away unexpectedly one midweek night in her sleep, tucked into a duvet with her clothes all laid out for the next day, her neatness being a sign of her respect for the small things in her life. The doctor noted the cause of death as a heart attack, but emphasised that there were no signs of suffering or drama. He said that her heart must have simply 'run out of beats.'

As Leonard was a shy only child of two shy only children, it was a small funeral. The front of the church was practically empty with the exception of Leonard, as people tended to underestimate their relative closeness to the deceased and sit several rows further back than they should. With no extended family to rely on, Leonard had to multi-task at the funeral: reading the prayers of the faithful, bringing up the offertory gifts, and taking care of all the other minor jobs that are usually done by cousins and in-laws. The priest's sermon was a generic one about death and hope, which was a relief for Leonard, as his mother disliked it when people summarised a dead person's life in a glib caricature. Had he had the courage, Leonard would have spoken up and said that his mother looked after everyone in her life as though they were her garden birds: that is to say, with unconditional pleasure and generosity.

At the crematorium, her coffin was launched through the red drapes on a set of rails in a slightly halting motion, fittingly reminiscent of the Ghost Train she so enjoyed at the funfair. With her fear of heights and contests, she had often found funfairs a bit of a trial, but went for Leonard's sake and enjoyed the Ghost Train as it was basically a slow drive through a dark fluorescent art gallery. As the curtains closed over the coffin to the strains of 'Nothing Rhymed' by her favourite singer, Gilbert O'Sullivan, Leonard wiped a tear from his glasses and headed back to the family home, now his home, as an orphan.

When an only child loses their second parent, the calendar of the generations turns a page. There are practicalities and arrangements to take care of, but there is also a more general facing up to things. Ready or not, here they come. The result is an alloy of sadness and bewilderment. It was in this state, with his mood tuned down an octave, that Leonard spent his first few weeks after the funeral: staring at a pie cooking in the oven; lingering over a bag of sunflower hearts at the bird feeder; or pausing sadly with a highlighter over an entry in the TV guide. If, during that period, you were to ask him what was on his mind or otherwise use the commonplace ways of snapping someone out of it—that is to say, interrupting them for no reason—he would have been at a loss to tell you, his mundane consciousness returning like a cat who walks in after being away for a few days without any explanation.

After dinner each evening, he would sit on the couch in that customary way of single men for whom time is something to fill rather than spend. He would open one of the historical biographies waiting patiently on his bookcase, several of which had bookmarks just a few pages in, the subjects yet to get beyond their childhood. He found book shops to be comforting places and book buying a comforting activity, but he was an absent-minded reader these days, the act of reading that much more solitary without his mother pottering around the house in the background. He would sit at the table and try to copy sketches from *A Birdwatcher's Year*—a Sanderling scuttling along the shore, or a Guillemot with its eggs shaped like a pear to stop them from rolling off cliffs—but, with nobody to show the sketches to, he became careless about the details on the feathers and the subtlety of the colours. And of course there was always the TV: supreme among alternatives, though strangely distant when there is no longer someone else on the couch to talk about it with.

Had Leonard been a different type of person he might have gone to the pub to meet some friends for an evening of darts, dominoes, cards or other prison games, but nothing made him feel lonelier these days than the thought of spending time in the company of extroverts. It is at times like this that we find out who our true friends are, or in Leonard's case, we call upon our only friend. And so, to avoid or fill that stale chapter of the evening, Leonard had made it a habit to take refuge in the company of Hungry Paul.

Chapter 2: 'PARLEY VIEW'

Hungry Paul still lived with his parents at the family home he had grown up in. He was now more than thirty years through his allotted three score and ten, and to an outside busybody it might have seemed that he had no 'go' in him, or maybe that he was hoping to outlast his parents en route to easy home ownership. But Hungry Paul was a man whose general obliviousness defied gossip. In truth, he never left home because his family was a happy one, and maybe it's rarer than it ought to be that a person appreciates such things.

His father, Peter, had worked for many years as an economist, but was now retired and living off a pension provided by the invisible hand of the market. He was bald, though it was as if his baldness had been caused by gravity, with the hair drawn from his scalp into his head, now tufting out of his ears, nose and eyebrows. Hungry Paul's mother, Helen, was a nearly-retired teacher, now down to two days a week. Helen had also taught Leonard for two years in primary school and used to praise his drawings, telling him that he had 'brains to burn if he would only use them,' which is the kindest possible way of calling someone lazy. Like any teacher who meets a former pupil as an adult, she always greeted Leonard with a genuine welcoming gladness.

She met Peter after he had stopped one day to give her directions to an art exhibition and then invited himself along. They fell in love effortlessly. Their initial chemistry broadened into physics and then biology, until they were blessed with Hungry Paul's older sister Grace as their first child. They then

6

had Hungry Paul after two difficult miscarriages and, understandably in the circumstances, they treasured him. As a couple, Helen and Peter continued to share the closeness of two people who have been through a lot together.

On Hungry Paul's suggestion they had named their house 'Parley View' after a French song that he had once heard at a rugby club. Helen had insisted on a bird friendly back garden and bee friendly front garden, while Peter handled what he called 'internal maintenance': hanging pictures, changing light bulbs and doing all the things you can do to a needy house without buying much in the way of proper tools. Grace had long since moved out and was preparing for her impending wedding, a project that was being managed with the help of nightly phone calls to Helen, whose role largely involved lots of listening, punctuated by interjections of 'I know love, I know' every now and again in a soothing maternal voice.

When Leonard arrived that evening, Peter answered the door with his usual smile and his bright happy-to-see-you eyes.

'Come on in Leonard, come on in.'

Leonard entered with a needless drying of his clean shoes on the doormat, a gesture of social respect rather than hygiene. In the front room Helen was doing a jigsaw on a tea tray. It looked like a picture of an impressionist painting but it was hard to tell with just the edges completed so far. Her tea was balanced on the arm of the couch in a way that Leonard's mother would never have allowed. Peter and Helen resumed their habitual couch positions, nestled in like two jigsaw pieces themselves.

'How've you been, Leonard—everything getting back to normal? I'm sure you've a lot to sort out,' said Helen, getting the sensitive subjects out of the way early and gently.

'Getting there,' answered Leonard, not specifically referring to the normality, the grieving or the sorting out.

'It's good to see you—help yourself,' she said, pointing to an Easter egg opened three weeks ahead of schedule, the guilt neutralised by sharing. Leonard took a big bit, tried to break off a smaller, more respectable portion, but decided just to eat it all once it broke up into his lap. The TV was paused in the middle of *University Challenge*, one of Leonard's favourite programmes. Peter's style was to sit in readiness and then shout machine-gun guesses once a contestant buzzed: 'Thomas Cromwell, NO, Oliver Cromwell, NO . . .' just ahead of an impossibly well-rounded twenty-year-old answering 'Cardinal Wolsey.' In contrast to Peter's machine gun was Helen's sniper rifle. She liked to work on something else—a crossword, Sudoku puzzle or, like tonight, a jigsaw—pretending she wasn't listening. And then, on some obscure question that had both teams stumped, she would deliver the correct answer from nowhere, hardly looking up. It was usually something unguessable, like an event that had happened in a leap year or that King Someone the Someteenth was a twin. She pretended not to enjoy how one of her coolly delivered correct answers could cancel out half a dozen of Peter's panicked guesses. One time, Peter recorded an episode and learned the first twenty answers just to blow her mind when they watched it later, which he duly did, although we'll never know if Helen truly fell for it, or just enjoyed the lengths to which he was still prepared to go to impress her after all these years. Above all, what held their interest in the programme was that the two of them genuinely believed in young people. They rooted for them and forgave them any overconfidence, seeing something pure and perfect in any bright young person who had made the most of a good education.

'How's the job going, Leonard?' asked Peter. He still retained a retired man's casual interest in how workplaces in general were getting on since he left it all behind.

'Not bad, not bad. Keeping busy.'

'What's the topic these days—dinosaurs? Ocean creatures? Cavemen? Greeks?'

'Close—the Romans. And especially their time in Britain

and places like that. Pretty interesting actually. The Scots gave them quite a hard time.'

Leonard wrote children's encyclopaedias and other factual books. While he actually wrote the words, he wasn't the author as such. That title—and the dust jacket credit—went to the academic charged with overseeing content. Leonard's role was really about making sure that the main concepts were conveyed in short memorable sentences. Some illustrators liked his way with nutshells and he had slowly built up a reputation as a fact writer with a child's eye. The job suited him as he was interested in pretty much everything interesting, and he preferred to play a minor part in someone else's story rather than being his own star. He also liked the underdog credibility that came from being unsung and uncredited, even if the money was a bit less than he would have liked for his stage of life. He worked alone in a big open-plan office shared with people from other companies and the admin people from his own company, who may as well have been from other companies. All this gave him the feeling and appearance of belonging to society, when the reality was that he worked alone and inside his own head most of the time. The illustrators, who were the real breadwinners, added their pictures after he had finished, so he tended not to meet them. His relationships with the overseeing authors were usually businesslike and distant. They gave emailed feedback and tracked comments with formal politeness that was friendly but without warmth. That was okay by Leonard. He wasn't looking to form professional friendships with the company's alpha dogs.

'You should take over the illustrations Leonard—you were always good at that. Then bump off the bossy supervisor and publish books yourself. Move to the Bahamas and write on the beach,' said Helen, who had spent her career lobbing encouragement in soft little underarm pitches for others to swing at.

'Maybe someday,' said Leonard. 'The problem is that all the factual books have been done over a million times, so it's hard to say something original. The illustrators are at the cutting edge; I'm just re-boiling the same old factoids. I suppose I'm happy enough—it's rewarding to think that kids are reading the books and getting excited by them.'

'There's nothing nicer than seeing a kid reading,' said Helen, 'I remember Grace lying on her belly reading on the rug, oblivious to the TV or the rest of us. I never met a child who didn't like reading, so long as they're given a *chance*. I used to have parents coming to the school telling me that their kids wouldn't read and my advice was always the same: if the parents read, the children will follow. If you want them to do it, do it yourself. I bet *their* parents were readers,' she added, pointing at the paused *University Challenge* students on screen.

'Speaking of gifted youths, I don't suppose there's any sign of your favourite son?' asked Leonard.

'Upstairs—he said to send you up,' said Peter, reaching for the remote. As Leonard left the room, the TV was unpaused and he heard Peter shout out 'Magnesium!' behind him.

Upstairs, Hungry Paul's room was unoccupied. Unsure of the rules for entering another adult's bedroom platonically, he paused at the doorway, lingering as comfortably as is possible for a man who can hear his friend emptying his bowels at a distance. He took the opportunity to scan the details of Hungry Paul's bedroom, a place he hadn't really ever been in before. Beyond the age of twelve or so, men tend not to see each other's bedrooms as it can be difficult to contrive a plausible premise for asking. The room was a mix of eras, with a general half-hearted adult gloss undermined by scatterings of boyhood fascination. Action figures stood in action poses on shelves where Hungry Paul's parents had surely hoped great books would one day sit. A homemade cardboard mobile of a Spitfire dangled from the room's only light. The walls were painted a pastel green, the shade you might choose for a nursery if you didn't know the sex of the baby. The curtains and bedspread were of a generic home store type: leaves and whatnot in graduated blues and greys. On the walls were some of Hungry Paul's own artworks, including a wobbly paint-by-numbers portrait of *The Laughing Cavalier* and a *Where's Wally?* jigsaw he had had framed and mounted as a testament to its difficulty. Though not untidy, the room had that random look you sometimes find among the bedrooms of former children who are still in residence.

Hungry Paul emerged from the bathroom wearing a white fluffy bathrobe tied with a white belt, tracksuit bottoms and flip flops with some tissue paper stuck to them. He was shaking his wrists and wore the look of intense concentration that is characteristic of a man with wet hands looking for a towel. The fact that he was in the unlikely position of wearing clothes made from the very material he needed might have tempted a lesser man, but, having already run the risk of doing a sit-down toilet while wearing white, he was not minded to capitulate under a lesser challenge. He resolved his difficulty by retrieving a t-shirt from the linen basket and drying his hands on it, his assessment being that clothes that were clean enough to wear only a short time previously were unlikely to have become too dirty to use in the meantime. There is much pleasure in relief and, as Hungry Paul noticed Leonard, he welcomed him with genuine warmth.

'Hi Leonard. They sent you up. Great, great. How are things?'

'Good thanks. What's with the bathrobe?' asked Leonard.

'Ah, I have begun training in the martial arts–how do I look?'

'You look like the real thing all right. What has brought this on? It's not like you to do something violent.'

'Oh, I haven't changed my mind about violence, but the martial arts are more about stillness in action. Calm in the midst of combat. It certainly is physical, but the mind remains still and peaceful. There is no mental violence; no ill will, which is the worst part of violence. And besides, it's judo, so there's no punching in the face or anything like that.'

'And how do you feel about rolling around with Neanderthals? I thought you didn't like people touching you, never mind twisting your limbs into a figure eight.'

'Well there is that. I actually thought it might help me with my personal space issues. As you say, it is one of the more intimate combat sports, hence we wear sleepover gear rather than, say, black tie. But to be honest, there is also my personal fitness to think of. I can't very well tackle a black belt if I can't even tackle stairs without panting.'

Hungry Paul then dropped to the floor and started a push-up on his knuckles. There was a cracking sound, followed by some oaths, and then he started again, looking like a break dancer doing the caterpillar.

'How many do you have to do?' asked Leonard.

'My sensei says I should keep going until I find my limit, and then go beyond it. To be like water. It was easier in the class with the spongy mats, but my wooden floors are actually quite hard. Maybe I'll try it with grippy socks instead of flip flops.'

'You look good in all the gear though. A white belt – that's pretty impressive. What sort of moves have you learned so far?'

'So far it's steady as she goes. The first thing they teach you is how to sign a waiver form, and then they teach you how to break a fall, so you don't get hurt, although I suspect whether I get hurt or not is as much up to my future opponents as it is up to me. Then we did some drills with the others. Most of them are a bit bigger than me, so I was mainly practising my defence.'

'I suppose it should be good for your mental strength too. The martial arts are known for emphasising oneness of mind and body,' said Leonard, who had actually written something on the martial arts in a children's encyclopaedia about the Olympics, though the combat sports got only a brief section at the back along with shooting, weightlifting and a fact box about steroids.

'Funny you should say that—I was actually quite light-headed after the class, which often happens whenever I try new things. Still, it's only my first lesson. I asked the sensei about my potential and he said that if I upgraded from my bathrobe and tracksuit bottoms to buying a *gi*—that's what they call the proper judo outfit—it would be a real sign of commitment. I can tell it will take many tournaments to win his respect.'

Leonard admired the way Hungry Paul had immersed himself in something that was so culturally alien, and, on reflection, he agreed that it was best to buy a proper *gi*, as the bathrobe probably looked a little too fluffy to intimidate any experienced judoka.

'If you're still practising, maybe I should wait downstairs?' suggested Leonard.

'Not at all. I can finish this later. Let's go down for a while and have a chat.' Hungry Paul tightened his white fluffy belt, using the same type of knot used for tying shoelaces.

Hungry Paul chose the kitchen rather than the front room, yelling 'We're in here' for the benefit of his parents, with Helen chirping 'Okay, love' from the other room. He flipped on the kettle and disappeared into the cubbyhole, an off-shoot from the kitchen which was probably intended to be used as a pantry, but which in this house was used to store board games. He scanned the battered spines of the stacked boxes like a sommelier looking for the right vintage. Within the time it took for the kettle to boil, he stuck out a disembodied arm from the cubbyhole and called 'This okay?' from within. He was holding out Yahtzee, a game they hadn't played in a very long time.

'Good choice. You're in a very Eastern mood this evening. Making plans to buy a *gi*, making yourself what looks like green tea, and now playing Yahtzee. Is this a new direction you are taking in life? Western civilisation no longer inspires you? Oh, and I'll have normal tea by the way please.'

'I think that I need to be a little immersive with regard to the cultural context for judo if I want to avoid getting beaten up by sixteen-year-old girls again next week. I think there was something important missing at my first lesson. I mean apart from things like balance and motor skills, I felt I was missing something of the essence of the judoka,' said Hungry Paul. 'Now, it's been a while since we played this. How does it go again?'

Hungry Paul laid out the bits and pieces: a circular playing area with raised edges, all covered in faux-Vegas red baize; four dice, which meant that one was missing; a black cup for shaking them in before rolling, which lent that characteristic hollow rattling sound to the game; and a set of impossibly complicated score cards, listing what the players should be trying to achieve.

'It doesn't look very Eastern' observed Leonard about the game, which was invented by Canadians and commercialised by Americans.

'Probably a prisoner of war game in Japanese camps during World War II. Do you recall how to play this? I'm starting to remember why we haven't taken this out in so long. I think the last time we tried this we gave up and ended up playing something less complicated like Risk, which is saying something.' Hungry Paul lived on a knife edge between a passion for board games and an aversion to instruction booklets.

Leonard explained the basics insofar as he could recall them. Hungry Paul, who himself lacked a Eureka face, nodded in false understanding.

'Why don't you just go first and then I'll see how it works. I'm sure it will come back to me. It's just the rules are all a bit like card games, which I can never understand. Oh, I had better get an extra die.' Hungry Paul disappeared back into the cubby hole and removed a die from another set, the board game equivalent of cannibalism.

The game got under way with Leonard rattling the dice cup, which is used two-handed as if the player were shaking cocktails in it. His first attempt was at a full house but he rolled five different numbers. Hungry Paul decided to try for a full house also and quickly popped a digestive biscuit into his mouth in order to free up his hands, having already dropped several crumbs on his judo bathrobe, which was opening at the chest under the pressure of the moment. He rolled two twos, a three, a five and six. He had no idea what that meant.

'Oh, I remember—do I call out "Yahtzee"?' he asked, for want of any better ideas.

'Not quite. You might be thinking of Bingo or Snap,' Leonard answered, before interpreting what Hungry Paul's roll meant and talking him through his next few goes.

As they both played board games regularly, and switched between them often, it was not unusual for games to start slowly whenever they changed to something new. It was perfectly normal to have a warm-up period, like the way a polyglot who has just arrived at the airport needs to hear the local language spoken around him before he can regain his own fluency in speaking it. Before long, the game settled into a steady rhythm of clacking dice and turn-taking, interspersed with uninhibited rallies of conversation between the two friends, both of whom were free thinkers with a broad range of interests.

Hungry Paul had always been fascinated by the world around him, viewing it as something fantastical. It was as if he saw the body of scientific understanding as an anthology of legends, something so wonderful and impenetrable that it might as well be a myth. He liked borrowing copies of *National Geographic* from the library, sometimes months in arrears, not that it mattered when he was reading articles about carbon dating or the Persians. In this way he maintained a lively interest in the wider world, while staying above and apart from what is generally described as current affairs. Leonard, very much the autodidact, held a subscription to *New Scientist*, which had been his annual Christmas present from his mother for many years. He also liked to read *Yesterday Today*, for all the latest developments in ancient history. For the two friends, the bleaching of the coral reefs was as current as the latest general election; the discovery of new dwarf planets was as relevant as last night's penalty shoot-out; and Marco Polo was discussed as others might gossip about the latest red carpet ingénue. Their conversations combined the yin of Leonard's love of facts with the yang of Hungry Paul's chaotic curiosity.

'Do you remember the Edvard Munch exhibition we went to last year, with all those haunting paintings of sick children?' asked Hungry Paul.

'Indeed I do. I see you still have the fridge magnet of *The Scream* you bought afterwards as a memento. It's not just any artist that makes it on to that fridge.'

'Well, I was reading an article about that very painting today and guess what? Do you want to know what the most fascinating thing about it is?' tantalised Hungry Paul.

'Okay, let me think. The orange background is related to the eruption of Krakatoa isn't it? Is that it?'

'Interesting but that's not it.' Hungry Paul was rattling his dice in the cup the whole time, adding to the sense of suspense.

'Okay, I give up.'

'The figure in the painting isn't actually screaming!' Hungry Paul spilled his dice on the board as he revealed this; a little too enthusiastically, as one of them had to be retrieved from under the table—a four, which did him no good.

'Really, are you sure?'

'Absolutely. That's the whole thing. The figure is actually closing his ears to *block out* a scream. Isn't that amazing? A painting can be so misunderstood and still become so famous.'

'Really? I must confess that I think I have made that mistake myself in several encyclopaedias. Never mind. It will be an interesting thing to include the next time we do a revised edition.'

Leonard rolled his go and completed his four-of-a-kind. He drank from his mug, but the tea had gone cold without him realising, leaving him to swallow a mouthful of nauseating leftovers.

'I don't suppose you saw the documentary about Edwin Hubble last night?' asked Hungry Paul, now entering a state of flow. 'Dad and I watched it after judo while Mam was on the phone to Grace. I must confess that, without television, I would never understand anything about space. Thank heavens for those enthusiastic Oxford dons doing all those BBC documentaries on the side—earning a bit of egg money I suppose. TV and space were made for each other. Dad and I were so absorbed that we ate a whole Toblerone between us—one of the big ones that you get at the airport.'

'I'm sorry I missed it. One thing I could never quite get right in my encyclopaedias, even after reading about it many times over the years, is the expansion and contraction of the universe,' Leonard confessed. 'I mean I couldn't begin to understand the physics of it, but the idea that the universe is surrounded by something that is not the universe, and which it expands into, or is it that the universe isn't expanding but space is expanding? How do you explain that to children without leaving them with a million unanswered questions? Never mind the idea that it will snap back like an elastic into a small little pinhead again, which would terrify any sensible child. How can we just walk around leading normal lives when we know that that sort of thing is going on above our heads? We'd all be a little less precious about our lot if we truly appreciated that the whole thing was going to end up as some sort of tiny full stop eventually. I suppose you just have to trust the science, but it is blind faith really beyond a certain point, at least as far as I'm concerned.'

Hungry Paul's brow became corrugated. 'I find the whole expansion of the universe disheartening to be honest. It's as though Mother Nature is trying to push everything away from everything else. Hardly maternal. The universe might well be expanding, but it's expanding to get away from *us*, leaving us more alone, and our world feeling smaller.'

The two friends then settled into one of the long pauses that characterised their comfort in each other's company. They could sit quietly for extended periods without the need to hurry back to whatever it was they were doing, allowing the silence to melt away in its own time. However, on this occasion, Hungry Paul's extemporising on astrophysics had struck a melancholy note inside Leonard. In the weeks since his mother had passed on, Leonard had noticed a distinct shrinking of his own personal universe. His evenings were less occupied, his social options had become more limited, and his mind seemed diverted inwards towards a vague, dreamy melancholy. As Hungry Paul got up to boil the kettle again and rinse the mugs, Leonard broached the subject.

'Maybe it's not just the universe that expands and contracts,' he said. 'Perhaps the same applies to us—you know, that as we get older, our lives start shrinking.'

'How do you mean?'

'The thing is, as a child the world looked huge, intimidatingly so. School looked big. Adults looked big. The future looked big. But I am starting to feel that over time I have retreated into a smaller world. I see people rushing around and I wonder—where are they going to? Who are they meeting? Their lives are so full. I've been trying to remember if my life was ever like that.'

Hungry Paul paused a moment. 'I think I know what you mean; but for me, the bigness of life was always the problem. I have spent over three decades hacking a safe path through the wilderness, as have you to some extent. The path may be a little narrow in places, but is that really so bad?'

'It's not just external circumstances,' answered Leonard. 'I feel *myself* getting smaller. I feel quieter and more, I don't know, invisible. There is this palpable sense of physics; that my life is being pulled inwards. One thing has led to another and now I feel that if I don't do something, I'll just carry on some minor harmless existence.'

'There is a lot to be said for that. As you know, I have always been modestly Hippocratic in my instincts: I wish to do no harm. My preference has always been to stand back from the world. Much like the Green Cross Code, I like to stop, look and listen before getting involved in things. It has stood me well and kept me on peaceful terms with my fellow man. It's certainly better than trying to make my mark on the world, only to end up defacing it,' said Hungry Paul.

'I am not about to start chaining myself to railings or throwing bras at policemen, if that's what you mean. There is no shortage of people willing to take that path. But I just can't help feeling that I need to open the doors and windows of my life a little.'

Hungry Paul hesitated, holding his biscuit over his tea just a fraction too long and despairing as a half-moon of digestive sank to the bottom of his mug. 'That may be so,' he said, 'but the trick is to know how much of the world to let in, without becoming overwhelmed. The universe, as Edwin Hubble taught us, is a hostile place.'

'Indeed. And sometimes it's difficult to know whether you want to scream or block out a scream,' said Leonard.

It was hard to say whether it was the Yahtzee talking, but both men had found themselves in one of those flowering conversations where one thought opens another. Perhaps they could have discussed the subject all evening, if only it had been hypothetical. Things being otherwise, the natural pause in the conversation gave them a moment to check themselves. Even among close friends, there are still some thoughts that ought to be allowed to ripen in private.

They finished their tea and reached an unspoken decision

that, after a pleasant evening's play, and with both their score cards looking a mess, they would call it a night.

Leonard popped his head into the sitting room to say goodbye. Helen had finished the jigsaw—Monet's *Lilies*, a painting Leonard had written about in the *World of Art* encyclopaedia—and was on the phone to Hungry Paul's sister Grace, discussing wedding DJs. Peter, with saintly patience, had the TV on pause again and said goodbye with a thumbs-up.

Hungry Paul saw Leonard off at the door.

'G'night then,' said Leonard.

'G'night Leonard,' said Hungry Paul, closing his judo bathrobe at the throat to keep his chest from getting a chill.

Without thinking, they both looked up at the inky universe they had just been talking about, as the big torchlight moon shone down on the snails criss-crossing the driveway. Leonard stepped over them and made his way home, carrying with him the things he had said over the course of the evening; things he hardly knew he knew.

Chapter 3: THE ROMANS

The next day at work, Leonard was trying to rescue a chapter about the Romans in Britain. The first batch of tracked changes had come back from the overseeing author as an assault of red and strikeout. When he accepted all her changes just to see what they looked like, his word count shrank so much that he could have fitted the whole thing inside a fortune cookie.

In one comment box she had written 'could we say something original here?' and in another she posed the question 'would someone really say this?' This kind of vaguely disappointed feedback was the norm from overseeing authors who were subject matter experts but who knew little about how kids' minds or writers' feelings worked. A game of tracked changes ping-pong required the ability to put up with a lot more than you should. Leonard often felt he was being paid for his patience. It was hard to do his best work when he knew that all his good ideas would be either rejected without being understood, or appropriated and credited to someone else. He tried to keep in mind the advice his mother had once given him, that he should take his work seriously but not personally.

In general, children's encyclopaedias about history weren't as popular or good as other factual books. The best illustrators wanted to work on dinosaurs (if they liked hand drawing) or books about space (if they preferred computer graphics). History encyclopaedias seemed to attract illustrators with more mixed talents. One guy could only draw people facing out from the page, staring at the reader, which made for farcical battle scenes.

Another couldn't draw different nationalities and so depicted everyone looking slightly cross, reasoning, not without insight, that angry people were the same the world over. The Romans themselves were a particular problem. Anything that goes from BC to AD is practically impossible to explain to kids. It sounds like you're going backwards in time to zero and then forwards, which is confusing for children who mark time by counting from birthday to birthday. Also, the Romans' long names made them hard to relate to, especially as Asterix and Monty Python had used up all the decent joke names, which was really the only way to get over that problem. Yes, there were the usual factoids about Latin, aqueducts, straight roads and slaves, but they had been overused and couldn't possibly compete with a Tyrannosaurus attack or a supernova explosion.

Leonard's real problem though was that the Romans were bullies. The Romans picked on everybody for four hundred years and were only eliminated when they got outbullied themselves by the Goths and Barbarians. To a kid, this is a worrying storyline. You like to think that a bully's upper hand is short-lived and his fall precipitous and permanent. The true tale of history was worryingly short of comeuppance.

Running out of ideas, Leonard took off his noise-cancelling/society-repelling headphones and went to the kitchenette for a mid-morning cup, even though he always disliked the awkward wait for the water to boil and the prospect of kettle-related time-killing small talk.

He checked his mobile and saw that he had a missed call from a private number, which was surely Hungry Paul's home phone. Hungry Paul didn't have a mobile and often left epic voicemails, spread over several messages, which at times sounded like one-man radio plays:

Leonard, hello. It seems that in a world where people compete with numbers, it is the numbers that always win.

Hungry Paul began cryptically and epigrammatically, like a first-time novelist.

Ordinarily, I like to discuss delicate matters face-to-face, but I think it best that I leave you a voice message rather than wait until I see you next.

Leonard noted Hungry Paul's typically impeccable manners.

My mother and Grace have talked things through about the wedding, at some length and in some detail, and the thing is, the numbers are tight. I mean if it's a wedding of 'about a hundred,' which is how they have put it to me, though I have no idea— *beep*

Leonard was used to Hungry Paul's lines over-running, with most messages being delivered in series format.

Apologies, I must get better at spitting it all out, so I hope this doesn't sound too brusque.

He delivered the last word with a lingering pronunciation, and in doing so ended a lengthy era during which he had pronounced it as 'brusk.'

A hundred is really just fifty each for the bride and groom, which is really just twenty-five for each of them plus the partners for each of those twenty-five. While it is perfectly acceptable for those on

*the outer orbits of the family to miss the cut, they,
I mean, 'we'—I was specifically told to say 'we'—
need to make the numbers work, as it were.* *beep*

As the next voicemail loaded Leonard braced himself for a demotion to an afters invitation, which meant missing all the nice parts of the wedding and attending only the late, drunken bits he disliked. It was unlikely that there would be scope for a commensurate downgrading of the wedding gift, at least not without creating the impression of hard feelings.

So I, or we, were wondering whether you had any plans for a plus one, because I have already confirmed that I will be unaccompanied on the night concerned owing to a confluence of factors, and if you were in a similar position then perhaps we could be each other's plus ones, thereby freeing up two spots which I am assured would be made available to guests without whom the whole wedding would be, I think the word Grace used was 'tense.' In the circumstances, and given that Grace has never asked me for anything, I'm inclined not to be difficult, so maybe you could think it over and call me back whenever you get the chance. I don't want you to think— *beep*

There were no further messages.

It was an easy non-decision to make. It had been quite some time since Leonard had been a plus one. In fact, these days he was decidedly not himself, so 'minus one' was closer to the mark. It had been something of a formality that they had him down for plus one at all.

Leonard rang back and got Helen, who was slightly embarrassed about the whole thing, but who made no effort to talk him out of agreeing to be Hungry Paul's plus one. 'So long as I don't have to wear a dress and dance with him— you never know, I could be your new daughter-in-law!' he chipped in.

'Thanks for understanding, Leonard. We weren't sure how to ask, so I'm glad you're okay about it.'

'Not at all, not at all. Give my best to Gracie—hope she's not too stressed. We're all on her side.'

Leonard hung up and took off the mask of easy conviviality. Standing there in the kitchenette, there was something about the sincerity of Helen's awkwardness that had brought it home to him. The 'plus one' on his invite, received several weeks ago, must have been intended for his poor mother. The thought stunned him gently for a moment as a man in chinos walked in and made disapproving noises at finding mugs left to soak. In a hurry to get back to his noise-cancelling headphones, Leonard put away the tea caddy and finished stirring his own palpable milky loneliness.

Chapter 4: GRACE

If there is one incident which best captures the relationship between Grace and Hungry Paul, it was when he received a fiver in a birthday card for the first time as a young boy. He stuffed it into that strange pocket-within-a-pocket that denim jeans have: a narrow, impractical feature barely wide enough for a finger. Grace, who was three years older, took him off to the shops to spend it on E numbers and comics. On the way, Hungry Paul spotted one of the neighbourhood boys, probably one of the football-playing jocks who normally ignored him or worse, and called him over, excited to have something to show off for once. In fishing out the note from his ridiculous pocket he tore it in half. The other boy gave a short derisive snort then kicked the ball ahead of him and chased it down the hill, leaving Hungry Paul standing there, frozen with baffled disappointment. Before he had time to compute this latest failure, Grace handed him a new fiver and took the old torn one. He ran after the boy with the ball, delighted with himself and forgetting to thank Grace, who hurried after him in case he went onto the road without looking.

Like all eldest children, Grace had been an only child for a time, and thrived under the warm lamp of undivided parental attention; but when Hungry Paul was brought home from the hospital after some delays for tests, she welcomed him with open sisterly enthusiasm. By the time he was a toddler, she was old enough to help look after him in little unsupervised ways, which usually involved rescuing him from himself, as he was a boy who tended to lean with his fingers in the hinges of doors, stick his head into railings and swallow wine gums without chewing them first.

In primary school she was clever, hardworking and well behaved, all of the things a teacher's child should be, though her natural charm and sense of fun largely protected her from the pitfalls of that role. It wasn't all easy. In the early years at school her best friend was a gentle, imaginative boy called Frederick, who devised fantastical games and babbled with inspirational enthusiasm about dinosaurs and outer space. (He pointed out that we didn't need to go to space as that's where we live: 'Where do you think the Earth is, dummy?') After a couple of years Frederick changed school even though his parents weren't moving house. Grace was bereft. Even worse, everyone else in the class had settled into little groups in the meantime, and Grace was left friendless. She dreaded lunchtimes, hoping to delay as long as possible eating her sandwich and fairy bun so that she had less time alone in the schoolyard. It is not hard to see how Grace became the family's slow eater—every family has one.

Loneliness begets loneliness. As an unattached kid she was not an exciting prospect for other children and so, without anyone doing anything in particular, it became a 'thing' that she was just someone who had no friends. She contrasted herself with Hungry Paul who she could see in his junior yard, alone as usual and wandering around inside his own head, except that he seemed at peace with his situation, protected by his own obliviousness.

During that period, which lasted almost a year but felt as long as the Ottoman Empire, Grace wandered around the yard on her own and at times, out of sheer frustration, she would run around as if to create the illusion of being chased. Once she slipped and fell on the stony old tarmac and grazed the width of her palm, the cut becoming a mix of light blood and small stones that would be painful to clean. Too embarrassed to be asked why she was running by herself, she hid it from the teacher and cleaned it later on at home herself, inexpertly. Helen asked her about it at bedtime but was deflected with vagueness, a pattern that would play out more regularly later, during the teenage years.

Grace's position turned on a tragic event. Gary Crowe, a nine-year-old wannabe fireman who sat at Grace's table in school, died in an accident at home. His father was a mechanic and had been working on an engine on a hoist in his garage when he went off to buy some spare parts. Gary had swung from the chain on the hoist and pulled the engine down on top of himself. Gary's death stunned the whole class. The shock of the story found resonance in the nightmares of the children who knew him, where it was all too readily reimagined at bedtime after lights out. Two dozen sets of parents spent the next month calmly explaining that there was nothing to worry about and that it was just an accident and that beds and houses and garages were perfectly safe places. For now, the kids were spared the true horror of imagining what Gary's parents were going through.

The tragedy galvanised the class and reset its social structure. The playground rules and cliques were shattered, as everybody played with everybody else, barely conscious of the survival instincts that were driving them to disregard their differences. Grace, who felt socially thawed by this change, immersed herself in what she felt might be a short-lived opportunity and laughed at other people's jokes, played their games and suppressed her own minor preferences in favour of her major preference for being included.

Those friends that Grace made at primary school were 'survival friends' rather than real friendships—none of them would be at the wedding—but they helped her to steady herself and begin to like herself again. They lasted her through secondary school during which time she started to individuate by immersing herself in student communism, Inspector Morse novels,

Judee Sill albums, and by taking long, long, long walks that would have any conscientious parent checking news bulletins. Her teenage years were exploratory and, broadly speaking, mild tempered. While there were some mood swings and a bit of door slamming, it seemed she was just trying all that out of curiosity, sensing that she had some wild cards that it would be a shame to leave unplayed.

Her relationship with Helen was at its most difficult during those years. Grace and Helen had always been close and had an intuitive communication channel through which they shared jokes, looks, hints and understandings, like a vaudeville double act that had learned each other's side of the routine to a transcendental level. During her teenage years, and without any identifiable starting point, Grace tuned out from Helen and instead turned inwards. She became hard to reach and connect with. Though not unhappy or sullen, she sought nourishment from within herself, in her nascent ideas and emerging preferences—it was simply not something Helen could share in. As the eldest child, everything new to Grace was new to her parents, and Helen perhaps suffered from the classic teacher's mistake of thinking that, when it came to children, she had seen it all. The more she tried to reach Grace the more she compounded her lack of understanding of her.

As is so often the case, when one parent struggles the other steps forward, parenting being a team sport played by individuals. Peter, who could be deep and introspective himself, became closer to Grace during that period. He had always been a friendly and warm presence in her life—biting the bruises off her bananas or letting her pluck the hair in his ears—but at times he had been guilty of acting as a deputy parent, aping Helen's approach rather than finding his own groove. He was naturally and happily introverted. Silences, solitary moments and stillness energised him. Loneliness was not something to overcome, but something to befriend and look into. And so,

Grace switched her connection from Helen to Peter during those years, as they were happy to share long silent car journeys together or read books at the kitchen table without feeling the need to have or share views about what they were reading. Though Grace wouldn't necessarily have agreed, it was generally said of her that she had turned out well. It had something to do with her talents being offset by being down-to-earth, and her achievements being the result of hard work rather than advantage. The compliment was part of a mentality found in people who believed in praise only when it didn't imply elevation. Had Grace been asked at the time, she probably would have said that she was neither happy nor unhappy, like everyone else, and that she was still trying to feel her way through life. One night at a friend's birthday party, during the college years when they were all still getting used to drinking, she was asked, while being recorded on a camcorder, what she would wish for if she could have anything in the world. Without taking time to think or be funny, she gave an answer which her friends said was 'pure Grace.' She looked straight into the lens of the now-obsolete camcorder and said 'I would like . . . whatever is good for me.'

Chapter 5: REGARDS

It had been a quiet few days for Hungry Paul since his Yahtzee conversation with Leonard, quiet days not being uncommon in his schedule. This had given him the opportunity to ponder the expansion and contraction of the universe as observed in localised form in the life of his best friend. Edwin Hubble, had he looked inside Leonard with his telescope, would have recorded that everything was just as the universe would ordain it. The thing is, for Hungry Paul the world was a complicated place, with people themselves being both the primary cause and chief victims of its complexity. He saw society as a sort of chemistry set, full of potentially explosive ingredients which, if handled correctly could be fascinating and educational, but which was otherwise best kept out of reach of those who did not know what they were doing. Though his life had been largely quiet and uneventful, his choices had turned out to be wise ones: he had already lived longer than Alexander the Great, and had fewer enemies, too. But he had now become awakened by the thought that, no matter how insignificant he was when compared to the night sky, he remained subject to the same elemental forces of expansion. The universe, it seemed, would eventually come knocking. And so it was that over a mid-morning scone he read a short article in the local freesheet with a sense of cosmic destiny.

The *Community Voice* was a paper delivered door-to-door on the generous interpretation that it was excused from the 'no junk mail' signs on the letterboxes of the community it voiced. Typically there was a picture of an old woman or young child in a wheelchair on the front page, holding up what we would be led to believe was a disingenuous letter from the Council. The outraged headline usually left limited room for the reader to draw alternative conclusions. Inside there were blatant advertisements presented as articles, pictures of medals being presented, an advice column from the local doctor, and a helpful chart showing which bins were to be collected on which Mondays, alternating between refuse and recyclables.

The article that caught Hungry Paul's interest had been written by the Chamber of Commerce, a group that he assumed had some relationship to the Chamber of Horrors at the wax museum, presumably displaying wax likenesses of entrepreneurs such as Richard Branson or Uncle Ben. The article posed what Hungry Paul considered to be a very modern quandary. In the world as we know it today, including in the business world where everything is more so, communication was now primarily conducted through email. Years of effort spent teaching the greatest business minds how to write template letters was coming undone, as the art of expression had not kept pace with technological developments. A lexicon of classic phrases, once thought perennial, was now facing obsolescence. The writer of the article—a Mr H. Means, Community Affairs Editor—had given the whole thing quite a bit of thought:

> *'To whom it may concern' has a certain letter-in-a-bottle sound to it, in that it seeks to engage the reader without specifying, or attempting to find out, their name, surname, title, gender or position. It also leaves open the possibility that the letter may not be relevant to the reader at all; the 'may' suggesting that this might all be the wildest of goose chases after the loosest of gooses.*

'Dear Sir or Madam' was originally agonised over as a concession made by the leather-bound gentlemen's clubs towards the inevitable possibility that some important letters were read by women. The either/or approach here also unintentionally opens the possibility that the recipient could decide to read the letter one day as a man and the next as a woman. In any event, as nobody is called 'Sir' these days, unless by a shop assistant who is unlikely to hold their customers in any sincere esteem, and addressing someone as a 'Madam' is preposterously formal to the point of stageyness, there is little of the phrase that is above criticism. Even 'Dear' suggests a letter between two darlings about to open their hearts in an epistolary confession; such a scenario is unlikely to have ever been common between affiliates of the Chamber of Commerce.

The real problem is a common perplexity and awkwardness around how to sign-off emails. In formal letters, 'yours faithfully' has been used by the Chamber of Commerce whenever the addressee is not identified, although some members feel that its suggestion of fidelity is somewhat at odds with the anonymous salutation: in effect they have been saying, 'You have my undying loyalty, whoever you are.' It was already amended once during the 1950s, when 'I remain, yours faithfully' was shortened because of complaints about its toady flirta-tiousness. 'Yours sincerely' was also a problem for some members who felt that an express statement of sincerity implied that they were the type of correspondent who was routinely disbelieved.

Emails, with their aspiration of chatty informality, have allowed local businesses to use more light-hearted sign-offs, none of which has made the leap from acceptability to satisfactoriness as far as the Chamber of Commerce is concerned.

'Regards' is the most common one, but some feel that it is a limp-wristed, lukewarm 'this'll do' type of sign-off. The phrase had actually started out as 'Regards to the wife and kids' but this was shortened by the Chamber many years ago as it moved with the times.

By way of international comparison, it is worth pointing out that in the United States of America, where they like their business correspondence to be snappy and rude, they have abandoned stuffy sign-offs altogether. Most letters and emails over there now end with the phrase 'Am I right or am I right?'

According to the article, all of this had the Chamber of Commerce in such a state that it had decided to throw it open to the public to see if they had any better ideas. In fact, they were holding a competition to identify a new sign-off that would be used by its members nationwide in all business correspondence. There was a cheque for ten grand and a statuette up for grabs. Hungry Paul, who had never had either, immediately recognised what was an almost vocational voice saying that he should enter.

Given that all good ideas have a natural buoyancy that forces them to the surface, he couldn't help raising it when Leonard was over later that evening for a four-player game of Scrabble with Helen and Peter, which had become something of a Sunday night ritual that helped to lighten that night-before-school feeling. Helen and Peter had played Scrabble for years, going back to when they first bought a house together and had no money to go out. They used to play high stakes games of Scrabble, with the loser providing carnal favours to the victor, a system which allowed them to explore both their vocabulary and their marriage at the same time. Naturally, this led to a certain sauciness in the choice of words played, with the result that triple word scores were sometimes foregone in favour of lower-scoring but more titillating alternatives. Once they became parents, this charming in-joke fell into abeyance, though they continued to keep board games (in their intended form) and the playing of them as a part of their household family routine.

The game on this particular evening, however, was somewhat frustrating, as four-player games often are, owing to the inability to plan more than one move at a time. Helen complained bitterly that Peter kept taking the spaces she had her eye on. Peter kept asking 'Is it my go?' unable to follow the complex sequence of turns among the four players, which went neither clockwise nor anti-clockwise, but was based on when players' birthdays occurred in a calendar year—a contrivance put in place years before to stop family rows about seating arrangements. Leonard seemed to get nothing but vowels all evening, which was neither good for him nor for anyone who needed them. Hungry Paul, as ever, was the referee with the battered Scrabble word book and a dictionary at his side. Some years ago, in response to what became known as the 'Za incident', they had introduced a house rule that you had to be able to explain the word you were using. Hungry Paul operated this rule with iron inflexibility, even though he himself was its most frequent victim, which surely speaks to his innate sense of fairness.

At one stage, following a controversial toilet break, Hungry Paul broached the topical issue of the day regarding the

Chamber of Commerce, igniting the interest of all those present. Straight away there began an outpouring of spuriously relevant ideas. While Helen confessed to using such banalities as 'Take Care' and 'Talk to you soon,' Peter said he was more austere in his habits and signed off simply as 'Peter,' in the style of such single-name legends as Morrissey and Prince. Peter and Helen then disappeared into their own married little wormhole about the length of his sign-off, making each other laugh with in-jokes that Hungry Paul was sure were only superficially clean. Leonard, ever the deep thinker, was provoked into a moment of reflection about how he signed off his own emails. He usually used 'Regards' but could immediately see its shortcomings. As he seemed to be the only one still taking the game of Scrabble seriously, a game he was losing, he took up the topic with some keenness.

'I think you're on to something there. I mean, technology has moved on so much and is now ubiquitous, so there must be a whole galaxy of communication conventions that need to be updated. Greetings, salutations, sign-offs, auto-replies, the lot. You don't even need a phrase that makes sense, you just need something that sounds right; after all, that is how it has worked up to now.'

'I like something friendly. Emails and texts are all so cold and impersonal. You need something to brighten the whole thing up,' said Helen.

'Darling, these are business people. You can't go suggesting emojis, smiley faces and the like. Why not go the whole hog and just wipe jam on the letters and write your age including half years at the end?' said Peter, joking recklessly and, in doing so, unwittingly exiting the good books he had just flirted his way into.

'If you won you could copyright the phrase and then earn some cash every time it was used. Even a small royalty per letter would add up if everyone uses it,' suggested Leonard.

'I'm not looking to make money from this. I want to contribute to society. Make a difference. That sort of thing.' Hungry Paul's pious clarification sent a shiver around the room.

'You could just give the money to charity,' suggested Leonard, not giving up on his idea easily.

At this Hungry Paul almost dropped his consonants. 'That's fundraising, not charity. Totally separate things. Charity transforms both giver and receiver for the better. It is rightly described as a virtue. Fundraising or donating to charity and all the other variations on that theme are something else: a tangle of mixed motivations and results, some good, some questionable. I want to make a clean, straight contribution to the world. Nothing sullied. Nothing that takes explaining. So no fundraising.'

During his working day Leonard was perennially in the role of unrequited suggester but found this negative feedback surprisingly hurtful, coming as it did from his dear friend and outside of business hours. Peter gave him a little look of support as if to say that he agreed with him even if Hungry Paul didn't, though he meant it more as an endorsement of the concept of market forces generally than of Leonard's idea specifically.

Just as the conversation was in danger of descending to the standard of a daytime phone-in show, where people outdo each other to come up with ever more banal angles on the topic, the landline rang with what everyone correctly assumed was Grace's latest round of updates and indecisions. Helen answered it and settled into the couch with her legs folded under herself, very much with the look of someone who was going to be occupied for some time to come. While it is theoretically possible to convert a four-player game into a three-player game, it is something that is just not done in the Scrabble world, and so the game was quietly abandoned without any attempt to tally who had been ahead.

There was a round of yawns and stretches, checking of watches and all those other unconscious preambles to the announcement of the evening's conclusion. Leonard cited the busyness of the day ahead of him tomorrow, which was neither true nor untrue, but as the visitor among the group he felt a greater onus to justify his exit. Hungry Paul would be up early the next morning on the off-chance of a call from the Post Office to do the Monday morning shift. Peter had no particular plans, but was used to feeling widowed by these regular calls from Grace and was keen to do something worthwhile with the balance of the evening.

Hungry Paul let Leonard out, joining him in the driveway for a brief scan of the universe to see if Jupiter and Mercury were visible that evening, which they were. They left each other with an understated goodbye, which is typical for friends who see each other regularly, as not all friends do.

Hungry Paul went in and filled himself a pint glass of water for his bedside, his stockinged feet cold on the tiles, and climbed the stairs to his room. Lying in bed, with one leg outside the sheets for coolness, Hungry Paul felt the ghost of inspiration enter the room. As he lay there on the threshold between reflection and sleep, an idea came to him from that special place that ideas come from. Swivelling to his left, he reached for the stumpy pencil on his bedside table and wrote out his competition entry in one perfect draft.

Chapter 6: GRACE BEFORE MEALS

Grace had taken a midweek half day off work to meet her parents for lunch and a walk. Now that they were 'getting on in life' she had started carving out portions of her calendar to make time for them, in compensation for her inattentive twenties and the many times she had squeezed them in rather than giving them the time they deserved. While they wouldn't exactly appreciate the 'getting on' bit, Peter and Helen were happy to spend time with their daughter on any premise.

Grace had a little time beforehand and popped in to a bookshop to pick up something for her dad. Peter was a heavy reader, but it was all newspapers, journals and magazines these days and not enough novels or improving books. She browsed the tables and saw books that she had read or wanted to read and almost bought one as an evangelical gift, wanting him to like what she liked. There was a section at the back of the shop full of books about history and other deadly serious subjects. It seemed to be some sort of crèche for older men who had been left there while their wives had gone off shopping elsewhere. Grace lifted up a whopper about Stalingrad and thought about how nothing says 'gift' quite like a great big hardback. Of course, she could always gamble on something exotic: short stories by an up-and-coming South American writer, or a debut novel by a young woman that had a bit of sex in it. In the end, she settled for a novel by an established middle-aged American writer, which was signed by the author, meaning that the purchaser was guaranteed millionaire status within a few short years. Still showing the born fairness of an eldest child, she also picked up something for Helen, which was easy: a cook book or something about the garden would do, books that she didn't realise Helen was sick of. She checked her phone briefly as she queued: a few emails she was copied in on, but nothing she needed to get involved in, she hoped.

She got to the restaurant early and sat upstairs. It was an Italian, chosen as a safe middle ground for everybody. Helen would try anything, but Peter was very much a man of his generation and was terrified of leaving a restaurant hungry. It was nicely busy, having just survived a period of buzz-driven fashionability. She waved across the room when they arrived.

'Hi love, I hope you weren't waiting long,' said Helen.

'Not at all. Great to see you both.'

'Hey Gracie,' said Peter with a gentle 'my girl is all grown up' smile. 'You look nice.'

Grace did look well. She still had a bright, natural complexion and was at a point in her career where the money was good and she knew which clothes suited her and she could afford them most of the time.

'Before we start, I've bought you both a little something. Now Dad, I know you're particular, but this one's supposed to be good and I think you've read one of his previous ones, the one that won the award, and I read the back and thought you'd like it. Mam, I got you this—it's Indian cooking, which I know you're not that into, but you might find something.'

'Ah thanks pet, you're very good,' said Helen. 'So how is everything? All okay with the flowers and cake or are they still being sorted out?' Grace had been let down with some of the wedding arrangements, which had taken several late evening phone calls with Helen to talk through.

'I think it's okay. I found this really nice florist. Now, he doesn't really do weddings, but he has enough stock to put together the bouquets and the altar flowers and then I'll just get some bows and stuff for the aisle ends. My cake man is still to get back to me. I must send him a quick text later on,' said Grace, putting her phone on the table. 'Sorry! I'm on a half day and they know not to call me unless it's life or death, but you know.'

'How's Andrew?' asked Peter, 'Looking forward to it all I hope. You can tell him I got my suit. Dark blue, so he can go ahead and get the crushed purple velvet.'

Grace smiled as she drank her water. 'Thanks all the same Dad, but I think we'll keep that for the honeymoon.'

'The two of you should come over this weekend,' said Peter, 'It's been ages since we all sat down together and had a chat. I was just saying to your mam that it would be good to see Andrew a bit more often now that he has negotiated your hand in marriage.'

'He's probably busy—all that travelling. When is he going to be home?' asked Helen.

'Not till next week. He's in Amsterdam. He has a few free days but it's not really worth it to fly home, so we just Skype in the evenings. I'll find out when he's back and we'll get together with you ahead of the big day. I can't believe it's only two-and-a-bit weeks away. I'm pretty organised though. It's really just the stuff that you can't do until the last minute that's left. How's my favourite brother?'

'He's fine. Still chipping away. He's entering a competition for the Chamber of Commerce. Trying to come up with a new way of signing emails. I'll tell him you send your love. He needs to get his suit sorted, I keep telling him. He's a funny size, so he mightn't get it in Marks. I told him to make sure his shoes and belt match. And we've sorted out the whole plus one business with Leonard, by the way, so that's all taken care of.'

'Ah, great,' said Grace, 'I'm getting really tight for numbers. I was slightly hoping some of the work crowd wouldn't come. I've never really mixed work and family before.'

'We'll do our best not to disappoint or be disappointed,' said Peter. 'Should we order some food? Are we having starters?'

The menu had plenty of crowd-pleasing dishes, but no pizza or Spaghetti Bolognese or that sort of thing.

'I'll order from the set menu,' said Grace, 'I know what I'm having. Actually, they've been really good to me at work. I've been spending loads of time on the internet and on personal calls. They're letting me get away with it, so really I shouldn't be saying I hope they won't be there. Sorry, I'm rambling—back to the business at hand. I'm going to have the asparagus and bacon to start and then the truffle gnocchi thing.'

'"Notchy"? I thought it was pronounced "G'knocky"?' said Peter. 'I think I'll have the soup and some pasta—the chicken one.'

'Same for me, except I'll order the bruschetta to start and then the mushroom risotto,' said Helen.

'That's not the same,' said Peter.

'I meant I'll go for the set menu too, but thanks for your vigilance.'

They ordered from an impossibly good-looking waiter, who poured on all the usual Italians-love-their-food stuff, recapping the order while looking into Grace's eyes.

'I think he liked you,' said Peter after he had gone, 'Might be a good catch—all those tips, tax free.'

'Maybe Andrew would let me take a second husband for when he's out of town.'

'One husband is more than enough for anybody,' said Helen, 'I can't believe you're actually going to be married. We're cautious marryers in our family. I had a good long look at the field before picking my man.'

'I knew that if I waited, all the good-looking girls would eventually drop their standards until they reached my level,' said Peter.

'It was weird when we got engaged,' said Grace, 'I didn't know what to call Andrew when I was talking about him. I couldn't say boyfriend, and fiancé just sounds so contrived. I remember being in a pub and queuing in the toilet for a cubicle and seeing the sign saying "engaged" and thinking, "aw, that's me." So silly.'

The starters arrived, brought by a waitress who didn't stare into anyone's eyes, not even Peter's when he asked for some salt.

Grace's phone buzzed on the table.

'I'll leave that,' she said, making a point of not dividing her attention, but still leaving the phone where it was.

'So, have you guys any plans for any trips? You should make the most of having some time off together after all these years,' said Grace. She was forever encouraging them to go on a few city breaks or take a sun holiday so that they could be together without Hungry Paul, something which she felt would do them and him the world of good.

'Nothing organised,' said Helen, 'We're all just looking forward to the wedding now. But we were thinking of doing something in September. July and August are too warm and your dad doesn't take to the sun.'

'All the same, I would like to get my skin tone up from its current shade of Art Gallery White to at least magnolia,' said Peter through a spoonful of unsalted soup.

'Have you thought about giving your brother something to do at the service? Nothing too central or anything, just, you know, to include him a bit,' said Helen.

'Yeah, of course. I'd love him to be involved, but I'd like to find something he'd be enthusiastic about. You know what he's like when he's going through the motions. He just drags himself around without meaning to. And I don't want him to spend the whole morning worrying about not messing up. I'm not being a perfectionist: I'm just happy we're all going to be together on the day.'

'What about getting him to do some prayers?' suggested Peter, his soup finished by the time the salt arrived.

'The problem is, he's not really a churchgoer—nor am I, if I'm honest—so he might be worried about when to bow or where to walk or when it's his time to come up. What if I asked him to bring up the offertory gifts? Slight risk of a spill or something, but he should be okay.' Grace was yet to eat the first piece of asparagus she had loaded onto her fork.

'It's usually the two mothers who do that. What about a reading?' suggested Helen.

'Same problem as the prayers with all the faffing about. Also, sometimes he just freezes when he's in front of a crowd, although I don't think it scares him one bit. He just gets a little mesmerised. It's like he realises how seldom you get to stand before a crowd so he just waits there and takes it in until someone ushers him off. I saw him do it at school once when he won a science prize. He just stood there like a waxwork. Maybe I'll get him to hand out the missalettes, you know, asking people if they're with the bride or groom, that sort of thing, like they do on TV weddings.'

'Maybe. It's not a bit *social* for him is it?' said Peter, looking at Grace's fork.

'How about if he does it with Leonard? A bit of moral support for him. They are plus ones after all. That has to count for something. Eat up love,' said Helen.

'So long as it's not too *peripheral* for him. I mean he's part of the inner circle with us three, so I want him to feel included,' said Grace, speaking with her mouth full, finally.

'Oh, I'd say he'll be happy with that,' said Helen, 'The whole day will be big for him, so I think we have that sorted. I'll tell him and I'll remind him again about the suit. Peter gave him some money for it which is still in his drawer, so he's no excuse to keep delaying. I'll get on to him about it when I get home. Any particular colour you'd prefer him to wear or not wear?'

'Just whatever he likes,' said Grace, 'I have certain colours I like to wear when I need confidence for an interview or presentation, so maybe he's the same. I'll leave it to him.'

'I'm not sure about that. He's not good with decisions unless it's something he cares about. Maybe I should ask him to pick the same colour as the bridesmaids' dresses, or would that make him look like the best man?' asked Helen.

The three of them often talked like this about Hungry Paul. They had always seen themselves as the bumpers along the bowling lane for him to bounce between, saving him from mundane dangers and guiding him towards his achievements, modest though they were. It was sincere, well-meant and maybe even necessary. And yet, when you love somebody it can be hard to know where the boundary of solicitude ends and interference begins. It was testament to their sincerity that each of them—quite separately and without discussing it—had begun to entertain their own private doubts on this question. How do you know whether you are a force for good? How do you ever know if the world would not in fact be lost without you? At what stage does a hand become a hold? The fact that Hungry Paul offered no resistance to their efforts was not necessarily proof that they were helping him. It could equally be supposed that his lack of independence was not the justification for their intervention, but the result of it. Helping someone can so easily become a habit for both parties and people are often more comfortable being the helper than the helped.

Peter had always said that Hungry Paul was Helen's 'sunfish.' Years ago, before they had kids, Helen and Peter visited the aquarium in Monterey, California. A preference for aquariums over zoos was one of the early examples of how the Venn diagram of their personal tastes often overlapped in idiosyncratic ways. Among the lithe coral reef sharks, alien jellyfish, and camouflaged rays, was what looked like a floating, severed head: a large, lopsided, sideways swimming fish, with reflective skin and a slightly lost expression on its face. It was a sunfish and Helen said it was her favourite. Peter looked at her when she said this. He looked at the concentrated sincerity on her face.

Usually he would tease her about being wilfully alternative in her choices, but even he knew that this was a very personal moment. Though she didn't say so, he realised that she had picked the sunfish as her favourite because she knew nobody else would pick it. It would have pained her beautiful heart to think that there was a living thing that would go through life unloved and she was compensating for that with a special, deliberate effort to love it. In the same way, when her son was born after two miscarriages and almost didn't make it, she had promised that if he survived she would not expect or ask any more from him for his whole life than that. And that is why she had accepted Hungry Paul as he was and let him follow his natural, meandering course through life as her sunfish.

Peter's own father had died when he was only nine and he had grown up without really knowing how boys and men were supposed to act, so he had always held back and looked inwards rather than trying to project his own unsure version of himself on to the world. When Helen was pregnant with Grace, they didn't find out the sex of the baby before the birth and Peter carried an uneasiness throughout that time that it might be a boy. He had barely enough maleness to get him through his own life, never mind imparting it to a son. When Grace was born he felt relieved that he would at least get some practice as a parent before having to face raising a boy. When Hungry Paul was born, there was little time for abstract problems, as the first few weeks were full of worry and sleeplessness. Later, at school, Hungry Paul always seemed a vulnerable child, who was small for his age and had few friends. Peter continually worried that his son would be bullied. This vicarious vulnerability made Peter feel guilty—was he worried about Hungry Paul or just worried about himself, that he wouldn't know how to handle it if his child was being victimised? When Hungry Paul left school, perhaps Peter could have done more to help him find a job he was good at—he had an aptitude for science and could think well, but he just had no ideas when it came to a career. But Peter had let Hungry Paul find his own way or, to be accurate, find no particular way at all. As his father, Peter had a nagging sense that through some paternal means unknown to him—man-to-man chats or fishing trips maybe—he should have prepared Hungry Paul for the world a little better.

When Hungry Paul was brought home from the hospital, Helen and Peter made a big fuss of Grace, about how she was a big sister and what an important job that was. A few years later, when Hungry Paul started school, Helen had a formal chat with Grace about the duties and responsibilities that fall to the older sister of someone like her brother. Grace had taken these conversations seriously: she was just as keen to be a model daughter as she was to be a model sister. Without anything further being said, and without her ever deliberately deciding anything, Grace had seamlessly continued to act as Hungry Paul's guardian angel through to secondary school and on into both their adulthoods. In fact, she had never even considered whether the duties assigned to her as a young girl had ever been lifted. As she planned her wedding and looked ahead to her marriage, she began to question whether she could move on to a new life without letting go of her old one. She found herself encouraging her parents to make Hungry Paul more independent, and to become more independent themselves. Somewhere at the back of her busy mind, she wondered who would look after Hungry Paul when they were gone if he couldn't look after himself. The thought of that role falling to her—she was the only realistic candidate for it—panicked her. She didn't want to become frozen in time with the boy she first met at the age of three, so she set about making other plans, committing herself to Andrew as a way of relinquishing her duty towards Hungry Paul.

And so, with such deep undercurrents causing undetected ripples at the surface, three people who loved each other very much, and who loved Hungry Paul very much, chatted over an Italian meal about the details of their lives. It was a long conversation, as Grace ate ponderously but with the approval of her parents, for whom every moment in her company was suspended in time. Over coffee they got to talking about married life, and Grace lobbed in the speculative question about what made Peter and Helen have such a happy marriage, a question that would be awkward for any couple who had had their fair share of private arguments over the years.

'There is one thing,' ventured Peter, fluttering his eyelids at Helen ostentatiously.

'Dad, I'm serious. I'd like to know. How come your marriage has lasted so long, when so many others haven't? Some couples split up after their kids leave home, or when they both retire and have to share their lives again after years of running a household, so you're never out of the woods I guess.'

'Well, if you only want serious answers,' began Helen, 'I think you have to put your relationship first. I mean really first, not just say that it's No.1 in Valentine's cards and things like that. I mean, you even have to put it ahead of your kids. Otherwise, you get sucked into being a parent and forget to prioritise your husband or wife and before you know it, you find yourself in the worst situation of all: married with children, but deeply lonely. As you both change, you will periodically lose each other. You need to find each other again and—here's the trick—instead of trying to rekindle what you had, you need to reinvent yourselves and your relationship. You have to keep starting new relationships with the same person. This won't make any sense to you now, but at some stage in your marriage to Andrew this may become very important.' Helen explained all this carefully, like someone who had learned it the hard way. Peter didn't even try and take the edge off the heavier tone it had brought to the table, realising that his darling wife was speaking very much from the heart.

'Thanks Mam. It sounds difficult. Sounds like something that's really easy to get wrong.' Grace was leaning forward with two hands on her glass of water as she spoke.

'You shouldn't worry ahead of time, love. Just trust your instincts even if they get buried by busyness. Anyway, this has all got serious all of a sudden. Why don't we go for a walk? I'm going to regret that cheesecake when I weigh myself at Silver Slimmers next week—at my age you pay for every dessert twice.'

Helen made the writing-a-cheque sign to the good-looking waiter and they began gathering their things before the inevitable fuss over who would pay, Grace pushing her dad's hand away from the bill.

Outside, the March weather had yet to make up its mind. After such a long, lingering winter, the sun—in the places where it fell—seemed brighter than it really was. They linked elbows, feeling overfull and squinting into the wind, as Grace's phone buzzed in the bottom of her bag.

Chapter 7: CASUAL MONDAY

Hungry Paul woke up just before the alarm at 6am, as he did most Mondays. Roughly three Mondays out of four he got a call from the Post Office to work a shift as a casual postman, covering for some malingering lush at the depot, and so he liked to be up early to answer the landline promptly in case it disturbed his folks. Helen and Peter usually liked to talk and joke in bed for ages after lights out, like two kids on a camping trip, so they tended to sleep in most mornings.

His first thought was to review what he had written the night before, to check that it had not curdled overnight. Though he was pleased with how it looked, he barely felt ownership of it. It had come to him as if from elsewhere, with no preceding stream of ideas and no trace of it in his thoughts afterwards.

He went to the bathroom to spit out the morning goo and gave himself a standing wash with a facecloth, the oxters and 'Adam and Eve' areas being the priority. It always felt strange to look at himself in the mirror, his reflection reminding him of how little of the world he took up. He was generally tidy in his appearance, especially in his postman's uniform, which was the closest thing that he had to a suit. If he didn't get his act together he might end up wearing it to Grace's wedding.

Downstairs, he took a moment to sit in stillness, listening to the silence and the gentle high frequency tingling in his ears that was barely audible except at quiet times like this. It was unclear whether this was a mild form of tinnitus from years of listening to headphones in his room or whether it was just the sound of nothing happening. The ambient music of air itself.

He supposed that the world was full of people who have never heard that sound. People with busy lives and even busier minds.

The bird feeders swinging in the garden were empty, so he took the fat balls and seed mix out of the corner cupboard, knowing that he would find it impossible to relax over his own food until the birds were taken care of. They were ravenous at this time of the year, their bodies bursting with reproductive urges. Chaffinches, great tits, starlings, collared doves, magpies and hooded crows all took turns at the feeder, quite literally in a pecking order. The larger birds looked like bullies at first until he realised the service they provided to the smaller birds in making sure that the area was safe and free from predators, small creatures being innately paranoid and with good reason. Hungry Paul was not a bird watcher as such. Though he loved looking at them and identifying them and being part of their lives, he never liked the collector mentality of birdwatching: all that ticking off lists and valuing the obscure over the everyday. He saw birds as part of nature, just like himself, and appreciated them with kindred interest.

Hungry Paul was a fan of routine and the way it had of bringing familiarity to one's life when so much else was new, changing or doubtful. As each day seemed to be fresh in its own way, he didn't feel the need to season life's innate variety with variety of his own. His breakfast was the same every morning: three Weetabix with banana chopped into the bowl using the side of the spoon, and a cup of strong, sugared coffee. Whereas people generally try to vary their lunch and dinner habits, at breakfast it is accepted the world over that it is better to find a system and stick to it. Hungry Paul felt that way about most things.

With the morning all to himself, he moved to the living room and sat by the phone. Above all things, Hungry Paul was a patient person. He saw patience as a way of allowing things to happen by themselves, trusting that things would turn out as they were meant to, not by design but because of the innate orderliness of things. Just as he started filing the side of his thumbnail with a matchbox, the phone rang and, after a very brief, very male, exchange of the barest information, he cycled to the Post Office, the wind blowing through his helmet. While it wasn't a career as such, he liked being a casual postman and was proud of the fact that he wasn't taking up a whole job, depriving someone else of a living. Like a small denomination stamp used to make up the balance due on a larger package, he simply covered the parts that needed covering.

When he entered the sorting area where his post bag was waiting for him, the large room was practically empty, the early rising full-timers keen to get their day started—or more specifically finished—as soon as possible. This was a busy place in a state of desertion, with a lingering atmosphere of bachelorhood and strong opinions. Hungry Paul started organising the post into pigeonholes, one for each street on the route, before ordering it by house number. Throwing up and setting in, as it was called. If you didn't know a street you didn't know how to order the letters. Some streets were best done in odds and evens, others in numerical order. In semi-rural areas, where houses had names but no numbers, it was all a question of local knowledge, which was unavailable to the casual postman. In most cases it would have made more sense just to leave the post until the next day when the regular man would be back, as hardly anything urgent went by post anymore, but they never did that. It was said that a clean bench was a clean conscience.

It had turned into a nice spring morning: bright and warm on the sunny side of the street, but in the shade there was a head cold waiting for anyone who thought it was an early summer and went out hatless. He passed kids going to school and vans running late with deliveries. It was enjoyable just watching the general distracted activity of that part of the morning, but once he got into the estates things were quieter. Postal workers weren't supposed to cross dividing walls, though many did, so he had to walk up and down the driveways, with each front gate having its own knack.

One heavy bloke—'stout' Helen would have called him—was leaning over his gate, his waist a testament to the sturdy stitch work of the sports jersey he wore. 'If they're bills, I don't want them.' There was an old couch in his front garden, and a Staffordshire bull terrier that was attacking a tyre hanging from a small birch tree.

'I'm just filling in; the regular fella will be back tomorrow.'

Further on, a young woman, still in her pyjamas, shouted after him from her door, something about bending her birthday cards.

'I'm just filling in; the regular fella will be back tomorrow.'

He had to get an elderly lady to sign for a package in the next street on behalf of her neighbour. 'They're never home. Poor kids in crèches all day. I'll drop it in later. You're a bit late today aren't you?'

'I'm just filling in; the regular fella will be back tomorrow.'

He didn't stop for lunch, as he always felt self-conscious sitting down and eating his sandwich while wearing the uniform. People didn't like seeing that sort of thing.

Hungry Paul continued on his rounds, his bag getting lighter and lighter, doing a job that has existed, largely unchanged, for hundreds of years. To any busy person, burdened with all of life's responsibilities and preoccupations, Hungry Paul's lot would seem a bearable one. He didn't have to decide which of a patient's limbs to amputate first, or where to invest the life savings of a company's pensioners. There was no pressure to report fourth quarter losses to the 'higher-ups' in HQ or force-feed cold carrots to a fevered toddler. His job, on the few days he did it, involved no agonising decisions or regrets that might spoil the conversation over dinner.

And yet, in modern vernacular, postal work is a profession

that has become synonymous with violent meltdowns. Why would this happen in such an apparently placid line of work, which involves chatting happily to the householders and performing a task that has, throughout history, been shown to be helpful in all ways? Most overworked middle managers would gladly swap their late evening conference calls with the West Coast for the simplicity of the postal worker, walking in the mixed March sunshine, alone with his thoughts. However, such white-collar fantasies fail to consider what it is that bends even the most pacific minds towards self-destruction. Though we may be a species that prizes great minds, we are also terrified of and by our thoughts.

In prisons, the most extreme and austere punishment that is meted out to errant prisoners—those whose behaviour exceeds even the diabolical standards of incarcerated society—is solitary confinement: the awful fate of being imprisoned with only one's thoughts for company. With no distractions, one thought billiards another, and an endless internal monologue drowns out the rest of life, bringing dissonance to silence, restlessness to stillness, and anxiety to forethought. A certain type of person, isolated and unsuited to long daily periods of reflection, will eventually think themselves to madness.

But Hungry Paul seemed to be able to maintain his peace where another man might have declared war on themselves and those around him. What did he think about? The answer is, quite simply, nothing. Hungry Paul had been blessed with a mental stillness which had become his natural state over the years. His mind worked perfectly fine and he had all the faculties of a healthy, if slightly unorthodox, man of his age. He just had no interest in, or capacity for, mental chatter. He had no internal narrator. When he saw a dog he just saw a dog, without his mind adding that it should be on a lead or that its tongue was hanging out like a rasher. When he heard an ambulance siren he just heard an ambulance siren, without noting its Doppler effect or wondering if it was a real emergency or just the driver running late for dinner. And it is in this way that Hungry Paul maintained a natural clarity throughout his day, and stayed apart from the trouble that the world will undoubtedly make for those who look for it.

At around midday he finished his deliveries and dropped his bag back to the depot. But there was one last letter to deal with before his day was finished. He took his competition entry out of his breast pocket and posted it in the box outside the sorting office, affixing a patchwork of smaller stamps that he had saved up in the back of his wallet. This was all done without any sense of excitement or concern about the competition; his entry was merely an offering. He didn't so much want to win as help. If some other phrase was selected, then that was fine too.

The house was empty when he got home. Peter and Helen had left a note on the fridge saying that they had gone off to buy a Buddha at the garden centre. Hungry Paul made himself a peanut butter sandwich and, having failed to find any treats in the cupboard, ate it alone in the kitchen on the seat where he had watched the birds only a few hours before, the feeders already empty again.

He decided to lie down on the couch and took off his shoes the lazy way, with the toe of one foot prising off the heel of the other, the laces still done up. His feet tingled now that the weight had been lifted from them after a long morning of walking. He dozed off, not minding that he would later wake with that drugged feeling that comes with a second sleep. All around him, the house stood in a state of empty, quiet equilibrium.

Chapter 8: DON'T USE THE LIFTS

Leonard had been cleaning the fluff out of his keyboard with a paperclip when he received the next set of comments from the author. He had sent her a stock piece of work about Roman noses and chariots as a sort of holding response to keep her off his case while he tried to rustle up some ideas. She loved it. Her covering email was gushing: 'Now we're finally getting somewhere,' like a teacher with a slow child who has just mastered a basic task that the rest of the class learned ages ago. Her comments and corrections were predictably about making it as much like every other Roman book as possible. It would be easy to keep her happy and to fill out the rest of the book on auto-pilot. Leonard didn't like churning out bland material but when the author took a different view he usually felt that there was no point campaigning. These were commercially produced books and he already had more artistic licence than he ever expected, purely because he backed down on anything important to the author and reserved his creativity for the bits the author didn't care about or notice. Whenever he lost some argument about content, he would try and make up for it by being more stylish or by sneaking in a phrase that he thought a kid might enjoy learning or asking their parents about, like 'eyeballing' or 'frogmarch.'

This time though, he felt less comfortable about capitulating and moving on. He wasn't satisfied with settling for some neatly-handled fact boxes, or digging out some obscure twist on a reworked apocryphal nugget. Whether it was his long-standing beef with the Romans or whether it was a response to the changes that had undoubtedly started to take place within him, he felt a new sense of impetus and creativity about his work. Some children might only ever read one book about the Romans and this one might be it. What if they were turned off history? Or worse: what if they were inspired by the example of the Romans to become their own little Caesars of the playground, making life difficult for the gentle, curious kids Leonard wanted the book to be read by? No, no, no, that wouldn't do. He couldn't dispute the Romans' undoubted success at dominating the continent, and he could not deny their unmatched contribution to ancient civilisation. But were they not achievements for historians and sociologists to write about? Leonard wanted to ignite children's imaginations about the world around them, and to inspire their curiosity. There would be plenty of time for them to learn the rough lessons of life, but shouldn't they first be allowed to develop very special ideas about the world? Wasn't it *his* role to catalyse the magic that happens when children read encyclopaedias, and especially so when they read them to their parents?

Leonard remembered getting a set of *Our World* encyclopaedias from his mother, one by one, every Christmas, birthday, special occasion and, sometimes, just because she wanted to cheer him up. With all his heart he had longed for the complete set: *Our Artists*, *Our Insects*, *Our Mammals*, and two dozen others. He loved getting a new encyclopaedia in the set without any idea what was in it. The notion that you could have favourites or could read some but not others was completely alien to him. Encyclopaedias were supposed to involve a sense of discovery, of openness to whatever came next. He read them in the back of his mother's car, at the supermarket, at the dinner table, and in his bed with a torch. Encyclopaedias were books you were meant to immerse yourself in. They created their own worlds with magical pairings of writers and illustrators, using short exciting prose with memorable tableaux, drawn in a way that was meant to look lifelike but not so detailed that a young seven-year-old couldn't attempt to copy the pictures themselves. Yes, they were factual books, but they weren't just books of facts. They were storytelling books that used the world around us merely as a starting point, as kindling for a child's imagination.

He had always pictured the author and illustrator as intrepid, inseparable friends who wrote the books about facts they had discovered themselves. The books were written and illustrated with such a personal touch that it was hard to imagine that the people involved had not actually seen all the animals and shared campfires with all the tribes in the pictures. As a child, they showed him what life could be like: an adventure undertaken in the name of curiosity alone. He had resolved to do everything in those books: climb Mount Everest, swim in a shark cage, walk on a tightrope over Niagara Falls, and pull himself out of quicksand.

But when he started working on encyclopaedias years ago as a proof-reader, he got his first exposure to the battery farm methods now used in the professionalised industry, the avuncular enthusiasts long since departed. Stock photos, dry facts, information with exclamation marks. It was still about getting kids excited, but now it was just sugar rush facts. Biggest this or that, gross-out facts, all written with an adult's sense of what a child would like. Books abounded on vehicles, space, dinosaurs, the human body, but sets of encyclopaedias were on an irreversible decline. You now bought books on things you were already interested in.

Leonard thought about his mother, who had always managed to find an encyclopaedia he hadn't read yet, and who must have had to scour bookshops to find them in the days before the internet. He thought about how, whenever he read something he wanted to share as a child, if only because he would burst with amazement if he didn't, she used the same phrase, a phrase that Leonard hoped every parent used with their children every day:

'Tell me.' With her attention undivided, he would gush with every last detail, urging her to share his awe, and pointing at the illustrations as if they were the only proof you could ever need that the world was indeed made of magic. In the past few weeks, as she started to retreat from his life, decades of conversation fragments like these had been stirred up within him. Random, unsorted mental echoes, not yet sweetened into nostalgia.

Leonard boldly tapped Ctrl-N, the keyboard shortcut that he hoped would launch the life-changing expedition he had always promised himself. He started filling the blank white rectangle with lines and lines of nascent ideas for his own encyclopaedia about the Romans, into which he would put all he understood about the world and the people who lived in it. If he wanted to do something special, and without front-facing angry people, he knew that he would have to illustrate the book himself. Though he was a little rusty, he had always been able to envisage epic drawings for the books he worked on, and often felt let down to see the stale, lifeless scenarios they used in the published works: battle scenes that looked like department store windows, warriors who looked like bored supermodels, and intrepid explorers killing lions while sporting a neat side parting and a Hollywood smile. Why not draw pictures that kids would want to pull out and hang on their walls, full of believable figures from other times and places, captured at their most heroic?

He wondered about Roman children and whether they were close to their parents. Were the Roman children born outside of marriage looked after in the spirit of Romulus and Remus, the storied founders of the city? He made a list of the toys Roman kids played with like kites and swords, all things that still filled toy boxes to this day. What did the shy Roman children make of it all—did they feel part of the Empire or did they have nightmares about Caesar? What about the public servants who actually designed and engineered the public works projects that the emperors took credit for; the unacknowledged geniuses who built great things and then came home to play with their kids, feeling exhausted and sore. He thought about the slaves who were smarter than their masters, who in a different era would have been as celebrated as Blackadder, Jeeves or Sir Humphrey. His mind became effervescent with pictures and stories of overlooked people who had simply lived their lives as best they could during the Roman Empire. Ordinary, kind, gentle people whose stories he had only ever considered telling in a generic way. Their details had only seemed relevant to him insofar as they typified Roman life. He had seen them as a topic, and in doing so he had made the mistake of dehumanising them, forgetting to make them into interesting people that kids would want to meet, or even be. All along he had been writing them as sort of historical mannequins, modelling generic facts about the period. Depicting them like that must be frustrating for kids, like bringing them to a toy shop where all the toys are in boxes. Kids needed to be able to put down the book, run off and grab their friends and bring the energy from the page into their play.

Locked away in his headphones, he bashed away at his keyboard like Mozart, writing his own alternative version of the book: a book about all the people who were invisible to history. He felt utterly connected to his work and creativity, timeless and free. It was as if the ideas were flowing from an imaginary classroom of children in his head, all with their hands up, asking him to write about their favourite subject.

It was like . . .

A hand waved in front of him.

It was like . . .

It continued waving in front of him like a windscreen wiper.

He looked up at a girl who was standing beside him and mouthing something.

Leonard took his headphones off with snappy overacted impatience.

'Can I help you?' he asked.

'Fire alarm. We have to go.' The girl with a green jumper and cherry-coloured hair was leaning to one side and double-pointing her thumbs in a direction she indicated was 'thataway.'

'Fire alarm,' she repeated. 'You have to get out of here. Run for your life. Please. If you don't mind.'

'Is it a fire or a fire drill?'

'Now, I'm not allowed to answer that question and even if I did answer it, it doesn't matter: you still have to get out of here. Those are the rules.'

'It's probably just a drill. They do them every once in a while.'

'Doesn't matter. You have to go. Women and children could be dying while I'm here talking to you.'

'I'm okay, I'll take a chance,' said Leonard, reaching for his headphones.

'Oh, no, no, no, no, no, no, no,' the girl sang the notes as a scale in the key of C. 'Sorry to pull rank on you my friend, but you don't have a choice.' She pointed to the hi-vis sash she was wearing which said 'Fire Warden.'

Leonard gave in and walked huffily towards the door. 'No need to thank me for saving your life,' she called behind him.

He pushed the button for what must be the slowest lift in the world and tried to trace back the thread of his thoughts about the book, getting the feeling that he'd lost a little momentum, like when a sneeze nearly happens but doesn't.

'Hey, hey, hey, you can't use the lift in a fire situation! Everybody knows that.' His fire warden friend had followed him out, pegging him for a trouble maker.

'How do I get down then?'

'Most people use the stairs, but you can also abseil or climb the outside of the building like Spiderman if you know how to do that. C'mon, stop being difficult. Disobeying a fire warden is seven years bad luck.'

'Shouldn't you be wardening the other floors?'

'Nope. I'm Floor 3 only. Other floors have lesser fire wardens so I imagine the body count on those will be pretty high. Look, can you not just go assemble yourself at the corner between the park and the museum with all the others. Please?'

Leonard did what he was told and as he walked off she blew a little whistle that was on a string around her neck, which startled him and gave her a giggle.

At the assembly point, the girl with the cherry-coloured hair carried a clipboard and counted up everyone, as the people from Floor 3 chatted light-heartedly, some wishing they'd brought coats, others wondering if they had time to get a coffee before returning to the building.

The girl cupped her hands into a megaphone and thanked everyone for their cooperation. As they all filed back to the building, some young guys joked flirtatiously with their colleagues about one last wish before they all perished in the fire. Leonard hurried back to his desk and started typing a few sentences, but the moment had gone and with it his inspiration. He decided to go onto the internet for a while, surfing aimlessly and brainlessly, before giving up and heading for a cup of tea.

He stood in the kitchenette and waited for the kettle to boil, checking his reflection in the microwave door. There was some stubble he'd missed during his preoccupied shave that morning, and, dumbest of all, he was still wearing his single-pocket, paisley pyjama top, having forgotten to change it in his rush out of the door that morning. Just as he was bending down, looking in the back of the bottom cupboard for some sugar, a loud peeping noise sounded behind him, taking two years off his life expectancy.

'Hi there. Glad you survived the fire.' It was the girl with the cherry-coloured hair.

'You almost gave me a heart attack. What are you doing?'

'Oh, just thought I'd come and say hello. A fire warden needs to know who she's protecting, you know, in case I need to notify next of kin.

'Actually, I think I kinda, sorta know who you are,' she continued. 'Are you Mark Baxter, BEd, the guy who wrote all the *Facts at My Fingertips* series? I've seen you working on them at your desk. They're great books. You're really good.'

Facts at My Fingertips was a series of mass-produced fact books that Leonard had worked on a few years ago, and which he had recently updated as part of a revised edition. It was supposed to be full of lists and records, with practically no original content, but Leonard had rescued it surreptitiously by pouring his creativity into it and making the series into what one industry newsletter called 'a future classic.' Mark Baxter, BEd, was the overseeing author and hardly lifted a finger on the whole thing. Interns from his office just emailed all the changes and feedback, while Mark was away on the conference circuit, presumably sleeping with more interns, the BEd in his title providing a clue as to where he did his best work.

'Oh no, I'm not Mark Baxter. He's the author of those books, I'm just the content supervisor. He decides what's in the book and I just write it up.'

'Oh, really? Is that a job?'

'I hope so,' said Leonard a little too sensitively.

'I don't mean it that way. I just think it's unfair that you do all the work and he gets his name on the book. You should at least get a co-credit.'

'It doesn't really work that way,' replied Leonard.

'You're kind of like a *ghost writer*,' she said in a haunted house voice, relentless in her cheerfulness.

'I suppose I am a bit. I prefer to be in the background. Anyway, better get back.'

'Sure thing. Me too. Find any sugar by the way? Ah, never mind, I'll just dip my biscuits in mine—would you like one?'

'No thanks,' said Leonard patting his slightly protruding

stomach and immediately regretting he had done so in front of a girl, of all people.

'Okay, talk to you next time there's a fire,' she said.

Leonard brought his tea back to his desk and faked some typing. Too much in one day: first the Romans, then a fire drill and now a conversation with a girl. In fact, that was his first one-to-one conversation with a girl in a very long time. As he sat at his desk he went through the whole thing again. When he was chatting to her he had been slightly out of body, still sobering up from the intense immersion in his book. He catalogued his mistakes with an amplified sense of embarrassment: the way he missed her humorous cues, his stilted aloofness, his patting of his stupid, stupid, stupid, what-was-I-thinking stomach. He wanted to bang his head on the desk. To take his mind off the embarrassment, he tried to start a piece about the children of gladiators, and whether they got to see their dads fight, but all he could think about was his own ineptness. It was not even that he thought she fancied him, he just wanted to give a good account of himself. She took his side on the whole Mark Baxter, BEd, thing—that was positive wasn't it? Why didn't he even hear the compliment that was buried in what she said? She had offered him a biscuit—a biscuit for God's sake. Why didn't he just say 'yes, thank you' or eat it from the palm of her hand or offer to eat it together until their lips touched à la Lady and the Tramp? And the pyjamas—of all the days to make that blunder.

Was he attracted to her? Or was it just that she was a girl and he should have taken the chance to notice whether she was flirting with him or just doing that woman/man office banter thing that he could never tell apart from real flirting.

He thought back to what she looked like. His shyness meant that he unconsciously avoided eye contact, which meant that he wasn't able to picture her clearly enough. A bit arty maybe—with intelligent but vulnerable eyes? How long was her hair—seemed to be about shoulder length, but was it a bit wavy or just messy? Her hands—nail varnish on chewed nails maybe? Rings or jewellery—Jesus, rings! He didn't even notice a wedding or engagement ring. How could he overlook such a thing? She was probably married. Married women can be overly familiar with men without being misinterpreted, can't they? How tall was she? Hard to tell: he was sitting down when they first started talking, then she was behind him and then outside she was standing on her own, so hard to compare, and then in the kitchenette she was sort of leaning against the sink, making her seem smaller than she was. She wasn't tall, but hard to say otherwise. Her accent—what was it—her voice was kind of, what? *Squeaky* maybe? She kept putting on funny voices. The haunted house voice and other jokey things—was she kind of quirky or was she being nervous or nice or just embarrassed to be in a position of semi-authority and telling grown-ups what to do?

He tried to get back to his work. The gladiators. Their kids. Come on, think Leonard, think. Every time he tried to focus, his mind drifted back to some other slip-up. He never even asked her name. What kind of rude, self-absorbed person would forget to extend a hand and ask her name? Idiot! He never even said his own name. All he said is that he wasn't Mark Baxter, which was true of pretty much everybody except Mr Mark Baxter, BEd, himself. And he never asked her about herself. What did his mother always say? 'Leonard, if you want to make friends, ask people about themselves.'

Maybe if he'd had some warning he might have handled it better. Had he known that today would be the day when a girl, a real-life, probably attractive girl, would talk to him, make *jokes* with him, he might have prepared a little. He wouldn't have worn a pyjama top. Instead, he might have worn a nice shirt, or knotted a jumper around his shoulders, like a winner. He would have shaved properly, or at least grown all stubble, or maybe even grown a big beard like lots of other guys in the office. And then he looked down at his shoes—black bloody brogues, with *jeans*. Good God!

Not for the first time, he longed for an 'undo' button in his life. He wished that she had met the very best version of himself. He always felt that he stood little chance with women, but on his best days—wearing his newest clothes, after a haircut and a good night's sleep—he just might be considered passable by some patient girl who could see past the superficial stuff and realise that he had the makings of an apprentice boyfriend. Not the finished article admittedly, but surely there was potential there. Hopefully she went to a mixed secondary school. If she went to an all-girls school he was finished. Those girls went out looking for the perfect man, their perfect man. At least girls who went to mixed schools had the attitude of 'just give me something I can work with.' He was certainly that. A nice, warm-hearted girl could possibly work wonders with him. Her friends would say 'where did you find this one—does he have any brothers?' While he didn't exactly have confidence with girls, he did have *hope*. He saw loads of girls and thought them to be way out of his league, but he had also seen lots of couples, where the girl, the *happy* girl, was holding hands with a guy from his league. A sort of okay-looking guy who made her laugh maybe, or who made her feel comfortable in herself. You just needed an *in*, so she would give you a chance. A chance to get to know her. Not to blow her away—he knew he would never be that type—but at least for her to warm to him over time maybe; to overlook him, only to realise he was what she was looking for all the while.

Leonard was getting overstimulated. Having gone through long barren stretches, his romantic feelings were now starting to awaken, with all their crazy body chemistry. It was exhausting. It was actually physically uncomfortable: all this genetic programming kicking in at once, while his poor fragile personality got run over.

Leonard had little to say on the Romans that day. He left a little early to meet Hungry Paul who was under instructions to buy a suit for Grace's wedding—'by sundown,' is how he explained it—and as Thursday was late night shopping, Leonard offered to keep him company and help him decide.

One consequence of Hungry Paul not having a mobile was that he was always on time. You could arrange to meet him six months hence at a certain time on a given spot and, without any reminders or last minute excuses, he would be there exactly as arranged. When Leonard arrived early, Hungry Paul was already waiting for him. They decided to try Marks, where Leonard had bought his suit for his mother's funeral, which he planned to wear again for the wedding, albeit with a different colour tie.

'So, what are you thinking of getting?' Leonard asked.

'I suppose I'll just see what they have. I hope I can find something that fits. I'm a little bit in-between, sizewise.'

'When was the last time you bought a suit?'

'Well, if you don't count the *gi* I bought for judo the other day, this is my first one.'

'So what size are you?'

'Dunno. Usually shirts that fit my shoulders are too long for my arms, and trousers that fit my short legs don't fit my waist.'

'What they call in tailoring, the *orang-utan problem*,' offered Leonard. 'Let's ask them to measure you.'

They looked around for a shop assistant, harking back to the days when shops actually employed people on the shop floor to help customers. Various middle-aged women in black clothes and name badges scuttled by:

'Sorry, I'm just with someone.'

'Sorry, I'm on my break.'

'Sorry, I don't work here.'

So they tried to figure it out themselves.

'What colour do you want?' asked Leonard.

'Not navy, as that's too much like my post office uniform. Not black, because I'll look like someone in a ska band. Not brown, because I'd look like a teacher. So, maybe grey, dark grey even?' Hungry Paul had given this some thought.

'What about this pinstripe one?' suggested Leonard.

'Nah, pinstripe is for a work suit, not for a social occasion. Besides, that's chalk stripe, which is different.'

'I'm impressed,' said Leonard, 'I sort of expected you to be hopeless at this, to be honest. How do you know so much about all this?'

'I think my mother thought the same. There isn't much to know. Men don't have huge variety in suits and I like to pay attention to what goes on, so after a while you notice who wears what, even if you're not interested in a wearing a suit yourself. Let's try the dark grey one.'

Hungry Paul put it on but was defeated by his own proportions.

'Maybe they could take it up, in and out?' offered Leonard.

'You mean that it would be a perfect fit if only the dimensions were all different. Hold on, here's one of the orderlies.'

Hungry Paul intercepted a male shop assistant, who looked about eleven years old and had 'stock room' written all over him.

'Do you have this one in any other sizes?' asked Hungry Paul.

'I think it's just what's out on the racks,' he answered.

'So what's in the stock room?' interrogated Hungry Paul, QC.

'There might be some other sizes, but I'd have to check,' offered the shop assistant in the spirit of Muhammad going to the mountain.

'Could I ask you to measure me first, just so it's not a wasted journey—it won't take a moment,' asked Hungry Paul.

The shop assistant found a measuring tape from somewhere and started measuring Hungry Paul, using what looked like a self-taught method he had only just invented that second. 'Eh, I'd say something around 36", short jacket and 38" short for the trousers,' he guessed, calling out the measurements for E.T.

'Maybe we'll just look around. Thanks all the same,' said Hungry Paul.

The young shop assistant went through some double doors to finish his adolescence.

Thanks to some methodical persistence, Hungry Paul managed to find a smart grey suit that fitted him well on top and which would fit him well in the trouser once it had been adjusted a little bit. He actually looked quite smart when he put it on, even though anyone trying on a suit in his stockinged feet (with protruding toes) leaves an impression tantalisingly short of the full effect.

'What colour shirt—blue maybe?' asked Leonard.

'It's not a policeman's ball,' said Hungry Paul. 'White, of course. And for a tie, let me see. I'll pick purple. It was always Grace's favourite when we were younger. It was the colour of the wrapper of her favourite sweet in the Quality Street tin at Christmas.'

'I suppose I better sort myself out too,' said Leonard, inspired by Hungry Paul's example. 'A white shirt, of course, and for a tie, I'll go for this nice green one—not too loud is it?'

'Not at all. It looks like the colour of birch leaves when light shines through them,' answered Hungry Paul, with a touch of poetry.

As they queued, both men became smitten with the days-of-the-week socks on offer near the register and bought a set each. Tragically they had not realised that, far from making sock selection easy, they would be an absolute nuisance, and that once the first wear was out of the way, each sock of a given day would never again be matched with its counterpart.

On their way home, with Leonard still in awe of Hungry Paul's hidden aptitudes, they started chatting about the generalities of life, their duty for the evening now discharged.

'So any plans for the rest of the week now that the suit shopping is done?' asked Leonard.

'My mam suggested popping in to the hospital with her where she volunteers, to see if I could help out a bit,' answered Hungry Paul.

'Very thoughtful of you to offer your skills as a heart surgeon for free. Do you have to bring your own scissors and glue?" asked Leonard.

'Well, I have your book *The Human Body* to help me—what could go wrong? Actually, my mam does visiting there. Just walks around the ward and asks people if they want a chat, so she suggested I join her. I'm not sure I'll be much use, to be honest,' said Hungry Paul.

'I never had you down for that sort. Talking to strangers isn't usually your thing,' said Leonard.

'I think I'll just sit there and listen rather than chatting much. I'm due to start doing it tomorrow. How about you— how are the Romans?'

'Okay, I suppose. I've decided to do a basic job on the main book, as that's all the author wants, but I've also started putting together my own ideas. I'm not sure what I'll do with it, but I quite fancy a go at writing my own book. In fact I'm spending most of the company's time working on my own ideas at the moment.'

'You've always been able to write but you've just never seen yourself as a writer—you've always held yourself back. You know more about encyclopaedias than anyone—why so much self-doubt? If I were a kid I'd much rather read your books than the regurgitations of some absentee author,' said Hungry Paul, with his mother's gift for encouragement.

'I was also going to mention that I was talking to a girl today. In work I mean. As part of a fire drill,' non-sequitured Leonard.

'The old fire drill romance, eh? What's her name?' asked Hungry Paul.

'I don't know.'

'Does she work with you?'

'Not with me, no. But she might be in the same company, I'm not sure.'

'What does she look like?'

'A bit arty I think, but I'm not sure.'

'How do you mean, not sure? Was she wearing a wrestling mask or something? Was it dark or foggy in the office today?'

'I just didn't get a good look at her.'

'Was it a hit and run—did you get her registration plate? How can you know so little about her—can you at least tell me whether she was a liquid, gas or solid?'

'To be honest, it was nothing more a chat. She was nice though, as far as I can remember,' said Leonard, retreating a little.

'I'm sorry, I shouldn't joke. All I can say is best of luck with it. If you need any advice on how to mess it up, just ask.'

'I will, old pal.'

The two friends parted company, swinging their bags and looking forward to starting with the Friday socks the next day. Hungry Paul had a nice grey suit that needed taking up and Leonard had a tie which was the colour of birch leaves when the light shines through them. Coincidentally it was the same colour as the jumper worn that day by Shelley, the fire warden on Floor 3, who is 5'5", has cherry-coloured hair, bites her red nails and is responsible for training and induction at a company called Physical Solutions Limited, which trains carers how to lift their patients without hurting their backs.

Chapter 9: THANK YOU FOR THE ROSES

The next morning Leonard got up early and made a special effort to iron his nicest, most contemporary, shirt. He matched it with some new cords he had bought but never worn, principally because they did not have the customary zip cover flap and Leonard was concerned that this might have some coded underground significance that it was best not to mess with. Shoes-wise, he was stuck with either his brogues or a pair of Adidas that he had intended throwing out. It would have to be the Adidas.

As soon as he got in to work he tried to see if he could figure out where the girl's desk was, but he had arrived too early and she wasn't around yet. His immediate priority had been to try and unwind their last two conversations and replace them with a new first impression, something he could only attempt if it was the first thing he did that day, before his self-doubt got the better of him.

He tried to pay attention to what the other guys in the office were wearing; in other words, he wanted to know what girls liked men to wear. Most of the men were young and whippet-thin, and could wear band t-shirts without looking like a deflating balloon. Some of them wore hats indoors; one guy wore a thumb ring, which surely couldn't be right. A couple of guys were actually wearing paisley pyjama tops—had Leonard started something?

When he got to his desk, hoping to make up for time lost the day before, there was a whole bunch of housekeeping emails waiting for him. A book he was finalising—*Nature's Factories*, all about photosynthesis and pollination—had come back from proofreading and needed to be checked. He made up his mind to do the responsible thing and work through the various requests and then maybe try and find the girl at around lunchtime. Maybe she didn't have lunch plans and Leonard might be able to mention casually that he was heading for a walk or thinking of seeing if there was music on at the bandstand in the park. He put on his noise-cancelling headphones and despatched a dozen emails, all signed off with 'apologies for the delay in responding.'

At one stage, when he was removing a paper jam from the printer, he saw the girl with the cherry-coloured hair across the open-plan area. She looked to be in a hurry and a little stressed. He tried to delay so he could figure out surreptitiously where she sat, and therefore who she worked for, and particularly whether she worked for the same company as he did, but she was too hard to track, disappearing between the modular furniture like a fish darting through rocks.

Things went a little slower than expected in clearing the backlog, as the people he emailed inevitably emailed back with further questions or asked him to do something else. By the time he had freed himself from all of that it was past 1pm and the window for his lunchtime plan was closing.

He tried to walk languidly over to where he thought the girl's desk was, planning to say something like 'No fires today, then?' which would help him to pick up the conversation right where had had left it. The idea was to shrug off their previous conversation, showing her the sociable, likeable Leonard instead.

When he got there, two other girls were sitting in a pod for four people. One was on the phone dealing with what sounded like a difficult customer; the other was grabbing up papers to go to a meeting or something.

'Hi there,' said Leonard in a sort of 'howdy' tone of voice.

The two girls ignored him and continued doing what they were doing.

'Hi. I was just wondering, is there a girl with dyed red hair who works on one of these desks?'

'Yes. Why? We're busy,' answered the girl who was going to a meeting.

'I was just wondering if she's around. She's the fire warden and I was hoping to get some safety advice. Em . . . just wondering . . . em . . . if it's safe to leave my phone plugged in overnight?' Leonard was definitely not good at this.

'Do what you want,' said the meeting girl without looking at him as she scurried off to the other end of the room.

Leonard, feeling abandoned but not yet ready to give up, decided to linger and wait for the other woman to come off the phone. He wasn't sure whether he should catch a bit of eye contact to let her know he was waiting, or just loiter invisibly to avoid provoking her. She made up his mind for him by slamming the phone down and then giving the handset a double middle finger, before swivelling her head and saying 'What do you want?'

'Hi, there. Someone told me that, I mean, I think I saw the fire warden here earlier, the girl who was fire warden yesterday that is, and I needed advice about a fire safety question, my charger sometimes gets warm, and—'

'Shelley is not in in the afternoon. Mornings only,' she interrupted.

'Oh, okay. Thanks. I'll let you get back to it. I'll try not to cause a fire in the meantime,' he replied, not yet ready to give up the potential for fire safety to be made light-hearted and conversational.

Leonard decided to go out for some fresh air and put in some preoccupied laps of the park. His stomach was too overwhelmed by exhausted butterflies to eat anything. He felt drained and

74

disappointed. Now he would have to wait until Monday to see her and explain things. Time had already crawled since the day before and now he had a long, slow weekend to get through before trying to talk to her again. Only now her two workmates had probably already seen through him. They would probably laugh about Leonard to her. It would be impossible for her to go out with someone her workmates thought was a joke.

He thought it all over, chewing his anxiety into his thumbnail. She worked mornings only. What was that all about? Is it just a part-time job? Does she have an afternoon job or does she need afternoons off for some reason? What did she do in the afternoons—hit the sack with her boyfriend, husband?

But he did get her name. 'Shelley.' Hmm. He said it to himself a few times. A girl who was eating a sandwich on a bench near the duck pond gave him a judgemental look. Had he ever met a 'Shelley' before? Was that even a real name? Was it Shelley, or short for Michelle or Rochelle?

As he circled the bandstand where members of a brass band were packing away their instruments, his thoughts continued to babble through countless leads as to who she might be, speculations to which there would be no answer until Monday at the earliest. His mind was like a bottle of cola that had been shaken and which now needed the air let out of it slowly and carefully. He got back to his desk, enervated and unfed, and tried to work on his book about the Romans, but his concentration was elsewhere. After a while he gave up and decided to ring Hungry Paul to talk through the confusion he was feeling, but when he tried to ring his good friend, the landline just rang and rang. It seemed that his confidant was out of the house. Leonard would have to struggle through the afternoon alone.

Hungry Paul was, in fact, on his way to the hospital to do some visiting. Helen had launched him on his first independent voyage in that direction on the premise that he was to deliver a tin of Roses sweets to the nurses on her behalf, while she was off getting her roots done. With all the enthusiasm of a man who has no choice in the matter, he set off for the hospital by himself and was almost at the park when he remembered that he had forgotten to bring the sweets. Doubling back to the house, he grabbed a tin of Roses from under the stairs and started back down the road for a second time.

He stopped at the corner and decided to cross the main street using the lollipop lady, who was holding back the school kids on the other side. She was chatting to an adult and missed several viable opportunities to initiate a crossing. As he waited for the lollipop lady from the opposite kerb, he idly inspected the tin of Roses and, as he did so, he noticed that it was out of date. In fact it was significantly out of date—by more than a year. His first thought was to marvel at how the universe, now knocking on for thirteen and a half billion years old or so, continued to operate through the medium of chance. Hungry Paul would not have noticed the date on the tin but for a delay at the lollipop lady, who would not have been on duty had it not been a week-day. And it was quite out of character for Hungry Paul to even inspect the date on a tin of sweets. He would normally assume all was well with such things and in fact was usually confused by the nuances between 'best before' and 'use by' dates, each of which seemed to be differentiated with unnecessary subtlety. However, the universe, being senior to Hungry Paul in its age and wisdom—by some degree on both counts—had seen fit to reveal itself through happenstance, and so he accepted the in-advertent discovery as a simple question of fate.

Had Isaac Newton been waiting for the lollipop lady that Friday lunchtime, he would no doubt have pointed out that every action has an equal and opposite reaction, and it was in this Newtonian frame of mind that Hungry Paul considered his next move. Having already gone back to the house once, he was certainly not minded to retrace his steps a second time. It was also clear that he could neither walk to the hospital and poison the workforce of St Matthew's ward nor arrive empty-handed after his mother had specifically said that he would bring in the sweets the next time he was in.

Hungry Paul, who was ordinarily a phlegmatic soul—slow to anger or bear a grudge—felt a loss of equilibrium. He was of course clear in his own mind that no blame of any sort attached to his dear mother, who was kind and thoughtful in motivation and deed in this case. His ire, his bewilderment, his sense of injustice, was directed towards the not-so-supermarket (as he sarcastically dubbed it to himself) where his mother had bought the tin of Roses in the first place. This corporate monster was clearly indifferent to the potentially catastrophic consequences that might befall the dedicated nursing staff who walked the wards of the nation's hospitals to care for its weakest and most vulnerable citizens. Hungry Paul (on behalf of his mother) wanted those brave nurses to be able to indulge in the modest luxury of a Toffee Barrel or a Caramel Dream without finding themselves doubled over one of Armitage Shanks' best pieces of affordable porcelain. The very thought of it was enough to unleash dark Shakespearian moods within even the most stable of temperaments. Hungry Paul was a man who normally stood as a weir, letting the world wash over and through him, but on this occasion he felt the pedantic sanctimony of one who is offended on others' behalf.

As he walked by the supermarket, disgusted by the empty customer service promises braying from the advertising hoardings in the car park, he stood and confronted the (admittedly innocent) building with a sense of destiny. He walked into the supermarket and accosted the first operative he encountered, but she brushed him off by saying she was going on her break. A second operative said she was with another customer, which Hungry Paul immediately recognised as a deflecting ploy.

Sensing that he would make better headway with a member of his own sex, he found one of the retail man-children that he often saw around the store. 'I'd like to make a complaint about this tin of Roses,' he said authoritatively, even rolling his Rs for some reason.

'Eh, I'm on tissues and paper towels. You need to go to confeckshunree,' he said, waving his hand vaguely yonder.

Hungry Paul, not wishing to unload prematurely on the wrong target, overlooked the limited helpfulness of the answer and made his businesslike way to said aisle. There he found another man-child unloading a trolley of Easter eggs, stabbing the wholesaler's plastic wrapping with the tip of his ballpoint pen.

'Excuse me. I'd like to make a complaint about this tin of Roses.'

'Eh. Okay. I'm not sure what the story is with that.'

'Well it's more than a year out of date. What do you think of that?'

'You can swap it for another one there,' he offered with instant capitulation.

'It's not just the sweets: it's the *principle*,' said Hungry Paul, emphasising the last word to indicate that there was very much a bigger picture here.

'Do you want to, like, talk to a manager?'

'Please. Indeed.'

The man-child disappeared behind the strange plastic doors that only supermarkets seem to use. He was gone quite some time. A woman who had been standing nearby, and who obviously had a keen sense of impending drama, approached the scene. She was wearing what looked like a self-knitted jumper and beret. Her trolley had several items of confectionery in it already, thereby establishing that she potentially had *locus standi* in what was about to unfold. 'What happened, love?'

'I bought this as a thoughtful gift for the kind nurses at the hospital and their suffering patients, or rather my mother did, only to notice that it is over a year out of date! I couldn't believe it. Something has to be done,' explained Hungry Paul.

'You're dead right love. That could have been a disaster. They don't give a damn here. Not. A. Damn,' replied the woman.

Another kindred soul, a heavy-set middle-aged woman who was wearing a tracksuit—Hungry Paul assumed she was a competitor in the shot putt or one of the other sports where it's an advantage to be stocky—added her voice to the chorus. 'I bet half the stuff here is gone off. They feed you anything. I'd never check the dates on chocolate. Bread or milk you'd have a look, but I'd never think of looking at sweets.'

'Yes, you did well to spot it,' added the self-knitted woman, though expressing through her body language that she was a different class of chocolate eater from the shot-putter.

The man-child returned beside what looked like a football pundit: a man in an ill-fitting suit with a gelled side parting, who looked like he used to be one of the lads when he was younger.

'Are you the man with the Roses? I'm the duty manager. How can I help you sir?' he asked.

'I bought these Roses, or rather my mother bought these Roses, as a thoughtful gift for the kind people at the hospital only to find that they are over a year out of date. The nurses and patients—some of whom already have stomach and digestion complaints—could have suffered untold miseries because of a moment of thoughtfulness gone wrong, through no fault of my own or my mother's I might add.'

'I bought bread here once, which was mouldy when I opened it at home,' chipped in the self-knitted woman.

'Yeah, I once bought a multi-pack of beer and when I opened it one of the cans was missing,' added the shot-putter with an example that was not quite on point.

'Are you sure you bought them here? Have you got the receipt?' asked the duty manager.

'Of course I'm sure. My mother has been shopping here for years. She never goes anywhere else. If it's evidence you want, we can produce that in court!' added Hungry Paul with a flourish to nods all round him. A small posse of busybodies had started to assemble, some of whom were disapproving facially to an oppressive extent.

'And have you actually eaten any of the sweets? Do they taste off? I mean sometimes these things are good even past their date, you know, the dates can be more of a guideline in some cases,' said the duty manager.

'Tasted them? Imagine if I had! I'd be writhing around on my bathroom floor, in a fever, clutching the bowl for dear life,' replied Hungry Paul, with uncalled-for vividness.

The posse was now circling tighter, as Hungry Paul started addressing his points to them directly, showing a new-found political aptitude. The self-knitted lady was also nodding and making eye contact with the rabble, adopting the role of chief witness in the scene.

'Do you mind if I taste one, just to see whether they're alright?' asked the duty manager.

'Be my guest,' answered Hungry Paul, sensing that a denouement was imminent.

The duty manager reached for the tin. Hungry Paul turned towards the rabble in preparation for their reaction.

The duty manager expected to see a box of sweets that were perfectly fine and edible, but he was wrong.

Hungry Paul expected to see sweets that were mushy and gone off, but he was wrong also.

The posse expected an ending and a resolution, which is what they surely got.

The duty manager prised the lid off, slowly popping around the rim.

Inside, it could be seen plainly that the tin was stuffed to the brim, not with chocolates in a state of perfection or deterioration or any stage in between, but with all of Helen's sewing stuff. The shot-putter burst out a braying laugh in which a shower of spit rained on Hungry Paul's jacket.

There were some other giggles, but mostly the posse broke up in hurried dismissal of Hungry Paul as an egregious timewaster. The self-knitted lady abandoned him in a sudden undoing of what she had only just started, a trick any knitter would know.

For one seemingly eternal moment, Hungry Paul stood still, feeling strangely out of body.

'Well, it seems that it's an honest mistake,' offered the duty manager nobly. Under normal circumstances, he might have felt triumphant at exposing a petty scam. However, the drained look on Hungry Paul's face, his frozen expression, his mouth half-moving without any sound, all told him that he was dealing with a man beset by tragicomedy.

'No hard feelings. Glad no harm was done,' said the duty manager cheerfully. 'Tell you what, why don't you take an Easter egg home? As a goodwill gesture from the shop. Here's a Buttons one. Hope to see you back again soon.' And with that the duty manager disappeared through the strange plastic doors.

Hungry Paul stood there at his most alone under the flickering tube lighting, holding a Buttons Easter egg and a tin of sewing stuff, while the man-child resumed stabbing the clear plastic with his pen.

Hungry Paul doesn't remember much about what he said next, how he left the store, or how he dreamed his way through the long walk home.

As he arrived back at the house, leaving his Easter egg, the tin and his keys beside the letters on the hall table, he slunk in to the back room where Helen, with her roots done, had his suit trousers out on the back of the chair. 'How are things love? How did you get on at the hospital?'

'I didn't get to go in the end. I'll go over at the weekend,' he answered meekly.

'Oh, okay. Don't forget to bring the sweets. Sorry for heading off without telling you where they were, but I had driven half way to the hairdressers before I realised I had them in the boot.'

'Not to worry. Probably for the best.'

'I was just going to take up your wedding trousers, but I can't find my sewing box,' said Helen.

'It's on the hall table.'

'Oh, great. I must have walked right past it. God bless your eyesight.'

Hungry Paul sat slumped in the sitting room and stayed there for most of the evening, catatonic with failure and looking out of the front window as car after car ran over a lost glove on the road.

Chapter 10: FILLING THE WEEKEND

That Saturday Grace's body woke up according to its week-day discipline. It was used to getting up early even when it needed rest and even when Grace willed it to decommission and go back to sleep at nine-minute snooze alarm intervals. She had gone for a drink with the work crowd the night before and, while she didn't stay out too late, she had missed dinner and fell into bed hungry, forgetting to ring Andrew at his hotel in Amsterdam as she had promised. There were no missed calls on her phone the next morning.

She got up slowly and walked around the house opening all the curtains and windows, letting the light in, the stale air out, and generally bringing the place back to life after it had been barely lived in during a week of long hours.

After making her way downstairs in her pyjamas, Grace carried the hunger from the day before into the kitchen and had a long, frank look at the shelves, which were in a state of neglected depletion. Unwilling and unready to break her cosy solitude, she decided against a trip to the shops, and instead sat at the kitchen table and took an improvised breakfast of tea (no coffee left), Weetabix (no granola left) and cracker bread (no bagels left), reading the news on her phone.

It was a bright, sunny morning, the good weather bringing its own pressure to make something of it. Grace would have really preferred an overcast day. A day of TV. A day of floating from one nothing to the next. The phone call to Andrew was hanging over her, as was the feeling of guilt at her lack of enthusiasm for ringing him. With the wedding approaching, she had started to feel pressure to be in love and sound in love when talking to him. Of course she did love him, but she just wanted to get back to the love being ordinary, everyday and natural, instead of the Disney love that she felt a bride was supposed to project to the world. The truth was, she just wanted him home to share her Plan B breakfast in silence and to let her sit there and watch a rubbish movie while he did something else in the background. That's what she really loved about him: his ability to ignore her and leave her alone until she was ready to include him and then, but only then, could she chat and laugh and goof off as part of a couple.

For the first time in weeks, the calendar was free of plans and arrangements. She hadn't had time to organise anything and had secretly looked forward to a quiet weekend, but now that it was here, it seemed to yawn in front of her. The unstructured easiness she had hoped for had turned into plain old restlessness. The house needed sorting out, but she had already worked too hard this week. Her body felt like it needed a run or a swim, but she felt lazy and was struggling to find first gear. The idea of kicking back with a vacuous film or book appealed to her, but she had no concentration and all the options bored her. Nor had she any appetite for galleries, cinemas, farmers' markets or whatever outdoor community-building thing was on in town that weekend.

In the past, she would have sat reading peacefully on the rug in the front room in Parley View, her dad and Hungry Paul shouting up and down the stairs to each other, asking where some random household item was and guessing its possible location at the top of their voices. After having heard enough, her mother would shout in the correct answer from the garden where she would be busy doing the work she loved. Grace missed being the quiet person in a busy house.

She sent Andrew a quick text, apologising for not phoning and saying that she was just going out and would ring him later.

Two kisses. G. Then she sat back into the couch and started picking a callous off the knuckle of her little toe, which fascinated her in its grotesqueness.

Her phone buzzed and a short text came in from Andrew:

> *Sorry, can't talk. Am in a cheese museum on a tour.*
> *Part of the organised fun. This is what I turn into*
> *when you're not here. XX A*

She gave a relieved little chuckle. Andrew had read, and read into, her text and understood her need for a little down payment of affection. Having broken her first smile of the day, she flicked the flake of calloused skin into the fireplace and rang her mum who said yes, of course, call over later after she got back from visiting at the hospital. With a plan now made, the day's long hours seemed to contract, so Grace took out the wedding to-do list and made a start on the million and one things that flooded her mind.

As Helen got off the phone, she again called up to Hungry Paul from downstairs that he needed to get a move on. Hungry Paul, who lacked the coordination to yell back and get dressed at the same time, paused the buttoning of his jeans, having already had to restart the task after matching the buttons to the corresponding holes and finding that he had one button left over. Helen had started to notice that he was going cold on the idea of visiting at the hospital after he had arrived home the other evening, his mission with the Roses unfulfilled. She didn't want to leave an extended interval before the next visit, which would only inspire him to excuses. For his part, and as so often happens, his disappointment about the Roses tin did not survive a night's sleep and he was even able to see the funny side to his mistake, though not to the extent that he felt ready to share the vignette with his mother, in case it was added to the library of family folklore where his past experiences were somewhat overrepresented.

The two of them left together in Helen's small Fiat Punto. Hungry Paul had the unusual habit of sitting in the back, behind Helen, even when it was just the two of them in the car and even though it made him look like a third world dictator and Helen his chauffeuse. He wasn't a fan of speed and riding up front just reminded him that their bodies were hurtling through the air at the speed limit. He also liked to drive with the window open in all weathers. When he was a child he was always baffled as to why marathon runners never seemed to run out of air, and had wondered how much air a person needed to run a marathon anyway—sacks and sacks of it, presumably. When he asked his father, Peter suggested that he should see how much air he could take in during long car journeys, which is a creative way of keeping a young boy quiet for a long time. Helen usually liked to have a chat while driving, but with Hungry Paul she tended to let him have his way and enjoy the incoming breeze without interruptions.

When they arrived at the hospital they reported to the duty nurse and Hungry Paul handed over the tin of Roses, explaining that they were for the nurses rather than the patients. The nurse thanked him for his thoughtfulness but put the tin away in an empty filing cabinet, explaining that the girls on the ward were trying to stay off sweets and get in shape during Lent.

The ward to which they were going was full of people who didn't look especially sick, except for the fact that they were all older ladies in pyjamas. The first patient they approached told them to 'go away' using vernacular language, and that she didn't want any 'religious bitch' touching her, apparently mistaking Helen for the Eucharistic Minister who came around to give out communion to those who wanted it.

The second woman was asleep and had a drip connected to her arm. Her skin was pale and her thinning white hair was like duvet stuffing. Helen lifted up the crossword that was open on the woman's lap, put the lid back on the pen and set it all down on the locker beside her, which had several cards and kids' drawings on it. She thought it was nice that such a fragile, sick lady had people who cared about her.

The third lady was texting on her phone and was wearing bright red trapezoid glasses. She had on a pair of pink silk pyjamas, with a pattern of herons and pagodas on it.

'Oh, hello. Are you bringing me down for the scan? I thought it wasn't until this evening?' the woman asked.

'No, actually. We're just volunteers, here to visit anyone who fancies a chat. Would you like us to sit down for a bit?' asked Helen.

'Of course. Make yourselves at home. There's only one chair, so you'll have to sit on the bed if you don't mind, love,' she said, addressing Hungry Paul, who sat near her exposed feet with toes that looked like tree roots.

'Aren't you all very good, visiting sick people stuck in here? It's great to have people like you in the world. My kids are all grown up, probably his age,' she said, pointing to Hungry Paul, 'but they're all away: London, Sydney, and one still travelling, not sure what he wants to do. I get texts and Skypes—my kids emigrating has brought me into the twenty-first century—but it's not the same as having them near you. Have you any kids yourself?' she asked Helen.

'I do actually, and I'm lucky they're still close by. This fine young specimen is my son,' Hungry Paul waved by way of introduction, 'and I have a daughter getting married at Easter. I'm Helen by the way.'

'Nice to meet you. I'm Barbara, or Bar; just not Babs or Barbie please. Easter wedding? I didn't think they allowed that. In the church I mean, although who gets married in a church these days? She's probably doing it in a nice hotel or something. Doesn't matter where it is, so long as they love each other.'

'Actually it is in a church,' said Helen, 'Although Grace is not religious, so I'm not sure why they're taking the trouble. The wedding is on Easter Monday, which they say is fine. We'll probably get Easter eggs with our meal. But enough about us: how long have you been in here, Barbara?' Helen was following the golden rule and asking the patient about themselves.

'Oh, let me think,' said Barbara, 'Since Wednesday and then I have to stay in for another day once I have had the scan, which is hopefully today. I don't mind it too much, but my back gets sore in the bed, and all these ladies like to listen to the TV up loud, which isn't really my thing. I try and get up for walks, to the shop or out into the sensory garden, but the day drags. All my life I wanted some downtime to read books and just relax, and now I'm here I can't settle,' she said. 'He doesn't talk much, your son, does he?'

'You're a good listener though aren't you?' said Helen, nodding her head to the side as if to say to Hungry Paul: 'C'mon, get on with it.'

'I like your glasses—are they designer?' he asked.

'Oh these. I got them at the optometry college—they design them whatever way you want and it only costs a fraction of the usual price. I designed them myself. I wanted to look like an architect, but I think I'm too fat and old to pull it off—you need to be a skinnymalink in a black polo neck for that sort of thing.'

'You must make some nice plans for when you leave here— maybe give yourself a night away in a nice hotel or go to a spa or something,' said Helen, showing her experience by trying to get the patient to make plans, look forward to things.

'I'm not so much into hotels since my husband died,' said Barbara, 'That was five years ago, my God, that's flown. But hotels are for couples really. No point sleeping in a big posh bed by yourself. I might do some shopping, though. Being here these past few days has made me realise that all my pyjamas and stuff are in rag order.'

'That set is nice. It looks Chinesey,' said Helen.

'I like the heron on it,' added Hungry Paul, who always suffered from writer's block when it came to small talk.

'Tom gave me these. My husband. We were in Japan at the time and he was sick of seeing me wearing his pyjamas, so he bought me this pair. I like the way that they look, but they're too light and keep slipping down—I don't want to give the old geezers on the corridor a heart condition.'

'What ages are your kids?' asked Helen.

'Linda is the eldest, she's thirty-five and is in Australia. She's a vet and she married a guy who runs his own business—he does sound at concerts and things. I've been out there to see them. The house is huge but I suppose there's no shortage of space in Australia. Joyce is thirty-two and is in London; works for a bank, but not a bank you've heard of. Joyce was always a hard worker. Ben is travelling the world—he's just turned thirty. He'd never been anywhere exotic, but then he went on a gap year and stayed on travelling when his friends came back. I'd say he's met a girl, though he tells me nothing. You're lucky to still have yours nearby. I hated them all going but you know young people, they all want to travel and you can't stop them. What do yours do?' she asked.

'I'm a postman. A casual postman. Fill in for sick days, that sort of thing,' answered Hungry Paul, speaking for himself.

'Ah, that's nice. Lots of fresh air and not too many dogs I hope.'

'If there's a dangerous dog in the garden you just write *dog-at-large* on the letter and send it back to the depot. The real problem is with the dogs roaming the street who like to chase after the bike.'

'What do you do with those?' asked Barbara.

'Pedal faster,' answered Hungry Paul, getting a laugh without meaning to be funny.

'And my daughter Grace works for a big American company,

though we're never 100 per cent sure what she does. She's explained it loads of times. It's something to do with computers, but she's not working on the computers themselves; logistics and project management are involved. The main point is that when you invite her over she's often late or gets interrupted by her phone. We're used to it, but I think she works too hard. Those companies expect you to give everything to your job.'

'And is your husband still hale and healthy?' asked Barbara.

'Yes, thank God. He's retired now. Peter is his name,' said Helen, sensing some sensitivity in the question.

'It's great to be able to retire together. Tom and I had loads of plans, but there are no promises in life. What I learned is that everyone in your life has an invisible number on their foreheads, which represents the number of times you will see them again. It might be zero or one, or it could be a thousand, but it's a number. We don't have unlimited time with people. I don't mean that in a morbid way. It's a lesson for us to appreciate people while we can. Don't put people off. Don't think you can make up the time later. I miss him terribly, but we always made time for each other. We travelled. We went to things. We spent lots and lots of time looking at each other's faces, so even though I miss him every day, I know I made the most of my time with him.'

'I couldn't agree more Barbara. Is there anything we can do for you before we go? Time's nearly up I'm afraid and we'll have to leave you to it,' said Helen.

'Nothing at all, thanks Helen. It was so good of you to come. Hopefully, I'll be gone home by the time you're next in, but it was a pleasure to meet you—and you too, young man. Do your best to keep the girls at bay so you can look after your mother,' said Barbara, winking at Helen.

'Women are usually respectful of my need for distance without being reminded,' he answered.

Helen noticed that the old lady with the crossword in the second bed was now awake and two young kids were climbing on her bedside chair, giving her rushed, loud updates on their lives, while their parents fixed up the pillows and de-cluttered the locker area.

As they left the room, the first lady shouted 'religious bitch!' after Helen.

When they got home, Grace was already there, lying back on the couch with her head on Peter's lap, being a daddy's girl.

'Hey there. How did you get on? No fatalities I hope?' said Grace, as Hungry Paul came over and gave her a kiss on the cheek.

'No. They only let us near the healthy ones. It wasn't too bad,' he answered.

'He was great. I think older people like you. You're a good listener,' said Helen. 'What are you two up to, lounging around like that?'

'I'm helping Dad with his wedding speech. Telling him all about my wonderful character traits and Andrew's deep, deep flaws. Although I am concerned that it might get a bit risqué in places—you know Dad and his sense of humour.'

'I'll be as dignified as I always am,' answered Peter in his own defence.

For the first time in ages, the four of them spent an evening together, sitting around, chatting and cooking. They shared a big mixum-gatherum of a dinner, before sitting down to watch *The Remorseful Day*, the final Inspector Morse episode. It was Grace and Helen's favourite, which they had watched together about half a dozen times over the years.

At the end of the night, even though it wasn't that late and even though her house wasn't that far away, Grace decided to stay over with her happy family and sleep in her old room. And there, wearing a pair of pyjamas borrowed from her mother, she rang Andrew, delighted to hear his voice as she whispered and giggled in her childhood bed, the first single bed she'd slept in in years.

Chapter 11: SHELLEY

It was as true for Leonard as it is for the rest of us, that we can plan and calculate as much as we like, but romance never enters our lives on terms of our own choosing.

Leonard had spent the weekend getting ready. He had been clothes shopping for the second time in a week and despite the indecision that comes with being early-middle-aged and therefore somewhat 'between looks'—too old for casual, too young for daytime formal—he had managed to update his wardrobe, albeit by buying different versions of the same jumper and jeans combination. While his look would not stand out as particularly adventurous or interesting, he would at least benefit from the confidence that comes from knowing that the forces of nature are generally on the side of those who try something new. Over the weekend he had run through a range of conversation openers and had thought ahead to how Shelley might respond and what sort of casual witticism would go down well in counter-response, though being careful not to come across as too smart-alecky or world weary. He liked her positivity and energy and wanted to try and match it.

When he got to his office building on Monday morning he went to the bathroom to stare at himself for one last practice at the right facial expressions before stepping into the ring. He had wanted to splash water on his face, but got it all wrong and ended up cupping water and throwing it down his front like a toddler. With few other options, he got down on his knees to dry off his chest with the hand dryer and then decided to let the warm air blow over his face as he shook his head gently from side to side, forgetting where he was. When the dryer stopped there was a young guy standing beside him with a beard and a paisley pyjama top, waiting to dry his hands, with his crotch at Leonard's eye level.

Leonard pressed the button for the lift with his hands still soaking. As the door opened, he could see Shelley at the back corner, wearing her cycling helmet and hemmed in by the other rush hour lift passengers. He gave her a wave with his wet hands, which just looked sweaty, and stepped into the lift. She gave a friendly little 'isn't this weird' smile back to him. The doors kept trying to close, but the lift was too full and all eyes were on him to step back out. Initially he tried to tough it out and press the button to close the doors, but there was nothing doing. They shuddered repeatedly, each time stalling and refusing to shut. And of all moments, that had to be the time when Leonard's phone went off and revealed that he was the last person in the world still using the Crazy Frog ringtone, which he had meant to change ages ago but hadn't got around to it. At first he tried to ignore it, but it seemed to go on forever. Instead of the voicemail kicking in, the person just kept on trying again and again. The deadlock was broken by the muffled voice of a man who seemed to have Leonard's shoulder in his mouth, who said 'Do you want to get that?'

'Oh really, is that me? Oh, of course. Excuse me for a moment folks,' said Leonard as he let himself out of the lift in a way that implied that he would be missed. Shelley tried to wave at him but her arms were trapped. As he stepped out, the doors closed easily, resolving once and for all who had been at fault.

He answered the call and killed off the Crazy Frog's inane revving.

'Leonard, hi, it's me,' said Hungry Paul. 'Guess what?'

'What?' replied Leonard with barely contained exasperation.

'I got through the competition. My sign-off phrase has been shortlisted by the Chamber of Commerce. I have to go to a prize-giving and everything. Isn't that exciting? I was just starting my shift when our local postman came across to me and got me to sign for a registered letter in my own name. I've never won anything. I came straight home to tell my folks and thought I'd ring you too before I head back out and do my route.'

Leonard's annoyance softened when he heard how Hungry Paul had thought to include him among the first to hear the news. If ever there was a measure of their mutual fondness, it was the enthusiasm with which good news was shared between them, each friend assured of the good wishes of the other. 'It's great news old pal. I'm delighted for you. Can we come to the prize-giving?'

'I don't see why not. We could wear our wedding suits maybe. I know you're busy at work, so I won't delay. Best of luck with your seductress today.'

'Okay, talk to you later. Oh, what phrase did you send in, by the way?'

'Ah, you'll have to come to the prize-giving to find out. I'll leave the big reveal until then,' he replied.

Leonard walked up the stairs to his own floor, finding himself short of breath. While others spent their evenings at the gym or in boxercise, he spent his playing board games and it showed in his general lack of fitness. When he got to his desk there was a Post-it stuck to his screen, written in the prettiest curlicue handwriting: *'Need any fire advice?'*

He set aside his general disapproval of affixing any type of adhesive to touch screens, plucked it off with a sense of possibility, and popped it into the back section of his wallet where he kept his receipts. He tried to look over to her desk, but it was blocked by a temporary partition that was used both as a social noticeboard and as a gallery of warnings about printing things unnecessarily.

He drummed his fingers on his desk. Was this it? Was this

the moment? Was this a signal, an invitation, or had she simply been left a message about his earlier contrived fire safety request and was following up like any dutiful fire warden? His stomach dropped like a lift falling through a lift shaft. His adrenal glands were revving like the Crazy Frog. Do something, do something, do something, he repeated to himself.

He couldn't walk over to her desk again could he? Her workmates would think he was a weirdo to keep showing up like that. What if he set off the fire alarm—was that a great idea or a terrible one? Was there a fine for setting it off mischievously, like pulling the cord on the train? Would it just make her mad at him? What if he moseyed over to the ol' notice board, to give off the appearance of someone with a full social calendar, just swinging by to see what's cooking for the month ahead?

This was where he always struggled. On the rare occasions over the years when he had started to connect with a girl he could never quite figure out how to jump the canyon between being a nice guy and making romantic advances. He was always terrified of getting it all wrong and coming across as some letch whose friendliness was a façade to conceal a calculating carnal monster. His weakness had always been that he was not a closer; he had let every half chance slip away from him. For a man who suffered from indecision over the smallest things—including walking out of the Cineplex because of his inability to choose between three films, all of which he wanted to see—deciding his next romantic move was a Homeric struggle. All his plans and preparations came to nothing. Like a striker who dries up on Cup Final day, or a tennis player who double faults on the cusp of their first Grand Slam, Leonard froze under the pressure to act.

But it is an underappreciated fact about encyclopaedia writers that even though they might never have rescued a mammoth from a tar pit, or captained a record-breaking maglev, it is impossible for them to remain unaffected by the bravery they depict every day. Leonard turned on his computer, but instead of entering the correct password (H1L30nard6!) he entered three random incorrect passwords and locked himself out. Straight away he picked up the phone and rang the helpdesk, who was Greg, sitting across the office, just a couple of Yucca plants away from Shelley's pod of four.

'Hi Greg. Leonard here.'

'Lenny baby. Laughing Len. Len will I see you again. What can I do you for?"

'I've locked myself out. Can you get me back in—I can call over if that's easier?' suggested Leonard.

'No need, my man, I should be able to do it from here—'

But Leonard had already hung up, left his desk and was marching over to Greg before he could say another word. As he arrived, he gave a friendly hello to Shelley who was on the phone, but mercifully alone in her four-person pod.

'Hi Greg. I thought it best to come over. Am just under a bit of pressure. Me and my fat fingers. Just need the password reset. Thanks. I know you're busy.'

Greg had been halfway through buttering a demi-baguette, and had just opened a tin of tuna that he was going to fill it with. It was not even 9am.

'Okey dokey. This will take just one minutae. Take a load off, compadre,' said Greg, unable to complete one conventional sentence.

Leonard pointed to an empty desk in Shelley's pod with a 'May I?' look on his face. Shelley made the 'Okay' sign with her fingers. She brought her phone call to a conclusion, saying 'No problem. Yes indeed. The supervisor will call you back this afternoon.'

'Another happy customer?' asked Leonard.

'People are already mad and upset by the time they get through to me. I'm at the nothing-can-be-done stage, so I really just give them listening therapy. So c'mere, I hear you have been converted to the merits of fire safety. Welcome aboard,' said Shelley.

'Oh, you mean my query the other day. No biggie,' said Leonard, using an expression he had never contemplated using in his life up to now. 'It's just that my phone charger gets hot if I leave it on and I didn't want to create any trouble for you. Or the other fire wardens I mean,' answered Leonard meekly.

'Google wasn't working then?'

'I tried looking it up but I just wanted to check there wasn't anything I was missing from a company protocol point of view. Et cetera, et cetera,' he improvised.

'I would say, in my professional fire warden opinion, don't leave it plugged in overnight. It's bad for the environment.'

'Absolutely. I use the green bin all the time. I'm always stuffing paper into it,' answered Leonard, 'although I'm also trying to reduce the amount I print,' he added, pointing to the warnings on the notice board.

Shelley gave a little laugh and decided to stop winding him up. 'I have a favour to ask of you, actually.'

Anything, anything, anything, he thought.

'Really? Nothing too compromising I hope?' he asked.

'No. Not really. Could you sign these for me? They're a bedtime favourite in our house.' She took out some children's encyclopaedias from the *Facts at My Fingertips* series, all credited to Mark Baxter, BEd, which Leonard had ghost-written. She held up three books on the human body, birds and capital cities, each of them with curly edges and spines wrinkled from reading and rereading.

'Of course. I have never been asked for an autograph before. This is nice.' He started flicking through them for the first time since they were published. She was right: they were good. Full of punchy little descriptions and stuffed with enthusiasm.

'How about a deal? If I sign these for you, would you possibly consider meeting me for lunch in the park today, unless you have plans, in which case that's fine. I mean, no offence taken and I'll still sign the books for you, but if you're free and you'd like to do it, then maybe lunch would be nice, and if it doesn't suit you today then maybe some other day or even next week, or after Easter, I mean I'm pretty easy either way. It's my treat, although if we're going to the park we could get a takeaway sandwich, or maybe you bring in your lunch, you know, salad or something. Maybe, think about it and let me know what suits.' Leonard paused for breath and to make sure he didn't just keep babbling forever.

'That would be lovely. I'm free today as it happens, though I have to be gone by two if that's okay,' answered Shelley.

'Great. Of course, you head whenever. Great, great, great,' said Leonard, unable to conceal a smile as relief swept through his body.

'Oh, the books. Who should I make them out to?' asked Leonard, going through the pretence of asking officially for the name he already knew.

'To Patrick, please,' asked Shelley.

'Em, okay. Patrick it is.'

Who the hell is Patrick? thought Leonard.

'He's my son. He's seven. We read your books all the time. Well, he reads them and then reads them to me. He couldn't believe it when I told him the guy who writes them works in my office. By the way, I just told him you were Mark Baxter BEd, so maybe best to sign it as him.'

'Right' answered Leonard, winded and wondering what was going on.

'Just kidding, sign your own name! God, wouldn't that be terrible to ask you to pretend to be that other faker. Honestly. My name is Shelley by the way. Pleased to meet you.'

She extended her hand in mock formality as if offering it for a kiss. Leonard hesitated about whether she actually expected him to kiss it, which he would have done, but then she laughed again and took it back.

'I'm Leonard. Not Mark. No BEd. So, I suppose I'll just sign these then. Let's see, I had better do a little message, lemme think.'

He signed the books to Patrick and gave them back.

'Here's your new password, Lenster,' said Greg, as he came over and handed Leonard a Post-it with *MOnkeyc0ck!* on it.

'Okay. Thanks Greg. Thanks Shelley. See you at one. I'll pick you up here if that's okay?'

'Of course. One at the pod. Thanks for the autographs. Patrick will be delighted.'

Leonard walked back to his desk and collapsed. Never had he made such progress in his love life in such a short period. It had taken a lot out of him. How was he supposed to find the energy for round two at lunch time?

And Patrick? Well, that explained the half days and the rushing off at 2pm. A girl with a son. He hadn't bargained for that. What if it all worked out? He could be a parent in a matter of weeks. This was all going very fast. Was the real father still on the scene? Was Shelley really interested in him, or was she just looking for someone who would get on with Patrick? It's a big leap from writing encyclopaedias to raising a child, at least without some intermediate stages in between. Okay: calm down, Leonard. One step at a time. Stay in the moment.

Leonard picked Shelley up at her desk at exactly one and offered to carry her bags for her. Like all people who cycle to work she carried far too much stuff and had even more crap under her desk. He tried to think of somewhere trendy to grab a sandwich that they could then eat in the park, already pretending to be someone a little different, as people tend to do in the early days. He chose a hipster sandwich bar called Bite Me! There was a long queue, with several bearded young men ahead, wearing paisley pyjama tops and ordering veggie specials.

'No shortage of vegetarians, that's for sure. No wonder they can fit into those jeans. Are those blokes wearing women's jeans? Good God!' said Leonard, slightly forgetting himself.

Shelley just smiled.

They reached the top of the queue, where a girl with *Cutie* tattooed on her neck waited to take their order.

'Let me see, I'll have the Meat Feast please,' said Leonard, ordering something which was basically a full barnyard in a wrap, although with hummus, inevitably. 'And what would you like Shelley? My treat.'

'Thanks. I'll have the veggie special,' she said, nudging Leonard, 'And I should also confess that I am wearing women's jeans—hope that's okay?'

Leonard apologised for the veggie incorrectness.

'I didn't mean anything by it. Sorry. Does it bother you if I eat meat?'

'You're fine,' she answered, 'I'm not sensitive about things like that. Why don't we go find a bench and maybe ask each other loads of searching personal questions?' she asked.

'Not too searching I hope. I'll start wishing I had some interesting secrets to tell,' he answered.

They chatted on the way and Leonard did pretty okay. His initial awkwardness actually teed up some banter between them, and he was happy playing the straight man to her goofy sense of humour, which he was starting to get the hang of. They found a little bench near the duck pond, though there were no ducks on it, just some moorhens and a couple of sleeping swans.

'Wanna bite?' she offered.

'No thanks. I don't suppose there's much point in offering you a bite of mine?'

'Indeed.'

'Although all the animals in this wrap are, or were, vegetarian, so that's a halfway house maybe?' he said.

'Nice to know there are no carnivores in it. No lions or tigers.' Shelley looked at the birds on the pond. 'Should we throw them some bread or wrap or something?'

'Best not to. There's no nutrition in it and it's not good for them,' he answered.

'Of course. I must remember you're Mr Encyclopaedia. You could probably tell me where they come from and how big their eggs are and everything. Go on. Tell me something I've never heard before.' She was actually excited.

'Let me think. How about that they'd actually prefer some defrosted frozen peas?'

'Ah!' she laughed, or rather hooted. 'I've got some of those! They're in my bag. Actually it's a mix of frozen veg. I bought them on the way to work and was going to cook them at home. How about we throw some in?' She reached into her bag and rooted around a bit, taking out a few things in order to find the veg: goat's milk, Quorn burgers, soya yoghurts and green lentils.

'If you like. What about your dinner?'

'Never mind. Patrick hates vegetables. He'll be delighted with sausage and beans.'

So they stood at the pond and started scattering the food. The carrots were not fully defrosted and sank; the peas and corn floated and were picked off. Shelley's sense of fairness came out as she weighted her throws towards the less pushy birds. After the bag was empty, she crumpled it up and asked Leonard straight out, while handing him a cupcake: 'So, is this just a lunch or a getting to know you or what?'

'I'm not sure what you'd call it. I'd certainly like to get to know you. If that's okay, I mean. I'm not writing an encyclopaedia about you or anything. I'm not just good at mining for facts. I'm also happy to feed vegetables to birds or just hang out.'

They started walking as they chatted, taking the edge off the intensity of her question. He told her his age, that he had grown up nearby, that he was an only child and then finally, in what seemed like a fitting detail to explain where his life was at just then, that his mother had passed away a few weeks before.

'Oh, I'm so sorry, Leonard.'

The first time she had said his name.

'You must still be grieving. That's so sad. You must really miss her.'

For Leonard, this was the first time he had really had a conversation about the whole thing. That he was having it on his first date with a girl he really liked was either a really bad sign or a really good one.

'I do miss her. I do,' he said, strangely unable to make light of it.

'Let me see.' Shelley took up the reins of the conversation. 'I'm twenty-seven, on the way to twenty-eight. I don't like my job or the customers, but I like the people I work with. I started art college but didn't finish it. I have a son, Patrick, who's seven. Feel free to feel weird about that. No "biggie" as you might say. He's about yea big, with curly auburn hair, green eyes and Star Wars glasses. As he says about himself, he has "a big imagination and a big heart," which is the truest thing I have ever heard. His father is not on the scene—let's just get that out of the way. I'd like to go back to art college someday, but for now I still draw for fun, though I have sort of plateaued in terms of my talent. I like noisy music but I like it to have good lyrics. Not necessarily clever lyrics, just lyrics that have some spirit.'

The hour until two o'clock when, as she put it, she would turn into a pumpkin, seemed like the shortest hour of Leonard's life. They chatted and chatted in what, if he wasn't mistaken, seemed like the start of something. Their conversation, though not smooth, seemed to bounce back from slow patches and find its rhythm easily. They didn't link arms or hold hands, but they did seem to walk quite close to one another and their elbows brushed without clumsiness several times. He carried her bag and she was the more confident of the two of them. As the time wore on, and ran out, Leonard had not only abandoned his plans and contrivances, but had forgotten he ever had them. He walked her back to her bike with the time approaching two.

'So,' she said.

'So, la, ti, do,' Leonard sang, falling off his tippy toes at the high note, hardly realising he was doing an impression of Shelley's sense of humour. Making her laugh was his new favourite thing.

'So, Mr Encyclopaedia, I've got to go.'

'Yes, of course. How do you think it went?' he blurted.

She laughed a little snot bubble out of her nose and immediately covered it up with her gloved hand.

'Ah, that's classic.' She did a sigh of recovery from laughing. 'It was really nice. Thank you.'

His move.

'Right then. Could we maybe meet up again? Another lunch or something?' he suggested.

'You men. Always thinking ahead to your next Meat Feast. I am free Thursdays, so we could do an evening thing if that's what you meant.'

'Great, great. I just wasn't sure how you were fixed with your son and everything. That's great. Yeah, Thursday is free for me.' As was every other night. 'How about I meet you in town at the clock tower at about, what, eight?' he suggested.

'Ah, the clock tower. You old romantic. Okay. See you then. I'll let you choose the activity. See if you can blow my mind with something.'

'Yes. Okay. Will do.' Hmmm, he thought.

'See you there and then.'

Was he supposed to try and kiss her, peck her on the cheek or something? What to do? What to do? What to do?

He leaned forward awkwardly as she was putting her helmet on and sort of hugged her platonically to the side, at her shoulder.

'Woah, Casanova. Easy with the judo moves. Here,' and she pecked him on the cheek instructively. It was a subtle way of establishing what they had both guessed, which is that she knew a bit more about that kind of thing than he did.

She gave him a little 'tring, tring' on her bicycle bell as she pulled away.

Leonard stood there and exhaled, waving to her back as she got lost in the traffic. 'Boy oh boy,' he said out loud. Boy oh boy.

When Shelley got home she looked at what Leonard had written in the encyclopaedias he had signed:

Dear Patrick,

Everything in this book is true. The world really is this amazing. Make sure you tell your Mum all about it.

Yours,

Leonard

(The man who really wrote the words for these books.)

Chapter 12: GRACIE LOVES ANDY

I t hadn't quite worked out as Grace had hoped. Andrew's flight was due in at about 8pm and she had planned to take a half day and have a relaxing bath, maybe pick up a new perfume or earrings and then cook a nice dinner-cum-supper. She had bought a Japanese cookbook at Christmas that she had yet to try, and was toying with the idea of making something in honour of their planned honeymoon trip to Kyoto, arriving in the middle of the blossom season. They had booked a week there and had a further two weeks off, which they would just plan as they went. It had been busy in the run-up to the wedding and most of all she just wanted time off with Andrew all to herself. They had both been working hard for months and keeping three weeks off for the wedding meant taking very little time off during the rest of the year. Apart from a few days at Christmas and two long weekends—which were eaten up by friends' weddings— they hadn't really been off together except for Saturdays and Sundays. With Andrew's travelling schedule—short in/out visits to Europe's financial centres to give and receive PowerPoint presentations—the weekends were often a time to catch up and recover. He would sleep in most Saturday mornings, his body jumbled by moving one time zone east, then another time zone west, leaving Grace to enjoy solitary breakfasts or to go for a run. They would start synchronising at around lunchtime on Saturdays and build their weekend from there.

As she prepared for Andrew's return from his last pre-wedding trip—an occasion which officially marked their entry onto the runway of married life—things started going wrong at work, as they usually did whenever she planned to leave early. There had been some misunderstanding that the numbers on an order had gone awry, which made the logistics people in the States freak out, so Grace had to wait for the time difference to catch up so that she could un-freak them, and explain that the numbers were cumulative, which is how they were supposed to be done, even if it didn't look right. The conference call to sort it out took longer than expected as everyone agreed that they had some thinking to do. The people who made the decisions were not on the call, so Grace had to rescue everyone's wasted time by saying that she would do numbers in both formats for now until a decision was made on the bigger picture. The conference call ended with her thanking 'you guys' who could now 'get back to your breakfast,' as she realised that the call had killed her plans for a bath, which she had been promising herself ever since she insisted that they get one in the house, and not just a shower room. Eventually she left work at that awkward mid-afternoon period, costing her a precious half day from her holidays, while still looking like she was breezing off early as others stayed behind working.

She was disappointed about her plans getting unpicked, and not just for Andrew's sake. The idea had been to make a fuss and to inject some energy into the strangely anticlimactic preparations for the wedding. After a busy few weeks, she was hoping that a nice evening would make her feel in love and dreamy and excited about the imminence of the whole thing. Instead she was just tired and so, so sick of the organising. All she wanted was to get to the wedding day so she could start being a bride and stop being an event manager.

Grace's whole job, her whole career, involved sorting things out and putting people straight, but that was easy by comparison. In work she had complete detachment. No matter how well-planned her projects were she always expected road bumps, and had said many times that if there were no crises she would have nothing to do. It was important to her to be good at her job, good enough to be above the need for praise. But when it came to the wedding arrangements, she found herself overreacting and becoming agitated about the smallest things. She was frustrated by the flakiness of invite printers, cake makers and other one-person wedding suppliers, and blamed herself for falling for their earnest promises and cutesy services. Then there were the blatant price increases she faced from caterers, hotels, bands and DJs, all milking the happy couple's wish for a special day. Most of all, she missed the buying power and corporate muscle that she had at the company; the threat of commercial force that stood behind her workplace successes. If she was honest, she was also frustrated and hurt that Andrew had left most of the arrangements, in fact nearly all of them, to her. Yes, she had told him she wanted to do it, and yes, she had very definite ideas about how she wanted things to be done, and she certainly didn't want him to invent opinions he didn't truly have just for her sake. But she would have liked, *appreciated*, him fighting for some role in organising the wedding, as a sign that the details were as special to him as they were to her. Instead, it felt like he was coming to *her* wedding.

Grace had promised herself not to start thinking about this stuff when she was tired. It just made her negative, and her negativity would seek out a target and, if she wasn't careful, she would meet Andrew from the plane and passive-aggressive the life out of the evening.

On the way home from work, Grace flitted around a couple of shops just to see if she could pick up a new top or a pair of jeans quickly, anything to reset her mood. But the wedding had made her Spartan and money conscious, stopping her from spontaneously splashing out on something nice just to make herself feel better. At one of her favourite boutiques she saw a beautifully-cut jacket that cost the same as the wedding cake and a bag that cost almost as much as her hair and make-up for the wedding day. Instead, she bought a magazine and a packet of popcorn to eat on the train on the way home.

Grace decided that she would go and meet Andrew at the airport, just like when she was at college and Helen and Peter would meet her off the plane after she came back from working away all summer. They would hold up some corny homemade sign with her name on it in bright colours. Then, when she arrived through the gates with her friends she would get so embarrassed, but still, she loved her parents to bits for doing it.

At home, she took a quick shower and she checked her phone to see if there were any messages from Andrew about delays. There was just a short text: just about to take off, see you soon, x.

They had met three years previously, at a badminton class. He was a beginner who had enrolled in an improver's class, with the attitude of 'How hard can it be?' She had played as a teen and should have been in the advanced class, but she was rusty after years of not playing and decided to take it easy in the improver's class. She thrashed him in a practice game during which he joked a lot, and then again in a game where he was clearly trying very hard. His grunting was no match for her technique. At one stage he overreached for a shot and farted through his shorts, which got them both back to bantering and the ulterior purpose behind the game. Inevitably, he asked her out and they stopped attending the badminton lessons, heading to the pub for drinks and flirtation instead.

Andrew had come from a good family, a good school, a good area and had a good job: the kind of things Grace was impressed by—maybe 'reassured by' was more accurate—in spite of herself. He wasn't specifically materialistic, but he was definitely in that game of trying to be thought successful enough to be above materialism. Grace had been inclined to needle him, not always innocently, especially as he had grown up with two older sisters and was used to being fussed over rather than laughed at. Early in their relationship, Grace caught glandular fever and Andrew could well have found reasons not to stick around, but instead he bought her new pyjamas and read Inspector Morse books to her—back when Morse drove a Lancia—and ignored the texts from his friends about the nights out he was missing. By the time Grace had recovered from the illness, their relationship had matured into something intimate and real, and all from just sitting around and talking to each other.

Sometimes she wondered whether Andrew was just a bit too conventional for her. He had no real taste in music, he read sports biographies, he enjoyed pubs and rugby matches, and his opinions on politics all amounted to other people pulling up their socks just like he did. At heart, Grace was still a student communist and had a hidden rebellious side. She prided herself on having taste: experimental Laurie Anderson albums that were smarter than any music the boys made; those Lucien Freud portraits that looked like depressed character actors; long, slow Satyajit Ray movies that broke, then filled her heart; and travel choices that avoided the obvious. It had crossed her mind more than once that maybe Andrew was too much of a jock to be a long-term prospect, and at times during those early months she pushed him away, almost willing him to acknowledge that their divergent tastes were a warning sign. But, in spite of these reservations, Grace loved that Andrew didn't need minding or looking after. He wasn't complicated or troubled and didn't have hang-ups or dependencies. He didn't even depend on Grace. She knew that he would have been able to find happiness in his life no matter how things worked out between them, and that liberated her. It attracted her that she had no extra burdens in the relationship; that she could look after herself within it.

For Andrew, Grace was simply unlike any woman, any person, he had ever known. He had always gone for perfect girls, girls who looked and spoke as though life's opportunities were just a matter of time. In Grace, he had met someone who saw through all of that. She was perspicacious without being judgemental; smart but doubting; consummate in whatever she turned her hand to, without ever being consumed by any of it. He liked that she read books, not to have opinions about them, but to find herself in them. There seemed to be a sense of urgency, a sense of mission, about the way she lived her life. Above all this, their love lasted because when it came to the important things, the deep stuff that actually sustains and propels a relationship, their values were inseparably braided. They both loved their parents and had happy, though not necessarily straightforward, childhoods. They both wanted to start a family. And they both prized their mutual understanding that it was perfectly fine to be intimately in love, while retaining some private, sacred space for themselves as individuals within the relationship. Grace didn't realise how much she needed that until she found it with Andrew, and he was the same with her.

They each had a history of serial monogamy, though neither had lived with any of their previous partners. While Grace had been through the pantomime of teenage romances, her first proper relationship was at college. David, she had always said, was the 'funnest' of her boyfriends. He made her laugh, he made her friends laugh, and was always impossibly *up* for things. He had rooms on campus and all that that implied. She didn't really take him that seriously and they just had fun together, the way that young people are supposed to but seldom do. During the whole time that they were dating, she hardly even called him a boyfriend. They broke up when he went abroad on a year out. It was only when she stared into a long summer alone that she realised how much she missed him and how much she had been trying to mirror his easy-going outlook, hardly admitting to herself the earnestness of her feelings. Her competitive side hadn't let her admit that she was the serious one in the relationship. Last she heard, he was travelling in India.

Jean-Michel was her other college boyfriend, a guy she went out with ostensibly to keep herself sane during her finals, but who ended up hanging around every bloody day and who kept asking her what she was thinking, which for her, was tantamount to ducking her head under water. She couldn't bring herself to dump him, not least because she thought that he would become even clingier in the pursuit of closure, so she just decided to be cold towards him instead so that he would dump her. That only provoked him into calling around for more 'chats' as he tried to become her counsellor during a difficult time. In the end she became so disgusted at herself because of how creatively mean she could be, that she cheated on him drunkenly at a party with all their mutual friends there. The poor guy offered to forgive her and 'work through it.' There were several long letters from him afterwards about how he didn't hate her and that he hoped she would be happy. It was a nice thing to say if he meant it, but Grace, who was at times a little ungenerous when it came to giving credit, saw it as a his way of holding out for a Hollywood ending. Last she heard, he was working in London and doing well for himself.

Geoff broke her heart good and proper. A clean knockout, no need to go to the judges' scorecards. They went out together for over a year in those anything-can-happen years in the mid-twenties, when they both started earning good money and had nothing to spend it on except themselves. They had epic weekend nights out, which were boozy and full of running to wherever the next thing was on. It was a stage in their lives where their social circle stretched like an empire. He had a real job doing something in telecoms, but was also involved in the underground music scene and seemed to know everyone. It was the first time Grace had been with someone who was in a different league socially. He was the guy with grass who knew how to roll proper joints. He had droopy eyelids and said 'man' without sounding ridiculous. He was creative and played guitar in half a dozen bands, who released their own music as part of a collective. They travelled together: city breaks to Rome and London; and the odd weekend in a rented house by the sea with a bunch of scenesters, discussing politics self-consciously. In the end the betrayal was purely sexual. He had been cheating unapologetically with several girls from the scene, saying something about it being 'just a physical itch.' The end was instant and definitive. Grace would have preferred it if she had just flipped and destroyed him in one devastating moment of denouement. Instead, she made a mousey, capitulating exit, dumbstruck by the blatantness of it all. And so she left the scene and the crowd and the energy and the whole period of her life behind her that one evening, as she took a heartbroken taxi ride home. His words chased her thoughts round and round in her head, as he had explained, with almost parental simplicity, that the love she was feeling, and which she thought would grow to take over the world, was just some silly puppet show that she alone had thought was real. She cried in every room in Parley View for over two months as Helen nursed her with the chicken soup of motherly comfort and Peter let her lie on his lap as he stroked her tense, ridged eyebrows. And every evening Hungry Paul—dear, dear Hungry Paul—accompanied her on epic Tess of the D'Urbervilles walks, taken in silence and at thinking speed.

In time, Grace recovered and relapsed and recovered and so on, until life resumed a more normal rhythm, but at a beginner's level. Everything had to be relearned. She never saw or spoke to Geoff again, though she had scripted every possible future conversation between them, from magnanimous letting go to exacting, equalising character assault. It never came to anything. She learned of his death a couple of years after the event from a girl who had been in a band with him. He had been waiting at a bus stop when a drunk driver mounted the footpath after falling asleep at the wheel. He left behind a girlfriend and two boys.

It may well be that if you truly want to open a heart, you

need to break it open. The deep hurt of her failure with Geoff had taught her what was at stake in relationships. Grace had made the error of giving him a surrendering type of love: devotional, adoring love that she had mistaken for the real thing. But now she knew and understood so much more. Even as she shrank down to her smallest, she could still feel the faint and plucky pulse of her devastated heart. It had continued to beat in the darkest part of her chest during her loneliest moments. Knowing that her heart was always, always alive, and did not simply come to life when she loved, gave her an invincibility. Her heart felt like a chapel that had survived a bombing blitz and took on a divine status afterwards.

In time Grace met other men and enjoyed a few dalliances, but held back from entering anything you might call a relationship. It wasn't that she had been hurt or that she didn't trust men—she had had a rough time, but didn't buy into the idea of living out of her past—it was simply that she had learned that she was a pretty special person who had a pretty special and durable heart, and that she could go through dark times on her own and survive them. She became less interested in guys who hadn't been similarly tested. Superficial men, who wanted to talk to her and blah blah blah all night now seemed like kids to her. And that's how she connected with Mark.

Mark was not Grace's type. He was nervous and awkward, and his style and sense of humour were all wrong. He was a computer guy: introverted and with a limited range of interests and friends. But he too was coming out of a life-defining break-up, where he had been loved and let down by a girl who was out of his league, and who had dumped him once she realised it. She was another cold-blooded killer, who was able to walk away from a happy relationship as if it never happened. Mark didn't have a supportive family or the same deep reservoir of feeling that Grace had, so he simply self-medicated with alcohol and a massive credit card bill. He knew enough to stop all that before his life was irreversibly ruined, but not before he had amassed a repertoire of anecdotes and near-death experiences. He and Grace had amazing, therapeutic conversations into the small hours until they would fall asleep together, fully clothed and talked-out. Of course, they both knew that their relationship would not last. This was a practice relationship with the stabilisers on, underwritten by an unspoken agreement not to hurt each other. It ended amicably, when Mark was offered a research job in Rotterdam and Grace urged him not to pass it up. They parted, classically, at the airport with a hug and peck on the cheek that was more like a sister packing her brother off to boarding school than two lovers separating. Mark is the only one of her past loves that she still has occasional contact from, albeit intermittently. He is still single.

Andrew had always been a little coy about his past. He had said that what transpired between him and his past girlfriends needed a little privacy for their sakes, but Grace had known him long enough for the general picture to emerge in fragments, which she had been able to piece together for herself, though without verifying it with Andrew. She knew that he had a long-term girlfriend while at secondary school, someone called Rebecca who seemed like a female version of Andrew— they would probably have made Prom King and Queen had they lived in the States. They broke up when they went to different universities and discovered whole new worlds. He had a few girlfriends at college but most of them seemed to have been a case of having someone on his arm, or someone to stay over with. In his twenties he seemed to enjoy long periods of bachelorhood, although two names had come up a few times, and some details had been prised from him.

The first was Rachel, who seems to be the only girl he went out with that he really liked, or possibly loved. Rachel was an ex-girlfriend of a college friend of his. She and Andrew seemed to have gone out for over a year. Grace never got the full story about why they split but she had guessed that it had involved infidelity on his part, judging by the way he always spoke fondly of that period, but glossed over the details of how it ended. He would only say that he made some mistakes in that relationship and that it forced him to look at himself.

The other relationship was with Lucy, which was the only time he seemed to have dated someone from his job. Apparently it started at a Christmas party and continued as a drunken and lusty relationship. Grace had got the impression that they didn't visit too many museums or meet each other's parents, but that they both had plenty of practice at getting good at the one thing a woman doesn't mind her future husband getting good at. The relationship burned out, and she left the company for a promotion elsewhere. Lucy was the one woman from Andrew's past that Grace certainly did not want him to keep in contact with.

Grace left for the airport, leaving it a little bit late and driving with a heavy right foot. She blasted music from the car stereo—Sparks' *Propaganda*—and opened the driver's window, the incoming rush of air like a leaf blower on her overstimulated brain. Even though it was rush hour, she got lucky with the traffic, which was all headed in the opposite direction.

She waited for Andrew in the arrivals hall and held up an A4 sheet on which she had written ROBERT DOWNEY JUNIOR in lipstick, as a fake airport pick-up sign; an in-joke about her No. 1 movie star crush who looked nothing like Andrew. Grace was early and stood leaning against a superfluous crush barrier, people-watching. The airport was quiet, with men in red polo shirts pushing empty wheelchairs and regular travellers getting a squirt of perfume or aftershave in the duty free area. A guy was sitting on one of the elevated thrones having his shoes buffed at the shoeshine station, a public shoeshine, she thought, being a luxury that could only ever be enjoyed by creeps. A sleepy shop assistant was sending texts at the luggage shop, possibly the most bored person at the airport; Grace wondered how many people arrived at an airport with an armful of clothes, looking to buy luggage.

Grace always felt anaesthetised by airports and was glad of some dead time to allow the day's agitated momentum to settle and subside. In her pocket was a phone that was displaying a series of missed calls and incoming emails, symbols of the fake urgency of impatience. She caught herself reaching for it, her hands habitually unused to idleness, but then checked herself and decided not to puncture the bubble of calm she was starting to ease into. Eventually, Andrew stepped through the arrival doors in his crumpled suit, looking tired but handsome and in need of a shave. Grace gave a little wolf whistle and collapsed into giggles. His face broke into an open smile of surprise at seeing her. Before saying anything they took a moment to have their first kiss in ages.

'Good to see you, wine breath,' she said.

'You too. I just had *one* mini bottle on the flight to help me sleep, by the way. The guy behind me had his knees against my seat the whole way. Thanks for picking me up—it's a lovely surprise. You spelt my name wrong, though,' he said, noticing the pick-up sign.

'Lucky you got here first. Had Robert Downey Junior not been delayed buying snow globes in duty free you might have missed your chance.'

'How have you been? I was dying to see you. God, it's so great to have all this business travel out of the way. I don't want to see any more bullet points until the afterlife. It's nice to think that my next flight is to Kyoto, with my wife!'

'If you're lucky—I haven't signed anything yet.'

They went to find the car, full of a couple's silly talk and holding hands the way Grace would have liked them to do more often. They pulled out of the car park and got a bit lost with the new road layout, eventually cheating their way to the exit by using a bus lane, and getting a reprimanding beep from a bendy bus for doing so.

They stopped off at Sakura, a Japanese takeaway, and ordered *cha han*, udon noodles, fish and vegetable tempura, and some sashimi; over-ordering on an empty stomach. They grabbed some wine and Pringles at the off-licence, and planned an evening on the couch.

'We went to this restaurant in Amsterdam after one of the long meetings, just to unwind and pick over how it went,' said Andrew, as they ate on the couch. 'They were doing road works near the canal and there was a mouse scuttling around the restaurant in plain sight. When I mentioned it to the waitress she just said: "Oh, they always do that" and then waved her hand in a sort of *forgeddaboudid* way and walked off. I couldn't believe it! The others didn't care. I was the only one freaked out by it and spent the evening with my trouser legs tucked into my socks. I mean, imagine what the kitchen was like?'

'Oh, you're giving me the creeps. I just couldn't do it. You should give them a stinky review online,' said Grace, fishing around the end of the noodle box with chopsticks and then switching to a fork.

'No point. If they don't care about mice, they won't care about reviews.'

'How was the cheese museum by the way? Did you pick me up anything?'

'I didn't, I'm afraid—it's strangely difficult to pick out cheese for a woman, as it turns out. I would have liked to look around to see a bit of Amsterdam actually, but the crowd I was with just wanted to go drinking. I never feel in holiday mode on these trips.'

'Yeah, right. Men always talk up the difficulty and hardship of business travel.'

'I'm practically monastic on the road, but I know what you mean. Some guys act like they are on shore leave. Especially the older ones. It's great to think I have practically a full month ahead with no meetings though. Just fun stuff. How are your folks by the way?' he asked.

'Good, good, good. I'm trying to encourage them to plan a holiday. Not just a city break with museums and stuff, but something epic. Dad still has his retirement lump sum, so he should use it to whisk Mam away. Go somewhere far flung while their health is good and they can enjoy it. They just keep resisting it. I think they're worried about my brother coping on his own, but he's a grown-up.'

'What if he stayed with us? I mean just for a few nights while they're away?' Andrew suggested, picking through the tempura vegetables for clumps of batter without the accompanying veg.

'But we're going away ourselves and even if we weren't, we have to stop babying him. We need to take him out of his comfort zone for his own sake. Who knows what the future holds? He needs to be able to cope by himself eventually. He's stuck on this little merry-go-round of a life: his job only keeps him busy about two days a month, he has no concept of money or responsibility and, worst of all, he keeps Mam and Dad frozen in time. They've done their bit as parents and are entitled to enjoy their retirement, without having him to fuss over.'

'Are you not being a bit harsh? He's not doing any harm to anybody, and your parents seem okay with the arrangement,' said Andrew.

'What happens when my folks get older and need help?' asked Grace. 'We're getting to the stage where, in a few years' time, it will be our turn to look after them. So, who will all that fall to? Saint Grace, that's who. You too, in fact. My brother will be no help and, if anything, we'll end up taking responsibility for him too. We should be planning our future together, building a new life, all that sort of stuff, but I know exactly how it's going to turn out. All the family trouble, along with its luggage, will present itself at our door. That's why we need to do something about this now. Otherwise the future is going to look very much like the past. By the way, they have invited us over for dinner on Sunday and I said yes without asking you because I know you love me and would do anything to make me happy.'

Grace paused with her chopsticks poised over the noodles.

'Sorry for dumping on you. I think when you're away this stuff goes around and around in my head. Don't mind me. I feel a bit better just saying all this instead of thinking it.'

'It's fine,' said Andrew. 'It's good training for when I'm your husband and I'm legally required to listen to you. And of course I'm on for dinner on Sunday. I haven't seen your folks in ages. I was thinking I must get your dad a ticket to come with us the next time we're going to a match.'

'Good idea. He needs to expand his social circle. He's got a couple of friends that he still meets from work, and he does a bit of volunteering here and there, but he has no regular outlet. He needs to join something so that he can meet some new people. You need to keep reinventing yourself in life, churning your friends, but he has just settled in to pottering about all day,' said Grace.

'Maybe I'll see if there's something I could do with him, but my Dad's the same. A bit of golf and a bit of helping out at the credit union, but really he is terrible for falling out of touch with people. My mother is much better. She volunteers at the church, helps out with the residents' association, all that stuff. It's funny, she stayed at home all those years, but she's much more businesslike than he is. I think he got used to having staff that did everything for him and that made him look more organised than he was.'

They chatted away and finished off the food. They should have got a second bottle of wine, but then maybe not: it was still a school night after all. They brought everything into the kitchen, tip-toeing over the cold tiles and just stacking the dirty dishes by the sink to be dealt with tomorrow, along with the unpacking and the missed calls.

Grace did the short version of her evening bathroom routine and hopped into bed beside Andrew, who was already dangerously close to sleep. She cuddled into his warm body—his high body temperature being one of his unique selling points when they first got together—and continued chatting with her cheek on his chest. While she did have to confess that one or two things from the next day's to-do list floated into her mind, she quickly let them go and settled into a cosy, sleepy state of contentment, zipped-up from the inside.

Chapter 13: MRS HAWTHORN

Hungry Paul woke with the feeling of being fastened to his bed by Velcro. His body ached with a painful stiffness that stretched up and down his spine and into his thighs and calves. At the previous evening's judo class, they had put the gentle beginners' exercises behind them early and moved on to the business end of the training, practising various hip tosses and shoulder throws. Hungry Paul had been paired off with a man who was built like a wheelie bin, had cauliflower ears and who wore tape on his fingers, like Michael Jackson. He was called Lazlo and he didn't speak any English, not that he left much room for small talk when he was tossing Hungry Paul around like a chef handling pizza dough. It was unclear whether the sensei had confused Hungry Paul with someone else, or just wanted to discourage him from ever coming back again, but it was clearly a monumental mismatch. Even when Lazlo stood still without putting up any defence, Hungry Paul could barely lift one of his legs off the mat, ending up with his arms and legs clamped around him like a randy corgi.

The evening had already started badly when Hungry Paul picked up what would become a black eye, not from combat, but from the stacked mats that were stored on a high shelf and fell off onto his face when he tried to pull them down. He then got a telling off because he hadn't cut his toenails and scratched the sensei's shin while he was demonstrating the moves they were supposed to practice. After seeing him get ragdolled all evening by Lazlo, the sensei came over and told Hungry Paul that he was improving but that he needed to fix his mind-set, pointing to the tea stains on Hungry Paul's *gi* as evidence.

Hungry Paul came home and went straight to bed for twelve hours, too stiff and tired to shower or brush his teeth. His body lay frozen the next morning as Helen knocked on his door to remind him about going to the hospital to do some volunteering that morning. He tried to shout out that it might be more appropriate to visit A&E as a patient, but even his tongue felt broken. Eventually, he managed to manoeuvre out of bed and make his way gingerly to the bathroom, walking like a stiff slow-motion cowboy.

His entreaties to his mother over breakfast were batted away. Helen, who never approved of the whole martial arts idea anyway, wasn't going to allow judo-related excuses to become admissible.

'Come on, you said yourself that charity has to involve a bit of sacrifice,' said Helen, 'You can't just back out when it doesn't suit you. The one thing about helping vulnerable people is that it's a bigger deal when you let them down. You've already missed one visit, so no buts, let's get going.'

'Your mother's right,' added Peter, 'and if you stay here you'll have to help me empty the attic and haul loads of junk to the dump. Not a nice task for an aching body—I should know!'

Hungry Paul gave up. He knew tough love when he saw it.

'Okay, but go easy on me. No lifting old ladies or moving beds around. My body is on strike today.'

'To be honest, I'm not keen on these judo lessons,' said Helen, 'You're going to have a nice shiner for your Chamber of Commerce prize-giving on Saturday. You'll look like a thug in the photos.'

'What photos?' asked Hungry Paul. 'They didn't say anything about photos.'

'Oh they're bound to have the local paper there or some

newsletter for the Chamber. Don't worry about it. You should be proud of yourself that you've been shortlisted. We're certainly proud of you, aren't we Peter?'

'I think it's great. I just thought it was a bit of fun, but you did really well to get to the last three. What was your entry?' asked Peter.

'You'll have to wait until the prize-giving. It's supposed to be a big reveal. I mightn't even win. I hope there isn't too much fuss,' worried Hungry Paul.

'Just enjoy it. It's not often you get to go to this sort of thing. We'll all be there to support you.' Peter was trying to stop Hungry Paul projecting forward and worrying about one of his least favourite things: a hullabaloo.

'Anyway, we had better be going. See you later, love.' Helen kissed Peter on the forehead, bald heads in general getting more kisses than the hairy kind, which is some small comfort.

When they arrived at the hospital, Helen made a suggestion. 'Why don't we split up this time? We want to make sure everybody gets a visit and we don't want to crowd the patients.'

Hungry Paul's shoulders dropped. His conversation game was a bit off and he wasn't sure he would be able to fill an hour with his usual repertoire of comments about the weather and questions about the standard of food at the hospital.

As they entered the ward, the lady in the first bed shouted 'Religious bitch—mind your own business,' at Helen, again confusing her with the visiting Minister of the Eucharist.

'Why don't you help that lady?' suggested Helen, guiding Hungry Paul with a gentle push to his lower back.

Before he had the chance to answer, Helen was straightening the pillows of the lady in the middle bed, who was asleep, surrounded by fresh flowers and homemade get well cards. Helen then moved on to Barbara, who still hadn't been sent home.

'Hello again Helen. How nice to see you,' said Barbara, 'I'm afraid my scan wasn't clear so I have to stay in for more tests.

I hope it's nothing untoward, not that they give you any clues. I'm bored silly with crosswords, so I'm glad to have someone to talk to. These two aren't up to much,' she said, pointing with her thumb to the other patients.

And with that, Helen and Barbara entered into what Peter called 'nattering': a seamless narrative of personal stories, asides and value judgements, delivered in a point/counterpoint style, with each woman taking her turn on the mic with a seamlessness known only to middle-aged women and gangsta rappers. Hungry Paul was left standing at the first bed with his coat on and his options limited. He tried to gain eye contact with the swearing woman in the first bed but she just stared straight ahead.

'Do you mind if I take a seat, love?' he asked, instantly regretting the 'love' bit as a misjudged imitation of his mother that sounded weird coming from a man.

He got no answer.

He pulled the chair aside and sat down, feeling rusty and sore. It was nice to be still and quiet. His mother and Barbara provided a pattering background noise that was easy to zone out from, but otherwise the wards were quiet. No nurses dashing around, no TVs blaring and no patients swearing or crying or asking confused questions. He sat there calmly, simply sharing the moment with the woman. Her chart showed that her name was Mrs Hawthorn. Mrs Olivia Hawthorn. Hungry Paul was good at this: just sitting, not fidgeting, not thinking particularly, and simply listening to the room. He never minded time. It neither dragged nor slipped away for him. He always felt *in* time. Just here, just being around. There was a gentle breeze blowing through the room and a faint smell of today's dinner, which was gravy-like and indeterminate. He just sat there without small talk or prompts; nothing to get the relationship going, but no bum notes either.

After about twenty minutes, Mrs Hawthorn reached over

and, without altering her straight-ahead gaze, took his hand. She gave it a barely perceptible squeeze. He accepted her hand gently, without trying to catch her eye or check her motive. Her skin was soft and thin. They held hands like that for the remaining forty minutes: silently and in comfort. When time was up and Helen came over, Mrs Hawthorn was fast asleep, still holding Hungry Paul's hand in restful silence.

'You two got on well by the looks of things. How did you win her over? She only gives me abuse,' said Helen as they walked to the car park.

'I didn't do anything. Nothing at all,' answered Hungry Paul, who tended not to overthink these things.

When they got home, Hungry Paul rang Leonard at work. They had arranged to play Monopoly that night, but Hungry Paul was still stiff and tired and wanted to suggest a more straightforward game like Connect 4 or Battleship.

'Hello my old pal. What's on your mind? Looking forward to the prize-giving I bet,' answered Leonard in a chirpy voice.

'My goodness, you're in good form. Unfortunately I am somewhat in recovery mode. I wanted to ask a favour, actually. I had a rough judo session last night and am a little bit less than my best so I was wondering if we could play something easier than Monopoly tonight—I was thinking Connect 4 maybe? I don't like to change plans at the last minute, but it's just that judo is tricky until you get the hang of it.'

'Oh, I see. Hmmm, this is awkward, you see—'

'If it's a problem, then I don't mind changing back to Monopoly,' interrupted Hungry Paul, 'I wouldn't want to let you down.'

'Oh, it's not that. It's just that, well, I meant to ring you about this. You see, I'm supposed to meet Shelley tonight, and I forgot that I had double-booked myself a—'

'Oh, I see. Well, that's different. So maybe it's b—'

'I mean, I'm really sorry and I hate to let you down, it's all my mistake, but it's just that Shelley doesn't always find it easy to arrange a night out because of Patrick, bec—'

'Who is Patrick?' asked Hungry Paul.

'Oh that's her son, he's about s—'

'A son! Oh, I never knew that. My goodness, you are jumping in at the deep end . . . eh, but I'm sure it's all very straightforward. So I guess we'll just have to do it another night instead maybe?'

'Any night you like. And thanks for understanding. As you well know, I'm not often in this situation and I would really like it to work out so if you didn't mind maybe we could meet tomorrow instead?'

'Oh wait, I think tomorrow is booked,' lied Hungry Paul, a little hurt, 'so maybe I'll just see you at the prize-giving on Saturday, if you're still free that is?'

'Wouldn't miss it. I'll be rooting for you. And next time, you get to pick which game we play. No arguments from me.'

After Hungry Paul had hung up, he gave the stubble on his chin a contemplative rub. His initial disappointment about the evening's play soon receded, as the wider import of the conversation took its place. Undoubtedly Leonard, to his credit, had started making his long-overdue 'one small step for man.' He had the Roman book that he was writing on the side, and now a girlfriend. The girlfriend had a son, who could become Leonard's kid if it all worked out. Imagine that. Even though Hungry Paul was happy for his friend, he couldn't help but notice that things seemed to be moving on without him. This hit him with an unexpected heaviness. He started putting it all together. Grace would be married soon and would probably start a family. His parents were all but retired and kept talking about taking some big trip and specifically, some big trip without *him*. Judo had turned out harder than he had expected. His job at the Post Office—such as it was—would eventually be taken over by drones or robots. What was he supposed to do? He couldn't spend the rest of his life feeding birds and holding Mrs

Hawthorn's hand. And he certainly could not play board games every night by himself. Most games were four-player and it was already a compromise to play with just himself and Leonard.

Hungry Paul stretched out on the couch and felt his own limits. His body was just big enough to fit between the two arm rests. Lining everything up together—Leonard, Grace, his parents, and his own circumstances—he recognised a familiar pattern. Connect 4. Game Over.

Chapter 14: HAPPY MEAL

When Leonard got off the phone he felt an uncomfortable mixture of guilt and betrayal, having let Hungry Paul down, his best and only true friend. A man who had stood by him through everything and who had always reserved a space in his (admittedly quiet) life just for Leonard. Their friendship was not just one of convenience between two quiet, solitary men with few other options, it was a pact. A pact to resist the vortex of busyness and insensitivity that had engulfed the rest of the world. It was a pact of simplicity, which stood against the forces of competiveness and noise.

The only problem was that Leonard had discovered a flaw in their way of life. It was fine so long as everything else stayed the same. With a stable home and work life, a life of depth and meaning, it was certainly possible to preserve a sanctuary of gentleness through their special friendship. But once life had changed, once the people in your life started slipping away from you, as inevitably happens, then north, south, east and west all move from their fixed points on the compass. You are left bereft, with a choice of whether to *enter* the world, with all the risks that entails, or retreating from it. Leonard's natural instinct was to retreat and to create a safe bubble. But the bubble feeds on itself. Solitude and peace lose their specialness when they no longer stand in contrast to anything. In a busy—or at least bus*ier*—life, quiet reflection provides resonance to experience. But to deprive life of experiences deliberately and to hide from its realities was not special. It was just another form of fear that led to a life-limiting loneliness that accumulated and accumulated until it became so big that it blocked up the front door, drowned out conversations and put other people behind soundproof glass. And anyway, Leonard was discovering that distancing himself from people didn't even bring peace. The more he separated himself from others, the more they become unfathomable and perplexing. The distance just made him lose perspective. If he wasn't careful he could turn vinegary and judgemental, like that man he used to see in the supermarket, muttering to himself with egg down the front of his jumper. In fact, he had discovered that he was less critical of people when he allowed them in. People, it turns out, weren't so bad. At least that was true of some people. And maybe that was the trick: to find the right people; to be able to recognise them and to know how to appreciate them when you do find them.

All of this left him in a quandary with his best friend. He wasn't sure whether Hungry Paul had made the same leaps. What if Hungry Paul just planned to womble from day to day for ever, unaware that his universe was shrinking? It pained Leonard to think that he might be outgrowing Hungry Paul, as though their friendship had become a reverse tontine, where the last man standing was the loser. The prize, a retreating life of diminishment.

But Leonard resolved that he would not let his own growth, such as it was, be at Hungry Paul's expense. Their friendship meant too much to him. He decided that he would not let his burgeoning romance with Shelley—which, after all, was still at a very early stage—interfere with their friendship. This would be the last time he would cancel or renege on Hungry Paul because of thoughtlessness. From now on, he would make extra efforts to include him in his plans and perhaps, in gentle, covert ways he hadn't yet figured out fully, he would try and guide his friend towards opening up his own life.

Leonard was also clear on one other thing: he recognised that he had an opening with Shelley that provided him with a small but sporting chance of becoming part of her life, and she part of his. He wasn't exactly sure of where he wanted it to go, and he had parked for now the difficult questions he had about her having a seven-year-old son, but he knew that he didn't want to mess it up because of dithering and self-doubt. This time, he would take his chances, and bear the risks.

He had been planning their first evening date all week, the plans coming at the expense of progress on his book about the Romans. Rather than trying something unusual, he had decided that he would book a nice restaurant, somewhere quiet and tasteful, but affordable in the event that she wanted to split the bill; no hipster spots. There was a nice little Italian that he often passed on the way home from work, and which had a few veggie options for Shelley, so he decided to book a table there. After dinner he'd suggest a walk and, all going well, they could go somewhere for a nightcap, some friendship, maybe more.

Though still very much a reluctant shopper, he had spent money on a new designer fragrance, but he had already splashed it onto his cheeks when he saw the words *pour femme* in tiny gold font at the bottom of the dark, male-looking, bottle. Perhaps she wouldn't recognise it and he could pass it off as unisex. The fragrance had fooled him, so maybe it would fool her too, he thought, his optimism gallivanting ahead of his realism.

Having rushed out of the house, he arrived at their meeting point almost half an hour early. There were several overdressed, over-groomed date night hopefuls already waiting there. It was cold and between his nerves and his new jeans, which were a little snug, he realised that his bladder would not find it easy to last until 8pm. He crossed the road to McDonald's, which seemed the nearest and most straightforward option. When he went to open the door for the bathrooms, he found them locked.

'Toilets are for customers only,' said a deep male voice behind and above him. Leonard turned around to see a security guard who was the size of Mount Rushmore.

'Oh, I see. How about I buy something then?' suggested Leonard.

'That's the general idea of restaurants. But you need to buy it before you use the bathroom,' deadpanned Mount Rushmore.

Leonard presented himself at the counter where a sunny cashier was waiting for him.

'Hi, what's your cheapest burger?' asked Leonard.

'That would be our regular hamburger sir,' answered the cashier.

'Okay, I'll have one of those then. And a 7UP to wash it down.'

'Sprite okay?'

'Sprite, 7UP, all the same, yes, that would be fine.'

'It's actually cheaper to get the meal deal, so do you want to go for that sir? You'd get chips too and it would cost you less?'

This was getting out of hand, but it was hard to argue with her logic.

'Okay then. Can I use your toilet now?' asked Leonard, starting to shift from foot to foot.

'Sure thing, the code for the door is on your receipt. The food will just be a minute.'

'Okay, back in a tick.'

Leonard returned from the toilet a changed man. The cashier handed him a tray with his meal on it. It turned out that he had ordered a kids' Happy Meal, with a toy from the latest Disney franchise included inside the box. Now that he had been to the loo, he no longer wanted the food, but it would be a shame to waste it, so he decided to have a couple of bites, while still leaving room for the restaurant food. Maybe it was a good idea not to be too hungry on the date anyway—he didn't want Shelley to think he was a pig or anything.

He took his seat and opened up the Happy Meal box. The burger was pretty thin and flimsy, and the portion of chips was small, so he didn't think he was in danger of spoiling his appetite. He had just started eating when there was a knock at the window beside him. It was dark outside and he could only really see his reflection so he ignored it and took another bite. Then there was another knock followed by a pair of vaguely discernible waving hands. He pressed his face against the window, and there, with her face pressed against his, separated only by the double glazing, was Shelley smiling back at him.

She had likewise arrived early and stepped off her bus to see Leonard tucking into a kids' Happy Meal in McDonald's of all places. She came in through the automatic doors, pausing to let some teenagers out, and joined him at his window table.

'I have to hand it to you, you know how to lay on a surprise for a girl. Is this where we're going on our date?' she asked.

'Absolutely not!' answered Leonard a little too emphatically.

'Okay, phew. So what's the deal? Are you having a double dinner day or were you just *dying* to see what toy was in the Happy Meal?'

'It's just some cartoon fish, it's from a D—'

'It's one of the *Finding Nemo* fish, or whatever the new movie in the series is. Patrick has a few of them. They're such landfill toys. No offence intended if you're, you know, *into* them or something.'

'Oh, God no. I know this looks weird but I just needed to use the loo, and then the Mount Rushmore guy over th—'

'The what guy?'

'Mount Rushmore—he's so big and blocky he reminds me of the Thomas Jefferson face in particular. He intercepted me and said I had to buy something if I wanted to use the toilet, so I just got the cheapest, smallest thing, but then I thought it would be a waste to just dump it—and I know you'd disapprove of a cow being slaughtered just to be thrown into the bin—so I said I would just take a bite, and as you can see, I've hardly touched it so, well, there you are.'

He took a deep breath and looked at her as she picked at his chips with a strangely uncomprehending look on her face.

'I get it, I think. This meal is cover for your bladder. I think I can live with that. So, can we start our date now?' she asked.

'That would be nice. Hi, by the way.'

Leonard leaned over and gave her a peck on the cheek.

'You smell nice. Kind of reminds me of a fragrance I have at home. Let's get rid of this,' she said as she binned what was left of the food and stuffed the *Nemo* toy into her pocket, for want of a better idea.

At the Italian restaurant, the waiter sat them in a little booth. There was a piano player on the far side of the room, playing romantic voluntaries underneath the healthy ambient sound of conversation between couples of all ages. The diners looked to Leonard like a mix of first dates, wedding anniversaries, and return visits by couples to their favourite spot.

'This is really lovely. Where did you find this place?' asked Shelley.

'Oh, you know. I've passed it loads of times and thought it looked nice. I've never been here before,' answered Leonard, when what he meant to say was that every time he walked by he said to himself, if I ever meet a girl, *that's* the place I'm going to bring her.

When she took off her coat, he could see that she had on a beautiful green sleeveless lace dress. Her hair had a slightly darker colour than usual and had been cut and pushed behind her ear, and she was wearing just a little bit of make-up, which he'd never seen her do before. As he watched her scan the menu, with her lips moving as she read, he said 'You look really beautiful, Shelley,' having only meant to think it.

She smiled with a little shyness.

'Thank you. You look very handsome. I like your jacket. Ooh, this is so nice isn't it?' she said, possibly referring to the restaurant, the date, or the whole thing. 'Well there are lots of veggie options, thankfully.'

'So, how come you're a vegetarian? Is it an animal welfare thing or just a health thing?' asked Leonard.

'Oh, no special reason. I got food poisoning from some re-heated mince a few years ago and the thought of eating meat after that just made me nauseous, so I gave up for a month or two and just never went back to it. I'm not a zealous veggie, by the way. I won't nag you if you order a big T-bone steak. Patrick eats meat—well, sausages, if you can call them meat—and if there's meat left over, I'll finish it off. As you rightfully said, I hate the thought of meat being thrown out—death in vain and all that.'

'How do you make sure you get enough protein?' asked Leonard.

'Ah, protein. I know how you meat eaters stay awake at night worrying about how much protein vegetarians get. Margaret, who works with me, lives on a diet of cigarettes, popcorn and Diet Coke, and the other week she starts giving me the whole protein speech. I just told her not to worry, that silverback goril-las are vegetarian and they get by okay. She had to do an image search to see what a silverback looked like and then she seemed to be satisfied. So, anyway, if I collapse during the date, feel free to run over to McDonald's and get me some protein.'

She had a lovely way of laughing and speaking at the same time, just keeping it together enough until the end of the sentence when she exploded.

'Okay, okay, fair enough. I'd love to cook you a nice vegetar-ian meal sometime. I often eat veggie at home,' replied Leonard, thinking about the oven chips and ice cream in his freezer.

They ordered their food: she was having a sun-dried tomato salad and the mushroom risotto; he was having gazpacho fol-lowed by a ragout of some sort, his appetite undented by his pre-starter in McDonald's. Shelley ordered a glass of Prosecco and drank it a little faster than she meant to, though he was glad to see that he wasn't the only one who was a little nervous.

He ordered a beer and was relieved to be spared the drama that comes with wine: the little taste to see if it's corked and then the Man-from-Del-Monte nod when it's not.

Shelley ordered another Prosecco and they chatted through the preliminaries about her family—two brothers and a non-identical twin sister—how he got into encyclopaedias, and about the weirdo she met on the bus on the way into town, who thought she was someone off the TV, which Leonard told her was probably meant as a compliment, though she wasn't so sure.

After the starters arrived, Shelley decided on a little quiz.

'So, Leonard my man. It's about time I found out a little bit more about you. I know where you work, that your desk is pretty tidy, and that you like meat and encyclopaedias. So maybe let's fill in a few gaps. And just so you know, this won't be painful and it won't be one-way. So, first things first . . .'

Leonard tensed up a little.

'You're obviously a book person, so what's your favourite book ever?'

'Let me think . . . *The Chronicle of the Twentieth Century*,' he said confidently.

'The what now?'

'*The Chronicle*. Oh, basically it includes all the newspaper highlights from the twentieth century. Each month gets a page, so that's, what, about twelve hundred pages. It's fascinating—all contemporaneous accounts of what was going on. I used to love it as a kid and I often read it these days, whenever I'm doing a . . . em, whenever I am sitting down comfortably. How about you? What's your favourite?'

'Wait a minute, I was looking for a favourite novel or some-thing. You know, something that tells me who you are. So pick something like that, not the phone book or whatever it was your first answer was.'

Leonard laughed. He took her businesslike approach as a good sign that she wanted to go places with this.

'If those are the rules, I'd say probably something like *Moby-Dick*. Yes, *Moby-Dick*. A classic. A monster of a book, but yes, that's the one.'

'Isn't that basically an encyclopaedia of whaling with a story stuck on to it?'

'In a manner of speaking I suppose you have a point. But really, I'm not being evasive. I just like factual books. You can hardly be surprised. How about you, what's yours?'

'I don't really have that much time or energy to read these days, I'm afraid. But I suppose the book that has stayed with me most over the years is *The Mill on the Floss*—or maybe it's just that I've always felt there was a bit of Maggie Tulliver in me,' she answered.

'I know what you mean—I mean, not that I have *Moby-Dick*, as a creature, within me particularly; I think he and I are very different people. I haven't read *The Mill on the Floss*, I'm afraid, although I think I have a copy of it at home somewhere. I wasn't expecting you to pick a classic actually.'

'Why not—do I not look *brainy*?'

'It's not that, of course not. You're just so, I don't know, *energetic*. I was expecting something else, I don't know what. Salinger or something buzzy and current, not that that's a bad thing or anything, it's just . . .'

'I have a deep side too, you know—and I'm not scared of footnotes.'

'I never doubted you.'

'Okay, so what next, favourite piece of music?' she asked.

'Easy peasy.'

'Go on.'

Leonard tried to think of a cool band, but went blank.

'Am I allowed to include Greatest Hits compilations?'

She turned her eyes upwards to appeal to the god of Italian restaurant ceilings.

'Just kidding, just kidding. For me it's the *Pie Jesu* from

Fauré's *Requiem*. A divine piece of choral music. You'd love it if you haven't already heard it.'

'Oooh, choral music is so pure. I'm not religious, but I love sacred music,' she said.

'I'm the same with art. I don't like Mass, but I like going into churches to look at the art in them. Much nicer than galleries. So what's your favourite piece of music?'

'Something less posh I'm afraid. It's PJ Harvey's first album. I always liked her. She's so smart and lyrical, but still a bit raucous. Not a bad way to be,' said Shelley, adding emphasis with her eyebrows, as she took a sip from her glass.

And so they continued like this, going back and forth with their preferences—a light-hearted bit of fun that nevertheless helped them to scout each other out. His five next answers were: *All About Eve*, Peru, steak, Leonard Bernstein, snakes and twelve; hers were *The Goodbye Girl*, Bhutan, marzipan, Shelley Duvall, moths and seven.

Over dessert, and with the alcohol starting to sink in, they waded into deeper water.

'So how come you left art college?' he asked.

'The short answer is that I became pregnant with Patrick. The long answer is that I loved art college. It was really hard to get in and my teacher at secondary school was lazy and uninterested, and told me my portfolio wasn't good enough and that they wanted to see more originality. I nearly gave up there and then, but my dad dug up a load of my work and put it together and more or less nagged me into having a go at it. Most importantly, he stayed off my case with my other homework, and in the end I managed to submit a pretty strong portfolio but wasn't really sure what the standard was, as nobody else I knew was going for it. When I got in it was the proudest day of my life. I remember running up to the postman in the street and practically diving into his bag to look for the letter. He said it broke the rules to hand out letters on the street, but he knew there was no point trying to stop me. My folks were so excited. My dad rang the school to tell my art teacher and I think he used some pretty, you know, triumphant language.

'My first year was great, surrounded by all these people I could relate to for the first time ever. Sparky, exciting, barking mad creative people. Full of ideas and energy. The social life was good too—lots of parties and gate-crashing and just general madness. Anyway, I started having a bit of a thing with a tutor in my fine art class. He was only a couple of years older than me—Stanley Prince was his name. He's actually quite an established artist now. I used to call him Prince Stanley. Whenever it got to the end of a night at a party we'd seek each other out and we got together a few times and, well, I don't know whether you did biology at school, but sometimes when a man and a woman love each other very much, blahblahblah. He sort of overreacted to the pregnancy and decided to leave his job and me and told me—from a distance mind you—that he'd help out in any way he could. You can imagine how I responded. Unsurprisingly, we have had very little contact since then. Some of my friends had a go at me because Stanley left, so the whole thing became very difficult. In the end I dropped out. My dad wanted me to keep at it, but my heart was just kind of broken and I didn't feel up to being superwoman, doing it all by myself. I ended up taking some time out when Patrick was born and only really got back to work a few years ago. Mostly admin and office stuff. At least having a son got me back into drawing. He loves drawing so we draw together—it's our *thing*. He likes drawing pictures from your books actually, we both do. Some are better than others. There are a lot of angry-looking people in your books aren't there?'

'Ha, ha! Yes. Some of them,' he answered. 'I'm actually working on something a bit different at the moment. A little personal side project, although I shouldn't jinx it by talking about it until I've made more progress.'

'Ah, go on, give us the skinny.'

'There's nothing to tell exactly. It's just I was stuck on this boilerplate encyclopaedia about the Romans, you know, chariots, straight roads—'

'—noses, aqueducts, I know the type, go on,' interjected Shelley.

'Exactly. So I decided to try and write something more human. A real children's encyclopaedia in that it's all about children. So, I'm trying to write about a Roman child and what his life is like. All factually correct, but with more of a storytelling approach. Maybe give him a name, a family, toys, friends. Talk about his worries and other aspects of his life that kids nowadays might relate to. I'm not sure if it'll work but . . .'

'That's a really special idea. You could do a whole series of them. Kids would really get into that. Oh, that's so great. Is it going to be published?'

'I'm not sure. You're the only one I've really told about it, to be honest. I've been trying to do the illustrations as well, although I feel embarrassed saying that in front of you as I've no real training.'

'Oh, don't be silly. You should definitely try and do something with it. It sounds like a really original idea and I can't think of anyone better to do a great job. Pursue your talent. Don't end up like me, with everything sitting in a drawer.'

'It would be great if you could get back into it. I'd love to see some of your pictures, if you felt like showing them to me,' said Leonard, only too happy to shift to focus of the conversation away from himself—he wasn't used to compliments.

'Well, we'll see,' she said.

As he listened to her he became gradually swept into the current of her openness and enthusiasm. Their lives had been so different. He really, really liked her. Without meaning to, he blurted out a question, asking her what she saw in him?

'I mean, I don't want to sound like a loser, but you know

what I mean. I suppose I'm asking whether you see yourself as getting involved, or whatever the word is. And if so, what about getting involved with me? Or am I just a friend or something disappointingly platonic like that?'

'Seeing as you are straight out putting it up to me,' she began, 'I suppose it is kind of weird that we were working on the same floor together for months without anything happening. I pretty much overlooked you for the first good while. I sort of recognised you but just, you know, for whatever reason, looked past you, I'm not sure why. But the thing is, I have spent a lot of time on my own with Patrick, and so I read what he reads and we read together, and your books, well, they're just not like anyone else's. They are magical really. He really gets excited about them. Your books seem like they're from a different era, like they're written with the kid in mind. They've just got real heart. So, when I pieced together that you were writing them, and given that you're a minor celebrity in our house—or at least Mark Baxter, BEd, is, but it's really you—how could I not take an interest in you? And then when I got to meet you, you just seemed, I dunno, really gentle, and after all the different things I've done in my life, and all the people I've met, including some really confident guys—no offence by the way, but you know what I mean, you're not about projecting something, you really are for real—and I suppose I realised how hard it is to find that, to find gentleness in the world. And you really are. I know it sounds like a platonic compliment, but I mean it in the most honest way I can. Does any of this make any sense to you, or am I just talking fluent Prosecco at this stage?'

He knew exactly what she was talking about.

'I'm really glad you see it that way,' he said.

'So, what made you interested in me?'

He paused for a moment to put his finger on it.

'I just think you're breathtaking,' he said, plainly and truly.

For whatever reason, it had been a long time since anyone

had looked Shelley in the eye and called her special without any calculation or contrivance. Leonard's sincerity, so free from art, had a perfection about it. 'Don't make me get teary,' she said.

They talked and talked over the knickerbocker glories they ordered for dessert and the coffee that followed. When the time came, she made the cheque-signing motion with her hands.

'I don't mind paying, by the way, unless it offends you that is?' he offered.

'You're okay. You've already had to fork out for a Happy Meal, so I couldn't let you get this too. But I tell you what, you can cook me that veggie meal sometime if you like.'

'Anytime. Anytime at all.'

They split the bill down the middle and overtipped, for good luck as well as out of generosity.

They walked and talked with linked arms as far as the taxi stand and then talked some more while they waited in the fresh sobering air. As Shelley got ready to get into her cab, all apologies about having to get home to her sister who was babysitting, she stood straight in front of him.

'This is the bit where you kiss me like a gentleman, by the way,' she said, looking up at him.

Leonard kept his promise about taking his chances.

'Bye then,' she said. 'Take it easy on the protein won't you?'

'Good night Shelley. And thanks for a really lovely time,' said Leonard.

She gave smiling waves out of the taxi, holding up the plastic Disney fish she had forgotten she had. Leonard waved back and watched the cab disappear down the street and round the roundabout by the Natural History Museum. Happy to prolong his mood, he decided to walk home on that cloudless night, with a light heart and nothing above him but the universe.

Chapter 15: TRAVEL PLANS

It is hard to appreciate now, but there was once a time before mobile phones and text messages when people communicated with each other by sticking notes to refrigerators using magnets. It got to be so commonplace that it became the secondary purpose of fridges themselves. Families would leave dinner instructions, teenagers would explain their whereabouts, and unhappy wives would initiate divorces, all using short Hemingway-esque messages affixed at eye level using coloured magnetic letters. In fact there was widespread panic in the refrigeration industry when text messages became popular. And then, when *free* texts became available, the National Association of Subzero Appliances (the other NASA, as they called themselves) brought a case to the Supreme Court, citing an infringement of their right to earn a livelihood.

It was by this vestigial medium that Helen had learned that Hungry Paul had got up early that Saturday morning to make his own way to the hospital to visit Mrs Hawthorn. It is the nature of the medium that there is little space for explaining motives, but Helen surmised that Hungry Paul had woken up early with anxiety about the Chamber of Commerce prize-giving that day, and wanted to find something to do to take his mind off things. As Helen had often observed, there is no better cure for one's own worries than to help someone else with theirs.

Helen picked the note off the fridge and folded it into quarters, turning it over in her mind at the same time. It had often been the case that whenever Hungry Paul showed initiative in this way she reined in her natural inclination towards encouragement, experience having told her that such sorties were usually undertaken with maladroit enthusiasm and mixed results. To his credit, Hungry Paul had overcome his wavering commitment and social awkwardness to stick with volunteering at the hospital. He and Mrs Hawthorn seemed to share a kindred peace, sitting together quietly holding hands like Larkin's Arundel tomb. Surprisingly, he had even found a groove with Barbara and all her garrulous energy, which verged on brassiness, and which would ordinarily make Hungry Paul ill at ease. Helen put it down to the fact that he was about the same age as her own grown-up absent children, and sometimes that can be enough to create a familiar set-up on which to base a pleasant half hour. Barbara, to her credit, had quickly figured out that Hungry Paul was happier when conversation was incidental to an absorbing activity like draughts or Travel Scrabble, free from eye contact and leading questions.

Helen had expected that she would need to harry Hungry Paul to keep him involved at the hospital, though she had no greater plan in mind than to get him out of the house to make himself useful. The fact that he had gone visiting of his own volition should have been a signal that the vessel had been launched and was now capable of continuing under its own power. But Helen had developed a habitual resignation to the fact that Hungry Paul would forever fall short of full independence. He might get tantalisingly close at times, which would give her cause for hope—a new hobby, murmurings about a full-time job, passing references to apartments available to let—but, like so many people, the ability to discuss his ambitions seemed to satisfy his need to pursue them. Ideas led to well-meaning effort, led to messy disappointment, led to retreat and an affirmation that maybe a change was not needed after all. It was a cycle that seemed to be renewed and repeated under its own momentum. Meanwhile, Helen and Peter were getting older. The house was no longer mortgaged and was too big for them as a couple. Nothing looks as much like old age as dead space that has been dusted and vacuumed meticulously. Helen and Peter had friends who had deferred their plans only to find themselves in ill-health or widowhood; others kept on working because they needed the money or couldn't face the anonymity and loss of status that comes with retirement. She and Peter, on the other hand, had always wanted to recreate the relationship they had had before they became parents. After years of struggling with money and worry, they had fantasised about getting their lives back when they retired, a carefree window of however many years before the inevitable worst happened.

And yet, there was part of Helen that wanted to hang on to Hungry Paul. He had been at home so long that he had taken the edge off any relationship tensions that she and Peter might otherwise have had. Two people rattling around in a big house have a habit of getting under each other's feet; an abundance of free time does not, as it turns out, provide a cure for impatience. Helen had kept working two days a week ostensibly to allow her to get to full pension age, but really she just wasn't ready to find out whether her fantasy of an open-ended, unencumbered life with Peter would stand up. Hungry Paul brought life to their routine and had become an amulet against that fine film of loneliness that can settle on a big empty house. His pottering and general availability for incidental chats and activities that are more fun with two people, all allowed her to give Peter the time alone he had always craved, while keeping at bay her feelings of exclusion.

'Good morning love,' said Peter as he came into the kitchen after his usual Saturday lie-in, a habit from his working life that he had retained in retirement. 'How did you sleep last night?' he said, kissing her head and standing behind her as she looked out over the sink at the garden.

'Fine, thanks love. Are you a bit congested? You were a little snorey last night,' said Helen.

'It's spring. Hay fever is probably on its way. Any sign of our son and heir? If he's sleeping in I'll go ahead and make the porridge for the two of us.'

'Go ahead. He left a note—he went to the hospital to do some visiting. All by himself.'

'I'm impressed—good on him. You might have started something there,' said Peter, measuring out the porridge.

They settled into their Saturday breakfast, still in their pyjamas, with Peter reading the unfinished bits of yesterday's paper. After a while Helen put on the radio just to have some chat in the background, something Peter could have done without.

Helen looked out at the back garden at the bird feeders that had been restocked by Hungry Paul before he went out. Some chaffinches were at the seed feeder, picking out the bits they liked and spilling the rest; a pair of jackdaws was marshalling the fat balls. 'Have you given any more thought to our trip?' she asked, 'I mean once the wedding is over, we're pretty open. Maybe we should do something a bit special.'

'You won't need to ask me twice. I'm game, but I thought you wanted to think over whether we bring His Nibs? He won't want a long flight.'

'I know, but I was thinking about what Grace was saying. Maybe it would be good for him and us if we just went ourselves,' said Helen.

'I agree. Amen. Where would you like to go? I'd prefer not to go on any snooze cruises or anything too sedentary. Outside Europe maybe? The States maybe or somewhere less western? Argentina? How about Vietnam?'

'Maybe not Asia. Grace is going to Kyoto so she'll think we're following her.'

'Asia is pretty big you know, even though it's only this size on the map,' said Peter holding his hands three inches apart and laughing.

Helen turned down the porridge to stop it bubbling over. 'Let me think about it. And we better not say anything for now. We don't want to upset anybody.'

Chapter 16: Chamber of ComMERCE

Hungry Paul returned from the hospital in a good mood. He dropped his keys on the hall table and sauntered into the kitchen to give his mother a kiss and hand her the small bunch of chrysanthemums he had bought in the supermarket. For his father he landed the Saturday newspapers on the table with a tomely thud.

The hospital visits had gone well. Mrs Hawthorn was asleep when he arrived, so he chatted to Barbara instead, the middle bed being empty but slept in. He told her all about the prize-giving and remembered to ask her about her grown-up kids, all while playing a travel version of Battleship that he had brought specially, having previously discovered that Scrabble could make her argumentative. When he was leaving, and though under some time pressure, he checked in on Mrs Hawthorn, who was still sleeping, though now with a drip in her arm. He sat in his usual seat beside her and took a few moments in stillness, her faint breath a little raspy in her chest. When she woke to see him sitting by her bed there was a look of lightness on her face and she reached out to take his hand weakly. There they sat for another twenty minutes or so, by which time she had drifted off again. Hungry Paul placed her hand gently on top of the blanket and moved her glass of water in from the edge of the locker before making his way home.

He left the hospital with a new sense of confidence and independence. This continued at home where he readied himself for the prize-giving, even whistling while shaving and singing random song-like noises in the bath—la-da-di, la-da-da—show tunes from no musical in particular. His black eye was also starting to clear up and was now at the yellow stage. But a man like Hungry Paul is a complex and sensitive sort, whose momentum can be soon overturned by the simplest thing. In this case, his gaiety was punctured on the discovery that the new shirt he had bought for the wedding—which he was trying out with his new wedding suit—had a double cuff. As it hung there on the wardrobe door, where Helen had put it after ironing, he saw the cuffs and was immediately winded by all the associated complications. Double cuffs meant cuff links, something that he didn't have and which would need to be borrowed from his father, with the concomitant fear of then losing them. There was also the faffing about to be considered, the general mechanism a near impossibility for someone like Hungry Paul who was all thumbs. He sat on the side of his bed in his pants and socks, wearing the shirt with its ridiculous flapping cuffs, a ghost of his earlier triumphant self.

Reluctantly, he had to walk down in this semi-dressed state to ask his dad for the cuff links, not being prepared to fish around in his father's private drawers himself. He then had to ask his mother to fasten the cuff links, a job she was only too delighted to help with, pointing out that it was no shame and that she did the same for his father. But it was no use. Hungry Paul's earlier confidence had escaped him like a nearly-knotted balloon that had slipped away and fizzed around the room. When they left for the prize-giving, he sat in the back seat of the car with the window open, quiet and devoid of social energy.

They picked Leonard up en route to the local centre where the Chamber of Commerce prize-giving was to take place at 3pm as the climax to an afternoon of what were described as 'community events.' Leonard locked his front door and joined them in the car, but he was in an agitated state of mind himself. In a spontaneous act of good humour, he had texted Shelley to ask if she wanted to come to the prize-giving. He was now sufficiently sure of his position as boyfriend to introduce her to the others, and show her off a bit. She texted back a cheerful but regretful 'no,' as she had Patrick to look after. Not to be easily discouraged, Leonard had suggested that she bring him along, as there was bound to be kids' stuff there. She texted back, with what he perceived to be strained patience, that she thought it was still too soon for Patrick to meet Leonard, and besides, she had made him other promises which were not easily unmade. Leonard gave a short, understanding reply and suggested that they meet for lunch on Monday, disguising his bruised sense of having been put in his place, a few rungs below where he had understood himself to be.

With both Leonard and Hungry Paul stewing in self-pity, they sat on the back seat together in near silence. As they each suspected some frostiness in the other because of the midweek cancellation of their Monopoly game, they misread each other's mood, and in doing so doubled their helping of unhappiness.

They arrived for the prize-giving a little late and the hall was already noisy and full of people. The event, which had pretensions of showcasing the greatest business minds in the area, had a feeling of general community randomness. Its main focus was on the promotion of local small and medium enterprises through the timeless medium of information stands. A local pizza restaurant was showing people how to roll dough, and an executive from a company selling Velux windows was asking two young girls to keep their fingers out of the moving hinge of the demonstration model. The far corner of the room housed a section for the council library and exhibited the winners of the children's art competition, who had been announced earlier in the day. The winning entries were a picture of a sad puppy looking out of a window, a lighthouse in a storm, Ronaldo, and what looked like a picture of the Mona Lisa, though in the image of the little girl who painted it. A lady in the opposite corner was doing face painting and balloon animals, and was having a devil of a time painting Spiderman on the face of a crying boy who probably just needed a nap. In the middle of it all there was a guy with a beret, whose face was painted white with a clown tear on his cheek, who was going up to random punters and mimicking their actions in mime. Dads joined in and laughed it off, dads in general being the good sports in any family. The mime artist came up to Hungry Paul's face and stared at him, hoping to copy his reaction. Hungry Paul stared back into the eyes of the mime artist, recognising in him a kindred enjoyment of the silent life. Eventually the mime artist pointed at Hungry Paul's name badge, which read 'Special Guest,' and when he looked down did that trick of running his finger up to flick Hungry Paul in the face, before running off in silent hysterical laughter.

Helen and Peter wandered around the stands, wavering between half-hearted curiosity and resistance to sales-based small talk. The organiser from the Chamber of Commerce scooted over to Hungry Paul: 'Found you! Come on over here, I want you to meet our new president—he has just been appointed. He's over there with the chains of office. He'll be announcing the winner in a few minutes, so when you see him take the lectern, just wait at the side of the stage.'

Hungry Paul was introduced to the Chamber President, a man called Mike Brine, who was also the owner of Mike's Bike's, an ungrammatical bicycle shop on the main street, near the station. Mike spoke enthusiastically about the competition, saying that it was not the number of entries that counted but the quality, in effect confirming that the only three entries received had all been shortlisted. Standing to his left were the other two nominees. There was a businesswoman named Carol who ran a beauty salon and who was also a member of the Chamber of Commerce. She had lobbed in an entry only because it looked like they had received no responses and she wanted to save the Chamber from embarrassment. Her entry—'Please feel free to get in touch'—was, the judges felt, 'practical and permissive, though not wholly original.' She saw it as being in keeping with her long-standing reputation as a safe pair of hands. The other nominee was a taxi driver named Dermot—and not a taxidermist as Hungry Paul had originally misheard—who had entered purely to win the money and who boasted that he entered every competition he could. The inclusion of his entry—'Don't be a stranger'—was controversial, with one judge's assessment being that it was 'short, direct and moronic.'

The organiser took the mic and asked people to put their hands together for 'our new president,' omitting the unnecessary clarification that she was referring only to the president of the Chamber of Commerce, and not the Head of State. Mike from Mike's Bike's launched into an extravagant overplaying of the inspirational nature of the event, saying that it would be talked about for many years to come, while also sticking in something about how community includes 'unity.' As he spoke, the mime artist stood beside him doing what looked like sign language, but which was actually just plain old mickey-taking. Mike, who was presidential in his obliviousness, did his best to create dramatic tension when introducing the nominees by announcing the results in reverse order.

In third place, unsurprisingly, was Dermot whose entry had earned him a hamper of bike-related goods, including a puncture repair kit and a pair of those tights cyclists wear with a cushioned section to prevent saddle soreness. In second place was Carol, who won a spa treatment of her choice from her own salon, something which President Mike described as 'a break-even outcome.'

A process of elimination helped Hungry Paul to deduce for himself that he was the winner, even before his name was announced. Helen and Peter had also 'done the math' and embraced him with evident pride. Leonard, with his writer's powers of perception, joined in, his double handshake and big smile being returned in kind by his old pal.

Hungry Paul climbed the steps to the dais where his winning phrase was unfurled on a banner that spanned the stage and which had been kindly donated by Perfecto Print—'Your Words, Our Bond'. It read:

'You may wish to note the above.'

It was classic Hungry Paul. It assumed that what was of real interest to the letter reader were the preceding paragraphs and merely pointed out their noteworthiness, while also leaving the door open if the reader felt otherwise. Most importantly, it added nothing new to the letter, and in doing so, got to the heart of the matter, in that sign-off phrases are merely a device to avoid an otherwise abrupt conclusion to the correspondence. The judges in the Chamber of Commerce had been deeply relieved that such an insightful and worthy entry had emerged from what was a limited field. There was a big round of applause and some cheering, as a few people stepped forward to inspect the phrase, while others repeated it out loud to themselves to get used to its sound. Some eager business people were already on their phones, asking their teams back at base to update their templates so that they could be first to the market with the winning phrase. The atmosphere in the room was one of levity and celebration, mixed with confusion, as President Mike had neglected to tell the non-Chamber attendees what the competition was about. The mime artist captured all this beautifully in a complex mime, which is hard to do justice here in writing.

President Mike handed Hungry Paul a giant novelty cheque for ten grand and a trophy, which depicted a severed hand writing with a quill. He then invited Hungry Paul to say a few words, as the mime artist stood by to translate.

Hungry Paul approached the mic and surveyed the faces below. He had never had the chance to see this view before, all these people so happy and lively, yet hardly following what was going on, cheering for the sheer fun of it. Hungry Paul stood there silently, staring out into a crowd that became progressively quieter as they waited for him to say something. President Mike, a born leader, who assumed that this was an attack of nerves, whispered: 'Just thank everybody and tell them to have a good time.' But Hungry Paul stayed there, calm and quiet. The mime artist sat down on the edge of the stage, scratched his head comically and looked at his watch. In the end, President Mike, a true pro, simply took the mic, thanked everyone and glossed over the momentary awkwardness by saying that the winner had been overcome with emotion.

As he stepped off the stage, Hungry Paul once again accepted the congratulations of his family, the Chamber members and other well-wishers. Leonard made a special point of expressing his admiration for the light touch used in crafting the winning phrase, which meant a lot to Hungry Paul, as Leonard was not only his best friend but a professional writer who knew what he was talking about.

A reporter from the *Community Voice* asked Hungry Paul for a quote he could use in an advertorial about the competition but again was met with silence. The mime stood behind him, signing as if to zip his lips, then strangling himself with a noose before chopping his own head off. The reporter asked: 'Is this a joke or what?' but Hungry Paul simply stood there, enjoying the moment like a warm bath. The following week, there was a two-page feature on the event in the *Community Voice*, including a large photo of Hungry Paul with the caption: 'A sentence speaks a thousand words.' It was accompanied by lengthy quotes from Hungry Paul about the great work being done by the Chamber of Commerce, which had been composed and supplied by President Mike in a follow-up email.

With the prize-giving over, the other community events

also wound down, as the hall was emptied to allow for a quick turnaround before the alcohol-free teen disco that was due to start a few hours later.

While Leonard helped Peter fit the giant novelty cheque into the boot, which required the removal of the parcel shelf, Hungry Paul sat on the steps with the mime artist, who had slipped out of character and was smoking a cigarette and chatting. They seemed to have a lot to say to each other and finished on a handshake, with Hungry Paul being given a business card. As Leonard decided to walk home to clear his head, Peter drove Helen and Hungry Paul home in high spirits as if after winning a Cup Final. The man himself, who was enjoying the breeze from the open window, sat in the back in his new suit, his mind feeling free and open, just like his double cuffs.

Chapter 17: FAMILY DINNER

After a strange day at the prize-giving, Helen, Peter and Hungry Paul arrived back at the house feeling full of cheer and silliness. With Grace and Andrew due over the next day for Sunday dinner, the original plan had been to spend that Saturday evening preparing the food and getting the house in order. Instead, they spent their collective good humour finding a spot to hang the giant novelty cheque, before popping open a tin of sweets and watching *Broadway Danny Rose*.

So, on Sunday morning there were no lie-ins, as everything was organised for a crisp, military start to the day. Tasks were assigned and time slots agreed, with a view to presenting relaxed tidiness and hot food to Grace and Andrew when they arrived that afternoon.

The key to the whole thing was, of course, not getting under each other's feet. Helen was in charge of the main meal and had driven off to the shops as soon as they opened to buy a small number of essentials, including salt and sage, the kind of things you buy so seldom that you never notice them running out until it happens. Peter was in charge of starters and dessert, the former being a goat's cheese and walnut salad that he would assemble in real time on their arrival, the latter being tinned fruit and vanilla ice cream, a throwback to childhood days which would delight Grace while also getting over the problem that Peter had watched the movie last night instead of making a Pavlova. Hungry Paul was on bins—including the small ones in the bedrooms and bathrooms—and setting the table, two jobs that had comprised his household responsibilities for most of his adult life. He also refilled the bird feeders every day, although he didn't count that as a chore.

Grace and Andrew had had a busy few days. Though they had intended to build some romance into their schedule, they had spent most of the time zipping back and forth in the car, picking up and dropping off all the minor bits and pieces that season a wedding day into a success. The to-do list included finding a thick, fragrance-free wedding candle; making bows for the aisle ends; buying a fancy pen for signing the register; drawing coloured signs to guide guests to the out-of-the-way church; and picking up the clothes they needed for the honeymoon in Kyoto, where the temperature, like themselves, would be in the mid-thirties.

On the morning of the family dinner, Grace had gone running on an empty stomach and ended up having to walk back to the house, feeling drained. She went back to bed for half an hour, but Andrew let her sleep on. This meant that she woke up too late to get ready in time, and had to rush around feeling grouchy and stiff. They ended up arguing in the car on the way over, as he blamed her for being late every single bloody time, and she blamed him for not bloody waking her when she had asked, especially when he had bloody well insisted there was no need for her to set a bloody alarm. They arrived thirty minutes late, having had barely enough time to pick up some wine and flowers on the way. But when Peter opened the door they projected a happy portrait of public unity, which Peter and Helen mirrored, having just had an intense moment themselves over the current state of play on the starters.

'Great to see you love,' welcomed Helen, as Grace handed her the flowers with a cheek kiss that protected their make-up. 'Oh, you're very good—there's really no need, but they are lovely. Hi Andrew love—thanks for coming over. You both must be so busy.'

'Lovely to see you, Helen,' said Andrew, accepting a hug.

'Sorry it's been a while—I've been travelling and you know how it is. How have you been?'

'Great, great. Come on in. Here—I'll take the coats. You're right to wrap up—it's still nippy out there, even with the sun,' said Helen, overloading the newel post of the banister with the coats.

In the front room, Hungry Paul had just sat down after all his jobs to read his *National Geographic* from the library.

'And here he is, the man of the hour! Here, give me a hug. I'm chuffed about your prize. Well done. So we'll be seeing your handiwork on the end of all our company emails now I guess?' said Grace, delighted to see Hungry Paul.

'Something like that,' he said. 'You look well. Hope you're not too busy with the wedding and everything. Hi Andrew, please do come in—how have you been?'

'All's good, thanks. Good to see you,' said Andrew giving a manly shoulder-to-opposite-shoulder embrace that was over before Hungry Paul knew how to respond to it. 'Congratulations on the prize. What was the phrase again: "Thank you for noting the above" or something? Congratulations. We'll all have to start using it now. You'll be famous.'

'I don't know about that,' answered Hungry Paul. 'Dad will be here in a minute. He's on starters, so he's inside manhandling some salad I think.'

Grace went into the kitchen and offered to help out, looking for the one good knife in the top drawer.

'You relax, darling. I'm okay here,' said Peter. 'I have your mother's watchful eye on me so I'll be fine. You can open some wine if you like. Open the nice one you brought, not the screw top your brother bought—it comes from Colombia! Whoever drinks wine from there?'

Grace took drinks orders from everybody and, in a quiet aside to Andrew, offered to drive if he wanted to drink, but he gave her a kiss on the forehead and said it was okay, he would drive, thus making everything as sweet as pancakes between them again.

'Places everybody!' called Helen, as the window for preliminary drinks had been blown by Grace's late arrival, which had also put Helen's timings for the chicken under pressure. They all sat around the table in no particular formation, except for Helen sitting closest to the door, which would be easier for serving. Years before, Helen had wanted to knock the dining room through to the kitchen to have an open plan downstairs, but Peter had pleaded with her not to, as he didn't want washing machines and tumble dryers in the background when he was having his dinner. She had relented, and now with much regret, the kitchen was cut off from the rest of the downstairs, which meant you couldn't chat while preparing dinner, and you had to bring the food the long way around. Peter didn't mind, as he was able to carry four starters in one go: one in each hand and two further plates balanced using his thumbs and little fingers, like they do in restaurants. He was an expert at carrying a lazy man's load and could open door handles with his buttock, close them with elbows, and turn on light switches with his chin. This time though, he got Hungry Paul to help, as he had already been closely critiqued by Helen and didn't want to be held further accountable if there was a spillage.

As they tucked in to the starters—everyone feeling hungry, having saved their appetites all morning—Grace and Helen caught up on the wedding arrangements.

'So basically, the cake guy says he's closed on Good Friday but I have to text him and he'll come down to the shop and open up especially, because if we don't get it down to the hotel on the Friday, we would have to do it on the Monday, as their wedding person is away for the weekend and I don't want to hand it to anyone else,' Grace explained.

'I can do that for you if you like,' offered Peter.

'You're fine, thanks Dad—I wouldn't mind checking if all's as it should be and having one last catch-up with the hotel person before Monday. The florist should have the bouquets done for Sunday evening, but as it is Easter he's not sure what time, because he says he has family commitments and overall, to be honest, he has been slow to get back to me. I'm hoping we don't end up using service station flowers on the day. I don't want to walk up the aisle reeking of diesel, like some trucker bride. Are you still okay to do the offertory gifts, Mam? You'll be doing it with Andrew's mother.'

'Of course. It will be nice to see your parents again, Andrew. We haven't met up with them in quite a while. It would have been nice to have them over beforehand, but never mind,' said Helen.

'They're looking forward to it, Helen,' said Andrew. 'Mam is a bit shy in big crowds so she's delighted to have you to talk to. You'll all be at the same table, so you'll be able to catch up there.'

'How's your dad?' asked Peter. 'Still playing golf with no sun cream?'

'Yeah, he plays a few times a week with his old business friends. He's always asking me to play but I never got into it. I should really go out anyway, but he gets very competitive, so it's not exactly quality time. Did you ever play, Peter?'

'I played crazy golf once with your mother. But I lost and had to pay a forfeit,' said Peter, smiling and nudging Helen.

'Stop it you! Our whole lives told in front of everybody. Don't mind him, Andrew. He doesn't like playing games he's not good at,' said Helen.

'It's true, too,' said Hungry Paul. 'We have a stack of games he's only ever played once. He prefers quiz-type board games, which aren't really board games at all. Trivial Pursuit and all that. Why not just sit an exam?' Hungry Paul was a purist and believed that you should only succeed based on your skill at the game itself, and that it was cheating to rely on knowledge acquired outside it.

They were all hungry and finished up their starters quickly, even the family's slow eater, Grace, who was also enjoying the wine she had brought.

Helen got up to get the chicken out, batting away Grace's offer of help and instead topping up her wine. 'Relax—you've been rushed off your feet all week. Take it easy today. Come on Peter, let's see how good your waiting skills are with the main course.'

'It's all ahead of you Andrew. Once they get the ring, you're just another staff member to them,' said Peter as Helen responded by giving him a whip of the tea towel. After they had left, Grace took another sip of wine and turned to Hungry Paul, who wasn't much of a drinker.

'Tell us about yesterday. Did you get a trophy or anything?'

'I did indeed. There it is over there—a severed hand!' he said in a spooky voice, pointing to the trophy on the mantelpiece. 'I also got some prize money.'

'Go on, how much?' Andrew and Grace asked together.

'Quite a bit actually—ten grand.'

'Flippin' hell!' said Grace, genuinely surprised. 'That's some serious money. Wow! I wish I had entered now.'

'I even got one of those giant novelty cheques. It's upstairs. Dad said he'd make me a frame for it. They're not real cheques—you can't cash them, which I didn't actually realise until the president came up to me and handed over the proper cheque when I was leaving.'

'The President was there?' said Andrew, impressed.

'Well, not *the* president. The president of the Chamber of Commerce, Mike Brine. He owns Mike's Bike's on the main street.'

'Is that the one with the illiterate sign?' asked Grace.

'That's the one. He's a nice guy actually. He has a chain of office and everything. They take it really seriously.'

'Obviously they do—ten grand is no bloody joke. Flippin' hell,' repeated Grace.

'So what are you going to do with the cash?' asked Andrew

'Oh. I don't know. I haven't really thought about it.'

'Really? Is that not why you entered? Isn't there anything you want to treat yourself to?' said Andrew, revealing just a little bit too much attentiveness to the question of the money.

'Not really. I wasn't trying to win. I just saw that they had a problem and thought I had the answer that could help them. I don't have many talents that I can put to good use—as you know—but in this case I thought I might be able to step in, and so it proved. The money was their idea really. They wanted to make a fuss, and you know what business people are like, the only thing that makes a splash with them is cash,' said Hungry Paul.

'Yeah, but you should really think about this. I mean it's a lot of money. You could do something significant.' Grace had already finished her second glass, the shock of the prize money making her gulp in more ways than one.

'I'm not used to money, so I don't want to waste it. I think I'll just put it in the credit union for a rainy day. You never know,' answered Hungry Paul, hardly giving it a thought.

'But, but, you need to think about this. I mean, in fairness Mam and Dad have always looked after you here, and they never really ask you to put your hand in your pocket, so shouldn't you think about someone else maybe? Perhaps do something nice for them? I mean, they don't charge you rent and Dad had to give you money for your wedding suit, and you don't hand up any of your post office money, and now that you have a few bob, you're just going to let it rot away in the building society or whatever—'

'—the credit union,' corrected Andrew.

'—thank you, the credit union,' snapped Grace, irritated at the interruption, 'I mean, shouldn't you take things a bit more seriously for once? We're all moving on. I'm getting married, Dad's retired, Mam *will* be retired in another year, but you're still living at home playing Guess Who? or whatever and working one day a week until, what? Is that ever going to change?

Will *you* ever change? You have a chance to pull up your boot-straps or whatever the phrase is.' Grace refilled her glass and shook the end of the bottle in puzzlement, as if it had been emptied by a leak or something. 'Just think about it, that's all. Promise me that, will you? Please, just promise me that?' She paused as she caught herself getting angry.

'Okay. I promise,' answered Hungry Paul. He wasn't sure what he had done to upset Grace and was taken aback at the edge in her voice. He was, by nature, a phlegmatic soul who seldom, if ever, took offence, always willing to give the benefit of the doubt and allow for circumstances. He had thought that Grace would be happy for him. All he had wanted to do was suggest a simple phrase that would help the Chamber of Commerce to resolve a problem that was perplexing them. He would have done so if there had been no money and no trophy. It was simply one of those rare occasions when he saw the answer, like when he spotted a gap on the Scrabble board that others had overlooked during their turn. Now that he had the money, which meant little to him, he would have been happy to give some or all of it to his parents, but it simply never occurred to him that they would have any interest in it. His dad had held onto his lump sum without touching it ever since his retirement. Apparently Peter had no idea what to spend it on, apart from travel, but even then, Helen seemed slow to commit to anything. Maybe he could pay for a holiday? Was that what Grace was on about? Or maybe Grace would appreciate some help with the wedding? They both had good jobs, but weddings aren't cheap and they had mentioned a few times about cutting back here and there, and the whole fiasco with the wedding numbers and plus ones must have been about money, mustn't it? Maybe that was it. In that case, he could see why Grace was so upset. She must be under so much pressure organising everything and now they had blown their budget. Of course. Well, as her only brother, he wouldn't see her short. He would offer her some money to get her through. Maybe give it to her as a loan, as she'd be too proud to take it otherwise. He'd then say nothing more about the money and, if she ever did try to pay it back, he'd just wave her away and say he'd forgotten all about it, and that she should too.

'Now then!' said Helen entering the room with a delighted look on her face, which was glistening from the heat of the kitchen. 'Sorry about disappearing like that, but I hope you all agree that it's been worth the wait.' She gave Grace and Andrew their plates first, with roast chicken, potatoes cooked in goose fat, root vegetables in butter, sage stuffing and a little bit of mushroom sauce on the side. Peter followed her with the other three plates before making a second trip to bring in the butter dish, which Hungry Paul had forgotten to set out.

'So,' said Helen, 'tuck in. Did you hear all about the prize-giving yesterday? We're so proud of him. All those business people tripping over themselves to shake your hand weren't they?' she said, turning to Hungry Paul, who hadn't yet fully recovered. 'We'll be reading your words for years to come. We'll always be reminded not just of your talent, but of the lovely day we had.'

Her chirpiness was genuine, reflecting the fact that her heart was singing to have her whole family together again after one special day, with another one still ahead of them. She wanted nothing more than to cook a nice meal for them, her two grown-up children who had turned out so well.

Chapter 18: HI MARK!

Leonard had finished the final edit on the company's book about the Romans. It had ended up as a competent compendium of dry facts and narratives, presented in a crisp but soulless style. It would, no doubt, launch hundreds of forgettable school projects that would be corrected by student teachers in their spare time, each one getting more or less the same mark as the others. Leonard was now free to work on his own book on the same subject, an advanced draft of which had been sitting in his top drawer ever since that happy day when Shelley had agreed to meet him for a walk in the park. In its current form the book was a depiction of the life of a young Roman boy. In reviewing his draft, though, Leonard realised that the boy was still stuck in some generic, stylised template, lacking in personality. He was hardly the type of boy that kids would want to travel through time to be or be with—he had no sense of fun or preferences, and was short on actions and details. Leonard needed to bring him to life. To do this he needed someone to write for, someone who would provide his motivation and act as an idealised audience at whom he could pitch little moments of humour and sensitivity. And so he had decided to write the book for Shelley's little boy Patrick, and named the Roman boy Patrius.

The book now seemed to open up into a range of Technicolour possibilities. Leonard thought about how Patrick would react to a book about his Roman self, which made Leonard want to pack it with interesting, exciting, lived-in facts; not merely dry bits of trivia to languish at the bottom of a schoolbag, but facts as vectors of life itself, as messengers from the past. Leonard drew him going to school in a toga, wearing a bulla to protect against evil, and playing with his toys in the years before Christmas and Santa Claus existed, if Patrick could even conceive of such a barren era. He drew him playing dice with real bones and included a two-page spread about Patrius' mother, who was freed after many victories as a gladiator. On the following page he included a fold-out section showing the inside of Patrius' lunchbox: a slice of emmer loaf, some dates, and a purple carrot. But Leonard also wanted to give Patrius normal traits that were less about Roman times and more a reflection of the type of boy who would have had someone as special as Shelley as his mother. Leonard wrote that Patrius tried hard and did as much work as was good for him, even if it was more than he would have liked. Patrius painted and sang songs every day. He asked lots of questions and answered his mother back, which he got scolded for, even though his mother took private satisfaction in observing that independent spirits do not skip a generation. While he hopped into bed a little late most evenings, he always went to the doctor when he was sick and was happy when his teeth fell out. The main thing to know about Patrius was that he shared his life with his family. Leonard drew him as yea big, with curly auburn hair, green eyes and—historical accuracy notwithstanding—*Star Wars* glasses. A fact box described him as having a big heart and a big imagination.

Leonard had worked on enough books to know that he now had sufficient detail to put together a pitch. His only problem was that he had never actually pitched anything by himself before. He usually handed that bit over to the overseeing author and only heard back when the book had been commissioned. After a few moments' reflection, he decided to take a chance and send his pitch and an extract to the only person he could think of:

To: himark@markbaxterbed.com

'Hi Mark,

I hope you're keeping well. I hear you're in demand on the conference circuit these days, so I'm sorry to trouble you, but there's this project I have been working on that I thought you might be interested in . . .'

Leonard did his best to pitch it to Mark Baxter, BEd, with all due deference, hoping to get his help to break through from backroom anonymity to full authorship credits. He had to handle this with some sensitivity, as he was in effect asking for Mark's help in bypassing him altogether, but he figured that Mark had been around long enough and would still negotiate a cut and a cover credit for himself, even if all he did was pass on the email. Leonard wasn't in a mood to drive a hard bargain. He signed off the message in conformity with the new company policy on email signatures:

'You may wish to note the above.

Leonard'

He pressed 'send' and felt as though he had just thrown a water balloon over a privet hedge. Now that he'd submitted the pitch he would have to go into overdrive to finish the book in case Mark Baxter, BEd, took an interest and asked to see a full draft. But first, he noticed that the four clocks in view—his watch, mobile, computer, and desk phone—all displayed different times, meaning he was either slightly early, on time or a little late for his lunch date with Shelley. Leonard had arranged to meet her out by the bike rack, to avoid any unwelcome office banter from Helpdesk Greg. He couldn't wait to tell her about his idea of writing the book for and about Patrick, and about how she had inspired him to send it to the famous Mark Baxter, BEd. She had brought nothing but goodness to his life ever since she entered it.

When he reached the bike rack, Shelley was already waiting for him. As usual she was loaded like a packhorse with all her cycling gear.

'Hey, how are things?' he said, 'Let me carry that for you. How was your morning, and your weekend, come to think of it?'

'Okay, I suppose. Just hanging out with Patrick. He was a bit bored from being inside, but didn't want to go out. He gets like that sometimes. Kids get tired after a week at school, but I couldn't just let him sit indoors playing Lego all day, so I promised him a trip to the cinema.'

'Anything good? Did you go see the film from the Happy Meal?'

'No, actually. I never thought of that. We went to see the latest *Fart of Darkness* movie. You know, the usual format with loads of jokes aimed over the kids' heads at the parents. I was a bit snoozy in the cinema and he sort of wanted to leave once he had finished his treats. He was just in one of those hard-to-please moods. How about you—how did your friend get on at the prize-giving?'

'Great, yeah, really good. He won actually. Got a trophy of a severed hand and a giant cheque for ten grand. We could hardly fit it in the boot.'

'Wow, what a prize! Can you cash those giant cheques?'

'Nope. They give you a real cheque too. He's getting the giant one framed.'

'What's he going to do with the money?'

'Hard to know. He's never really had any money and he's not hugely interested in it. His sister is getting married on Easter

Monday, so he was talking about maybe helping her with that. She's booked the reception at Whitethorn Castle, which can't have been cheap. They've had to keep the numbers tight, so I've had to surrender my plus one, I'm afraid.'

They walked on a bit but the conversation petered out. With Hungry Paul, Leonard was able to surf over any silences, but things were different with Shelley. Getting the conversation going sometimes felt a bit like a hill start.

'So, where are we going by the way? Any ideas?' she asked.

'How about the bog bodies?' suggested Leonard.

'Okay. I haven't been to see them before. Are they scary?'

'Oh no, I shouldn't think so. It's just these leathery old bodies in bits and pieces. You can see all of their features perfectly though; some even have hair.'

'Okay. It sounds interesting, though I'll hold off scoring it for romantic potential until I see them,' she said, trying to raise a smile but not quite managing it.

The conversation went quiet again. He noticed how Shelley was often the pace setter between them. When she was bubbly and positive, everything was great, but when she was quiet, they struggled.

'Everything okay?' he asked as they approached the exhibition.

'Hmmm. Sort of. Well, not really. There's something I wanted to ask you. But it's kind of awkward.'

There was a feeling of a ghost walking across his abdomen. 'Ask away,' he said.

'It's about Patrick. Me and Patrick anyway. I'm really enjoying our time together, you and me I mean, and I like the way we are taking things slowly, but I was just wondering about what you said in your message about meeting Patrick. It kind of took me by surprise. I wasn't sure what you meant really. So, I dunno, I just wanted to ask you about it.'

'Oh, I see. I hadn't really thought about it to be honest. I just wondered whether you might like join us and, if you were minding Patrick, he could come too. Nothing more than that. All at face value, et cetera, et cetera.'

They were standing at the door of the exhibition. Leonard felt he was being tested but didn't understand the question.

'Patrick is my world, Leonard. I have put my life into looking after him. I don't want to mess him around.'

'Oh, of course, of course.'

'What I mean is that I can't introduce him to just any man I have met for a few dates.'

The characterisation was brutally clarifying for Leonard.

'Oh, I see. Of course. I mean, I never meant to interfere with you and Patrick. I was just trying to be nice.'

'I know, I know. I'm not criticising you. It's just that I can't tell him who you are, that you write his favourite books, and then let him meet you and then if things don't work out, he'll just feel abandoned and rejected, and I don't want that to happen. I can't just bring him along without explaining who you are. Not just your name and that you write the books, but who you are to me, and specifically, who you are to him. Do you understand? Do you understand that that's important to me? And why it's so important?'

A tour group of Italian students pushed between them, all wearing puff jackets and skinny jeans. It took a few minutes for the babbling line of teenagers to file past. Shelley looked at Leonard through the gaps in the crowd with a sad and gentle expression on her face. When they had all passed, Leonard might have said something, done something or otherwise conveyed to Shelley that he understood, truly understood, what she was getting at. She was sending a distress signal to him that was bouncing back to her unread. Leonard knew that something important was happening, but he was just too unsure, too inexperienced for the subtlety that was expected of him.

'Right so, should we head inside then? These bog bodies will be getting impatient!'

He could feel the echo of his own ridiculousness all around him. A big kid in an adult conversation. Found out.

'I'm going to go, Leonard.' Shelley gave him one last deep look with those sorry, sad, soulful eyes.

'Oh, okay. Maybe another time then,' said Leonard, panicked and paralysed. Out of his depth.

Shelley took her cycling gear from him.

'Bye Leonard.'

He stood at the door of the exhibition, watching her go through the most uncinematic rigmarole of putting on her cycling gear. She gave him a small, heroic smile that she would do her best to keep from turning tearful until she had faced around and was on her way. He stood still, dumbstruck with the significance of it all, watching her cycle off into the traffic and away from him.

Feeling undone and in need of somewhere quiet to gather himself, Leonard drifted into the exhibition, where he sat alone in a dimly lit room. Alongside him, a two-thousand-year-old bog man lay prostrate in a display case, preserved in the pose he held at the very moment his life changed.

Chapter 19: THE GAME OF LIFE

Later that evening, after dinner, Leonard hauled his heavy heart to Parley View for some uncomplicated friendship and board games. The good people at Milton Bradley were early pioneers of the kindergarten movement, and many of the classic games that bore the MB brand name over the years were designed with a gentle edifying purpose in mind. This was especially true of the Game of Life, a cheerfully competitive board game that sought to prepare its players for the boons and forfeits that Messrs Milton and Bradley saw as the reality of life. For Leonard the game had a new and special resonance. In recent weeks, he had lost his mother, inherited a house, embarked on a new career direction, and had met, and probably lost, the most special girl he had ever known. As he pushed his playing piece around the board—a car with an empty passenger seat and no blue or pink pegs in the rear—he could see a familiar pattern of ups and downs playing out before him.

Hungry Paul, who respected the privacy of a man's thoughts, and who ordinarily enjoyed extended calming silences with his friend, nevertheless became concerned at Leonard's abject mood. At one point Leonard reached past the chocolate and fancy biscuits to take a ginger nut, a sure sign that all was not what it should be.

'Anything up?' ventured Hungry Paul.

'Sorry?' replied Leonard from amidst the fog.

'Anything up, I said. It's just that you don't seem yourself. You've passed up two chances at buying a status symbol, as well as forgoing the opportunity to sue me for damages, and you seem content to fork out for an unsuccessful South Pole expedition and munch on ginger nuts which, to be honest, seem to me to be on the turn.'

'Oh, yes. I'm not quite myself this evening. I had hoped that I would perk up, but I'm sorry, I've had a difficult day.'

'I see. Roman trouble?' asked Hungry Paul.

'No, the Romans are not doing any damage. That whole project is actually going quite well. It's Shelley. We had a bit of . . . a bit of a problem and I think I may have lost her.'

'Oh, I see. What happened?'

'I don't know.'

'What do you mean?'

'I mean I don't know what happened.'

'If you don't know what happened, how do you know it has happened? I don't understand,' replied Hungry Paul. 'And if you don't know and I don't understand, then neither of us is really up to speed on any of this. Should we try again? What did she say to you?'

'She said that I didn't understand,' replied Leonard.

'Well she's right there.'

'She said I didn't understand about her and Patrick.'

'And do you?'

'Do I what?' answered Leonard.

'Do you understand?'

'You see, at the weekend I suggested that she might come along to your prize-giving but she was minding Patrick, so I thought that she could bring him along. She didn't want to do that because, for one thing, he would want to know who I am and all about the situation with Shelley and me. Between all the complications, I think Shelley wanted me to say or do the right thing at the right moment, but I just didn't know what she wanted me to say, so I ended up making a mess of things and now she probably thinks I'm hopeless and that it was blessed relief that she found out when she did, even if it hurts her feelings in the short run.'

'The short run can often be full of feelings,' observed Hungry Paul, sagely.

'The thing is, she's a sensitive person, even though she's quite positive in her outlook. She just has so much more at stake than I do. She has to think of Patrick and the future, whereas I only have to think about whether to bring her to a nice restaurant or to the bog bodies.'

'Bog bodies?' asked Hungry Paul, taking his turn.

'Yes, we had this discussion on the way to the bog bodies. She went home before we got a chance to go in.'

'That's a pity—some of them still have hair, you know. So where do you stand on the whole Patrick business? Going from long-term bachelorhood to becoming the father figure in a ready-made family is not straightforward, I would imagine.'

'I don't know. I hadn't thought that far. I just wanted to get to know Shelley, find a place for myself in her life, and her in my life, and then deal with the rest whenever it came up.'

'And what's wrong with that?' asked Hungry Paul, who landed on Jury Service and had to miss a turn.

'I don't know,' replied Leonard, 'But it turns out that it is wrong. It turns out that it's actually quite a hurtful thing to do.'

'I see. It's true that it's hard not to hurt people. Even doing nothing, you can end up hurting people. It seems that on the question of whether you are damned, there is an 'x' in both the 'do' and 'don't' columns. Your turn.'

'I don't even know what I am supposed to do in the meantime,' said Leonard, spinning the wheel. 'I mean, is she waiting for me to ring her or send her a message or what? I wouldn't even know what to say. But I sense that every minute I let it pass she is slipping further from my life. What would you do in my situation?'

'This is not my area of expertise, I'm afraid. Although if you do decide to send her a text I could suggest a very handy sign-off phrase.'

'Sorry to keep talking about myself. How are things going with the wedding? Did you get your suit cleaned after the prize-giving?' asked Leonard.

'The wedding plans are going fine I think. Some trouble with an organist driving a hard bargain, but all seems well. Grace is a little tense and judgemental these days but Mam's trying to offer moral support. To her and to us. I'm not able to get my suit cleaned just yet: I need it for Wednesday, for an interview.'

'What interview?'

'Sorry, I never told you. Yes, I have an interview. I was talking to that mime artist at the prize-giving—he's Dutch, his name is Arno—and he is involved with the National Mime Association. He mentioned that they are looking for a spokesman and he thought I might be suitable, so he asked if I would like to do an interview. He's moving back to the Netherlands and they need someone to fill the job quickly before he goes. He thought I might bring a bit of profile to the post because of the competition, and that I might get along with the mime community.'

'Well if it's silence they are after, their talent scouts are to be commended for finding their man. How does the National Mime Association have a spokesperson? I thought they didn't speak.'

'That's just the thing. They feel that mime is going out of fashion and that all anyone remembers is Marcel Marceau and his walking in the wind, good though it is. These days the guys who just stand as still as statues in the main street are much more popular.'

'Is that not mime?' asked Leonard innocently.

'Good God, no!' answered Hungry Paul, laughing. 'The statue people are pretty much at war with the mime artists. There have been a few incidents and the whole thing could blow up any day.

The problem for the mime artist is that life is so noisy now, they are being left behind. We live in an age of cacophony. Everyone talking and thinking out loud, with no space or oxygen left for quiet statements and silence. In a way, it's not just about being a spokesman for the National Mime Association, but a spokesman for silence itself.'

'What are you going to say at the interview?'

'I was thinking of asking them if I could still have Mondays off so that I can keep my promises at the post office.'

'Will that be enough to secure the position?'

'Possibly not. What kind of things do they usually ask? I've never had an interview before—I got the post office job through Dad.'

'In general, they usually like to know if you're a born leader, a visionary and a can-do sort of person.'

'I suppose there are probably lots of things I *could* do if I were to try them, but generally I don't try them, so maybe I'm more of a could-don't person?'

'I guess it's a start. Don't overthink it. These mime artists probably prefer someone a bit, you know, quiet.'

'Indeed,' pondered Hungry Paul. 'Indeed.'

Chapter 20: FATHER OF THE BRIDE

Peter hadn't written anything down yet for his speech but he had allowed a healthy collection of ideas to build up over the preceding weeks. He had asked Grace to meet him for a walk just to run through a few things, but also to check in with her in case she was having a meltdown from the pre-wedding stress, which was certainly Helen's view of the whole situation.

Peter had spent his career as a peripatetic economist, starting out as a researcher, then lecturer, before trying a disastrous turn as the in-house economist for a bank and then, finally, on the off-ramp of his career, returning to an academic backwater doing what he had liked doing most all along: teaching economics to interested young people. He had seen the economics profession change over the years. When he started, they were all idealists who believed that they held the missing piece of the puzzle in solving societal problems. Over time, the job seemed to change from one of understanding and decoding the market, to advocating for it. It had become a job devoid of ideological diversity and ambivalent in its methods: disdaining the soft centred humanity of the social sciences, but not quite committing to the disciplined empiricism of the physical sciences. Instead, it ended up as an add-on to arts and business courses, or else dominated by maths graduates who found it easier than real maths.

Throughout that time Peter had always been good at presentations and lectures. He knew how to build a narrative and drop in what seemed like effortless pieces of prepared spontaneity. Over a long career, he had amassed a tidy repertoire of humorous anecdotes and self-deprecating digressions—sometimes featuring Helen or his children, though not by name—which meant that he was able to keep his presentations fresh enough to entertain those of his colleagues who heard him speak regularly. It always made him marvel that introverts made the best speakers, perhaps taking themselves less seriously than the showboating businessmen who usually took the 'appearance fee' slots at conferences. Peter's trick was simple: he never made it about himself. He never put his fragile ego or reputation at stake, instead letting the subject be the star. For all his easy-going delivery, he prepared meticulously, and placed great emphasis on maintaining what he called a 'boxer's mind': relaxed enough to deliver what he needed, but alert enough not to get punched in the face. As good as he was, it took a lot out of him. He recalled a conference some years previously where he had given a lengthy talk to a ballroom full of international climate economists, after which, feeling exhausted, he had shut himself inside his hotel room for the rest of the evening and demolished two large chocolate Santas.

His Father-of-the-Bride speech would be a little different. Peter knew that he needed to go beyond a performance and finishing with an 'awww.' He wanted to dig inside himself to find the most sincere thing he could say. Though it wouldn't be easy, he had to mine past his obvious love and affection for Grace, into the molten core of their relationship, where deep connections had been forged between them. Most of all, he wanted her to embark on her new life with his full blessing, to know that her marriage was not a case of moving on or letting go, but manifest proof of her mastery of her own life. The very fact that she had, by her instincts and judgement, uncovered the path to her happiness, was the culmination of her own self-taught apprenticeship.

Peter had seen many Father-of-the-Bride speeches given over the years, including by his friends and colleagues, and they were the one aspect of the big day that never went wrong. At worst, the speeches could be a little unoriginal, or could end up as a two-person tango between the father and his daughter, but there was never anything inappropriate or off colour in them. Men of his generation were generally good judges of tone on these occasions, recognising that the bride and groom were entitled to a little dignity on their special day.

He liked Andrew a lot. When he and Helen first met him they wondered whether Grace had gone for a trophy boyfriend: good-looking, seemed to have a few bob, polite to the parents, but without the creativity or edge they had always assumed was part of Grace's taste in men. Her job surprised them similarly. They had always thought she would end up working in a creative field, though at the practical end, as a gallery curator or literary editor. Instead she had become successful at what Helen called 'a big job' with a US multinational. Incrementally, her job had grown into a career that took over her time like ivy, even though she had not yet given up on restoring some sort of balance to her busy and serious life.

Over time, they saw Andrew's deeper side, the sincerity of his feeling and, above all, his devotion to Grace. Grace spent so much of her life being 'together' that she needed someone she could trust, around whom she could regress a little bit, and be a flake. Andrew seemed to understand her better on that level, that aloof side to her personality that was still something of a mystery to her parents, in particular Helen.

Peter always remembered the cheerful loyalty that Andrew showed in the early days when Grace was sick with glandular fever. It was probably hard for Grace to allow herself to be looked after by a new boyfriend before she had had a proper opportunity to set out her own terms for the relationship. But when you see a young man—too young to know how young he is—taking care of your daughter and doing it well, and, most amazing of all, her letting him do it, a father realises that nature is taking its course.

Peter had arranged to meet Grace at the magazine section of the newsagent in the village, so that whoever arrived first could wait in the warm and dry and busy themselves with some aimless browsing. Peter got there early and opened the *Economist*, which he noticed was still recommending Economics 1.01 for every crisis the world over.

Grace arrived a few minutes late and kissed him on the cheek before saying hello.

'Oh, your cheeks are cold. How are things?' he asked.

'Good, good, sorry I'm a bit late—couldn't get parking. Where do you want to walk—stay local or head off somewhere?'

'Well, if you have parking let's stay local. Up around the back of the golf course maybe?'

'Okay. We can sell any golf balls we find to help pay for the wedding.'

They walked along with Grace linking her dad's elbow. A chilly April breeze had taken up and there was a little bite in the air now that the sun was sinking. Grace put her woolly scarf over her head and Peter took out his Thinsulate hat, neither of them taking any chances with a head cold so close to the wedding.

'So, how are all the arrangements going?' he asked.

'Oh fine, fine. Usual schmusual.'

'I hope you're getting to enjoy the build-up and that it's not getting on top of you. You always push yourself too hard.'

'Thanks *Mam*. You can tell her that I'm fine and that I'm even starting to relax a tiny bit. Andrew and I met for lunch today and we didn't even discuss the wedding arrangements. He just sat there and stared at me lovingly while I ate his pizza.'

'I'm no doctor, but I think if you eat someone else's pizza, it still counts towards your cholesterol. Seriously though, is there anything bugging you that I could help with?'

'I have to confess that I am looking forward to a time—hopefully not too far away—when people are no longer asking how I am, how things are going and whether I am all excited. I don't mean to sound ungrateful, and people are just being kind, but it will be nice to retreat back to being an ordinary participant in the conversation. You know me, I don't like a fuss and I am doing my best to play up to the occasion, but it's getting a bit tiring and my battery is starting to bleep a bit.'

'I know what you mean. That sort of thing puts some people off weddings altogether. When the day comes you'll just get a burst of positivity. I wasn't keen on a fuss when your mother and I got married, but I remember looking out at the church and realising that I'd never been to a wedding before where I had had personal one-to-one moments with everyone in the room. I actually got quite emotional. I hope you feel something similar. At least you have a lovely holiday to look forward to afterwards.'

'I can't wait for that. I hope I can rest on the flight and that I don't get flattened by jet lag on top of the wedding tiredness. How about you and Mam—have you given any more thought to going on a trip yourselves?'

'We talked about it a bit. She seems to be a little keener than she was, but not quite ready to make a decision for definite. She's ruled out Asia because you'll be there.'

'Ha! Aw my God. What an excuse!' scoffed Grace.

'She's not daft, she knows you won't bump into each other, she just doesn't want you to think she's tracking you everywhere.'

'So, what's holding her back? She doesn't have to do a long flight if she doesn't want to. You could go to some European capital or something.'

'I think she's still unsure about your brother. He's making a real effort with things, what with the hospital volunteering and the competition and everything, but he still has his moments.'

'But Dad, he's a grown man. He needs to stand up for himself. Yes, I know he has his struggles, but now is the time to get him going under his own steam. In fact it would have been great to have done it ten years ago. Now he's got used to bumming about and relying on the two of you. You've done everything for him. You need to start pushing him a little bit.'

'I know, I know. We just want to be careful, that's all. And your mother just wants to be sure. I suppose, you'll be away and then you have your own life to lead, so we're just not sure what happens if something goes awry. I think your mother would feel better if there was a Plan B. You know, just in case of emergencies.'

'If that's directed at me, I'm afraid I'm going to have to disappoint you. I can't spend my whole life as his babysitter. I need to move on, Dad. So do you and Mam. We need to take off the stabilisers, for his sake as much as our own. Did he say anything about the competition money? You know he tried to offer it to me for the wedding? I said no—of course we're over budget, but only because we're spoiling ourselves. I told him that he should think about doing something for you two. Has he said anything more about it?'

'Not as far as I know. But we don't need the money. Why complicate things? We just want to see him set up and we need to get ready to make that leap ourselves. I think I'm ready, but you know how your mam is. She'll try and support him but she wouldn't relax if she didn't think it was all figured out.'

'But you and Mam really need a break. Don't become one of those couples who leave it too late to travel and do all the things you have earned for yourselves.'

'We're not finished yet, chicken, but I know what you're saying. Just be patient okay? Especially with your mam. I think the wedding has kept her mind off the future, but she'll start to wonder about all that once you've tied the knot good and tight.'

They stopped at the end of the loop and began the walk back, the turnaround resetting the conversation topic.

'So tell me about your speech,' asked Grace, hugging into Peter a bit now that they were facing back into the wind on the return leg.

'I haven't written anything down yet, but I think I'm in the zone, so I need to start deciding on what I'm doing. Are you going to say a few words?'

'I'll see on the day. Not a speech, maybe just a few thank yous.'

'Word of advice. You can improvise a speech, but you shouldn't improvise thank yous—you're bound to forget someone and you won't get a second chance, so write them down. I made that mistake at my own wedding and forgot to thank your aunt Sarah, who had made the cake. She was so nice about it, but I knew that I had hurt her feelings.'

'If I can make one request for your own speech: keep it classy. No digging up embarrassing stories or poking fun at Andrew.'

'Good Lord, of course not. I may be an idiot, but I'm not *that* type of idiot. You know that I think the world of you and that I love you and that I'm so proud of you. This could be the only chance I get to say all those things in front of people. I need to find the right words so I don't choke up. I can see my throat getting lumpy if I go too deep.'

'Lumpy is fine. Lumpy but classy is what we're aiming for. Why get so upset? I moved out yonks ago and I've been with Andrew for a few years, even living together. Nothing changes you know. It's just a ritual.'

'I know you say that, but it does matter. Wait and see. Once Andrew is your husband things will seem subtly changed. There's a new type of closeness you feel, even if there's no logical reason to feel different. Part of me looks at you and realises that our family is changing. It's all good and natural, and I'm not getting soppy about it, but it seems like the end of a long first chapter. Your favourite brother, who you say is so hopeless, actually put me straight about the whole thing. He's very wise in his own way. I was talking to your mother about how we were losing you and all that sort of stuff and he just pipes up: "Everything you're talking about is already past." He just drops that on us while looking in the fridge for something. And I suppose he's right. Everything I'm holding onto is already gone. Memories feel real but they're not. Your brother just snapped me out of it. He never seems caught in the past. You never hear him talking about it. He never seems to look back, or at least he never seems stuck in something that has happened. Watch him the next time you spill something. His whole attitude is that it has already happened, and he just moves on to cleaning it up. He's all about what's going on now. I'm not sure if that's the cause or effect of the way he is, but he can be great for bringing a little bit of clarity to things. One time I was going on about work and how I was overlooked for promotion and how ageist it all was and he just cuts me off and says "That's just a story." Nothing more. Just like that. "That's just a story." And the thing is he was right. It *was* just a story I was telling myself. When I stopped telling it, it went away.'

'I'm sure it's nice to have a live-in sage,' replied Grace, 'but even sages need to fend for themselves in the end.'

They arrived back at the car, their chins frozen, but glad to have squeezed each other in.

'Do you want to come back to the house? Your mother would be delighted to see you.'

'Sorry. Send her my love. I promised I'd crank up the old laptop at home with Andrew and start booking tours and stuff for the honeymoon. Thanks for the meeting, Dad. It's not all in the past by the way. Tell our little guru that I'm not finished with you all just yet.'

Grace got on her tiptoes and gave him a kiss on the chin, kidding around. She climbed into her car and pulled away with a little 'beep-beep' of farewell, leaving Peter to nip back into the newsagent to buy the copy of the *Economist* he had been browsing earlier, just for something to read while he thought about his speech.

Chapter 21: MIME INTERVIEW

Hungry Paul arrived at the headquarters of the National Mime Association a little early. It was in a theatre that used to be the mews house of a larger property, and which had to be accessed through a back lane. Outside there was a mural showing a white-faced mime artist with a surprised expression, and a poster advertising a show that had taken place the previous year. Beside the entrance there was a painted picture of a doorbell with a sign above it saying 'Please Knock.' The ticket desk-cum-reception was unattended, so Hungry Paul let himself in, but decided not call 'hello' into the empty room in case that was against the house rules. The theatre was small, with about fifty foldable metal chairs, and looked like a screening room, which is what it had been before the National Mime Association took it over.

Earlier that morning, he had left Parley View without telling his parents where he was going. He didn't want their expectations on his mind when he had such mixed feelings about the interview in the first place. If he failed the interview, or was offered the job and turned it down, he didn't want to have the whole drama of discussing it over the dinner table afterwards, with his parents gently pushing him along with a 'how about this?' and a 'what about that?' If Hungry Paul was being entirely honest about it, he was a little fuzzy on why he was doing the interview in the first place. It had all started when he was enjoying Arno's routine at the Chamber of Commerce prize-giving as he entertained the congregating well-wishers by making jokes about the giant cheque (which he pretended to saw with his hand) or by playing with the President's chains of office (which he pretended to spit and polish). Afterwards, he saw Arno sitting down, smoking a cigarette and eating a normal sandwich normally, and was a little disappointed to see that mime artists did regular stuff too. They got chatting, with Arno seemingly under the impression that Hungry Paul was a successful—i.e. rich—businessman who was a big noise in the Chamber of Commerce. Arno opened up and explained how he had started studying drama and dance, and then got into mime when his college put on a musical version of *Mr Bean*. From there, he moved to Paris and studied with the last generation of master mime artists, who by then had become resigned to the decline of the silent arts. He became involved with the National Mime Association after they had advertised for a creative director. Though they had little or no money to pay him, he was able to live rent-free in a small bedsit behind the stage of the theatre. He managed to make enough money from teaching and corporate work to keep himself and the Association going, provided he was able to rent the theatre out for yoga classes twice a week and to a film club every second Friday.

The problems were not just financial. Morale in the mime world was at an all-time low. Some of the most talented mimes had switched to doing the whole living statue thing as a form of street theatre. However, when that proved to be quite lucrative it began attracting a number of charlatans, who dressed up but wore masks and were even happy to move around and do a thumbs-up for photos with tourists. Arno decided to put a stop to this, and while he would hold his hand up and say that he had made some mistakes and that some things were said which perhaps shouldn't have been, overall his intentions were true in that he wanted to preserve the integrity of the great art of mime, which had been handed down to him by the masters. But it had been a divisive move, which alienated some of the best members of the troupe and which discouraged the new joiners who had got involved with the theatre for drama of a different kind. The National Mime Association needed to repair its public image and Arno accepted that he was not the man to do it, so he was moving back to the Netherlands and leaving the creative direction of the association to his young apprentice, Lambert. And so began the search to find someone from the outside to bring fresh ideas and act as their spokesman in restoring their reputation in the real world. He figured that Hungry Paul, with his connections at the Chamber of Commerce, could be just the man to lead the National Mime Association to a better place. The fact that he was also a skilled performer—which Hungry Paul later worked out was a reference to his silent acceptance speech at the prize-giving—seemed like a gift from the muses. Naturally, there would have to be a process for filling the job, as the post was being funded in part by an Arts Council bursary, so Hungry Paul needed to do an interview if that was not too unreasonable a request.

In the days since Arno had laid all this out for him, Hungry Paul might have wondered what it was that stopped him disabusing Arno of his mistaken assumptions, and why his usual instinct to recoil from new opportunities had not been triggered. But Hungry Paul was not a man to ponder endlessly the whys and how comes of life. He simply assumed that silence, like yawns and itches, was contagious. The gentle pull of interest which arose within him, unbidden and unexplained, was the awakening of his inner silence in resonance with the powerful external forces of mime.

Hungry Paul sat himself in the front row of the theatre and waited quietly and patiently. He was wearing his wedding suit but with the shirt from his postal uniform underneath, that being the only other shirt he had which didn't have double cuffs. In fact it was short-sleeved and didn't have cuffs at all; whenever he took the jacket off, the combination of short sleeves and a tie made him look like a manager in a fast food restaurant. With no mobile phone, he was not tempted to scroll through his texts or refresh his social media feed. His freedom from restlessness meant that he didn't explore his nasal cavities or fiddle with his zip. His mental stillness left him untroubled by the passage of time or the spooky run-down emptiness of the place.

Standing behind the stage curtain, hidden and peeking through a gap, were Arno, Lambert and the chair of the interview board, Mr Davenport from the Arts Council. They marvelled at Hungry Paul's composure and were humbled by his profound inactivity. After fifteen minutes of observation they were in no doubt that they had their man. They exchanged notes excitedly among themselves and agreed on the outcome, which Mr Davenport had pointed out was no mere formality even though there had been no other candidates.

The three interview board members emerged from behind the stage curtain and congratulated the successful candidate. Hungry Paul greeted Arno with a handshake, to which Arno responded by miming as if it had been a bonecrusher that broke his hand and made him dizzy. As he lay on the floor, Lambert tried to revive him, before acting out an improvised last rites service and doing a digging action to bury him. Mr Davenport tried to join in, but soon found himself out of his depth, utterly outmimed by the other two, who wore their years of training lightly indeed.

For obvious reasons, the practicalities of signing the contract and coming to terms was not done through the medium of mime, as labour law did not yet allow for that. The initial contract was to be for eleven months, but Mr Davenport hinted strongly that these things were often rolled over if everything went well. The Arts Council would fund half the cost of Hungry Paul's salary, with the balance to come from the National Mime Association's own resources, including corporate and yoga income, as well as gate receipts, if any. Hungry Paul was also offered the bedsit behind the stage once Arno moved out, which was counted as an executive perquisite. He had asked to see the bedsit he was being offered, but this had not been possible as Arno's girlfriend was still asleep in there, which may or may not have been the reason why Arno had suggested to Mr Davenport that they should conduct the job interview in silence.

The job spec, which had been prepared in order to get the Arts Council on board, envisaged a panoramic range of responsibilities. Hungry Paul's main job was to motivate and inspire enthusiasm nationally for mime and the silent arts, excluding living statues and *tableaux vivants*. He was also to represent the perspective of the mime community in public discourse, as well as answering any mime-related questions that came in to the Arts Council helpdesk. While the Chamber of Commerce prize money meant that Hungry Paul was not particularly concerned about the paltry pay that came with the post, he could still drive a bargain when he needed to. He insisted on two conditions: first, that he would keep his Mondays free so that he could continue to honour his obligations to the Post Office; and secondly, that he would not be required to carry a mobile phone. The National Mime Association and the Arts Council agreed on both counts, as they were only offering the job on a three-day week and besides, they hadn't the money to pay for a phone.

With the deal made, Arno left Lambert to brief Hungry Paul on his new position while he showed Mr Davenport to his car. Lambert, unsure of how much time he had before Arno came back, was all brevity and candour. Arno's return to the Netherlands, he confided, could not come soon enough. The National Mime Association was in a complete mess. The theatre had not put on a show in over a year; what little money came in, went straight back out again; and mime as an art form no longer caught the imagination of the general public, with the younger generation scarcely aware of its existence. The theatre had become no more than a cobwebbed store room, with boxes and old posters lying around, such that even the yoga teachers had started to wonder whether the low hourly rates were worth it. With no sign of Arno's return—a fact noted knowingly by Lambert—they walked towards to the bike stand where Lambert had parked his black-and-white striped bicycle, which had a bell with the clanger decommissioned. Hungry Paul liked Lambert, and waved him off with the reflection that there was something special about the way that quiet people just seemed to find each other in life.

The day had been a hectic one by Hungry Paul's standards. Job interviews can be draining, so it was not surprising that he fell asleep on the train home, his temple vibrating against the glass. When he arrived at Parley View, his mother was on the phone to Grace about the table settings for the wedding, and his dad was on the laptop writing a letter to the editor of the *Economist*. As Hungry Paul paused at the doorway, reluctant to interrupt them, the urge to break the news about his new job seemed to pass and the announcement slipped back down his throat.

Tired but satisfied, he decided to go upstairs and hang his good suit in the wardrobe, just in case it got crumpled. He took off his Docs and lay back on his bed in just his pants and vest to reflect on the corporate complications he had just inherited. It seemed to him that the mime theatre, in its state of disrepair and irrelevance, had come to mirror the fate of silence itself. But how could he even begin to restore the position of mime as a unifying and humanising force in the world when the silent community itself was divided?

Hungry Paul stared at the stippled ceiling and bathed in the quiet all around him. He tuned his ears to listen to the ever-present silence itself, rather than the bubbles of noise that floated in it. He began to appreciate its profound scale. All major spiritual and philosophical traditions throughout history had emphasised the value of silence. The universe, whether expanding or contracting, does so amidst a vast ocean of it. The big bang sprang from it and will one day return to it. And yet, silence, for all its ubiquity and timelessness, had found itself at odds with the clamorous nature of modern mankind. This noisy opinionated world had made an enemy of silence: it had become something unwelcome, to be broken or filled.

Staring at the Spitfire mobile on his ceiling, it was as though the answer had been with him all along and was simply waiting to be noticed. He realised that before the public could be persuaded about mime they would first have to be put in contact with silence itself, for the power of mime lies in the its ability to touch the silence within us all. Feeling inspired, he lifted the stumpy pencil from his bedside table and sketched the following:

Sunday Night Quiet Club

One Hour of Sitting Quietly
at the National Mime
Association Theatre

Free admission – All welcome

First Sunday of Every Month at
8pm

(You may wish to note the above)

Its simplicity was its perfection. It had taken someone with the special insight of Hungry Paul to realise that the answer to the problem, strange though it seemed, was to get people to do nothing. He also decided to invite the statue artists to attend in full costume and to perform in silence for the duration of the Sunday Night Quiet Club meeting. He hoped that the request, made with deference and a degree of artistic sensitivity, would be enough to persuade them that a new era of close collaboration was being offered by their friends in the mime world.

As he heard his parents starting to make dinner noises downstairs, he snapped out of his executive preoccupations and looked for something comfortable to change into after a very adult-feeling day. Though this was all still quite new to him, he could see that making big decisions was just as consequential as not making them. Either way you were committing to something. We are never entirely outside of life's choices; everything leads somewhere.

Chapter 22: PYRAMID EGG

It had been a long and difficult week for Leonard. Shelley had been off work since Monday and had not been in contact. He wasn't sure whether she was avoiding him because of upset or awkwardness, or whether she was just at home with Patrick for his Easter school holidays. Perhaps she was even off sick with a tummy bug, or otherwise back to living her life in all the ways that didn't include him.

Several times he had drafted a hands-off, solicitous text just to check in, only to think better of it, a misjudged text having been the cause of all this in the first place. He had hoped that, at the very least, she wasn't mad at him, and that she understood that his clumsiness was not born of insensitivity but inexperience. In time, perhaps they would even be able to enjoy the odd platonic walk in the park or maybe she would tell her future boyfriends that, while Leonard was all wrong for her, at least he was one of the good guys. A mere week ago, he had considered himself to be Shelley's boyfriend, but now he doubted whether he had even got that far. How would she have seen it? By his own standards, it had been a major relationship, the furthest he had ever got; but perhaps, for a woman of Shelley's experience, it had ended too soon for him to be considered anything at all. 'Just any man have I met for a few dates,' she had said. A 'no contest' in boxing, a spoiled vote in a general election. In his imagination—which was located in his chest as much as in his head—he had already skipped forward a few chapters in their life together, but now he realised that they would be written without him. There was a palpable humiliation in having to pack up his ambitions and his fantasies and settle into a new type of dismantled normality.

After another lonely day at work, Leonard sat at home doodling in his sketchbook at the dining room table, his mouth in the twenty past eight position. He was too restless to concentrate, yet too listless to do anything worthwhile. The one thing that was on his mind would neither leave him be nor resolve itself. He still had many unfinished sections in his book about Patrius and the Romans, but it had become the last thread connecting Shelley to his life. His sadness over the break-up had become a secret new problem that was haunting the completion of the book.

For some it is the smell of a wet duffel coat at the radiator, for others it is the melting of a madeleine on the palate, but for Leonard it was the simple mistake of sucking the wrong end of a pencil. No sooner had the taste of graphite, so alien and unfoodlike, registered on his tongue, than he was transported back to the first time he had made that very same absent-minded error. It was a time many years ago: a time of power cuts; a time of milk bottle tops being pecked by blue tits; a time before kids' car seats or Playstations. Doing homework in his room, he got distracted by the shouting of some boys playing outside and accidentally sucked the pointed tip of his pencil. Disgusted by its flavour, he ran out to the bathroom to rinse his mouth using soap, which was a mistake. Muttering a child's curses, he comforted himself by sitting on the tiled bathroom floor with the *Our World* encyclopaedias, forgetting the time, or time itself, and nursing himself back to contentment in those pages. Closing his eyes, he swam inwardly towards the memory, not of the books, but of the *feeling* of reading the books. There, buried amidst the melancholy, he found the original charge that had animated his imagination all those years ago.

He began typing and sketching, transcending the space between his adult self and the young Leonard. A rediscovered magic energised and propelled him, as pages upon pages of imagination poured out of him. His touch for drawing came back to him, as he created tender scenes of Roman boyhood: the subtle expressions of wonder on the face of Patrius, as he pulled a frog from a well; a great double-paged scene of the boy's mother sitting on a chair in her gladiator gear, watching him practising his handstands; and a carefully shaded look of sad awe on the boy's face as he heard about his brave paterfamilias, who had loved him very much before he went off to fight the Goths all those years ago. Leonard emptied himself into those pages, smashing open his personal experience to release the universal experience within. He finally finished the book during that time which could be called very late at night or very early in the morning, and collapsed into bed with a feeling of sublime but exhausted calm, as if after a vomiting fit.

The next morning, Holy Thursday, the office was quiet. Leonard intended to sit at his desk for a few hours before packing up and going home to sleep through the weekend until the wedding on Monday, after which he had no idea what he would do with his book or his life.

He logged on and saw an email from Mark Baxter BEd:

From: himark@markbaxterbed.com

Hi Lenny,

Love, love, loved the pitch you sent me. Totally cooking my man. It needs a bit of work, so I think I'll need to wave my usual magic wand over it, but we're definitely on to something. I'm always into being innovative and disruptive. Let's blow the whole Roman scene open, that's what I say.

I'm off to the coast for the weekend. Some of the girls on the team managed to talk me into teaching them how to surf. I agreed as it's a good teambuilding exercise. You and me are the last two good guys left Lenny! If we don't give the girls a break it isn't going to come from the bozos at Factorial Publishing, that's for sure! I shouldn't trash talk them though, they're okay – they've got some really good guys over there. Real innovators, huge into disruption. I've actually got them lined up for a call on Tuesday – I think they're going to love our book my man!

You may wish to note the above,

Mark Baxter, BEd

Leonard started clearing through the other unread messages that he had been ignoring all week. Not a single email was from someone he had met personally. A handful needed a response, but they were mostly just memos about internal procedures. There was a lengthy email thread between two people who had a professional disagreement about some editing point—Leonard was among the spectators in the cc line. Inevitably, there was a series of emails about the expensive, bipolar accounts system, which was down for a few hours, then back up before finding itself back down again.

Leonard ran off a mock-up of the book on the good colour printer, just to see how it looked. As he sat back in his ergonomic swivel chair, he read through it slowly, page by page. It was the most beautiful thing he'd ever done, even if it nearly broke him to do it. He put all the pages in order and sealed them in an envelope with 'Shelley' written on the front. He wanted to leave it on her desk, along with a pyramid-shaped Toblerone Easter egg for Patrick.

Her desk was unoccupied, as he expected. Helpdesk Greg had a cereal bowl in front of him and was chopping a banana into what looked like dog food. He was wearing a paisley pyjama top.

'Hey Len. Long time no see. I've been checking through your internet history. Just a standard audit. We can talk more privately next week unless there's anything you'd like to confess now, just to get it over with.'

'Hi Greg. I see Shelley is still out.'

'Woah! You didn't know? Trouble in Eden? Oh, I'm sorry my man. Still, at least we have each other. Do you want me to mind that Easter egg? And your little A4 love letter in the envelope. You can trust me with your life, you know that.'

Leonard thought better of leaving the book and egg on Shelley's desk. Margaret, one of Shelley's colleagues, came running back to her desk repeating a series of expletives.

'Hi, I w—'

'What? What is it now—and shut it you,' she said, pointing to Greg without looking at him.

'Hi, I was just saying, do you know if there's anywhere I could leave this for Shelley? Somewhere private maybe?'

'What is it?'

'Just some personal gifts.'

'Is the Easter egg for her?'

'No, that's for her son. The envelope is for her. Well, and for him too.'

'Give it here.'

Leonard handed it over, not sure if he was doing the right thing.

'Okay, thanks. Will it be okay like that?' he asked.

'I'll see her over the weekend. I'll give it to her.'

'Okay, okay. If you don't mind. That would be great. Thanks.'

'That all?' she asked, looking at her screen, printing something.

'That's it. Happy Easter.'

He turned to say goodbye to Greg, who was mixing up a protein shake on his desk. Greg showed Margaret the Star Trek gesture for 'live long and prosper,' before swivelling it and flipping her the bird.

'Happy Easter, Greg,' said Leonard.

'Hey Mr Encyclopaedia. We're going to have a history lesson next week. Internet history. Don't miss it.'

Leonard packed up, went home and slept like a corpse for sixteen hours.

The next morning he felt rested and lighter. He got up to a new sense of clarity and equilibrium. He went through the house opening all the windows, like Yoko Ono in the *Imagine* video, only wearing paisley pyjamas and orange Crocs.

For weeks, the house he had lived in his whole life had unsettled him. He had felt homesick, its emptiness betraying him. But now, walking through each of its rooms, he felt ready to make friends with his own home again. Its space felt comfortable. All throughout there was an ambient sense of familiarity.

Leonard wore a new feeling of peace. He had always associated peace with the idea of happiness, as if it were some sort of steady state that happiness turned into when it was for real. But now he realised that peace is independent of any one feeling. The deep peace that he now felt was in a minor key. It was not blissful, but melancholy. It was a profound acceptance of things as they were, devoid of superficial preferences. The weight of effort that it took to be happy was lifted from his bones.

Before preparing his own breakfast, he stepped out to his neglected back garden where the bird feeders had been swinging for weeks, all empty and cobwebbed, and stained with the birds' dirty leavings. Leonard scrubbed the feeders in scalding water to disinfect them, and dug out the tub of birdseed from the cupboard. He filled the seed feeder up to the brim and put out some fat balls for the bigger birds who couldn't balance on the seed feeder's small perches. Feeling generous, he also scattered some seed on the ground in open space, so that the less pushy birds could have something to peck at. As he stood filling the kettle at the sink, he could see through the back window that two blue tits were already getting stuck in.

Heading into his living room with his breakfast on a tea tray, Leonard had a look at his bookshelves for some of the paperbacks he had bought recently, which had been stacked in the horizontal unread pile ever since, vertical alignment being reserved for those he had already finished and enjoyed. He found the copy of *The Mill on the Floss* that he had bought months before and forgotten about. He knew it would be a test to read it without flinching from whatever traces of Shelley he found there.

Upstairs, he pushed open the door to his mother's old room and sat on the bed, as he had often done to keep her company over a bedtime cuppa. The room was tidy and unfussy. It had already lost the characteristic freshness she had always brought to it, as much by her personality as her scent. In its place was the generic smell of dust undisturbed. On the bedside table stood the photo of his father that she had kissed with her fingers each night before going to sleep. Leonard hadn't yet gone through her personal effects but there would be plenty of time for all the organising and charity shop donations. She really was gone. There would be no more chats or shared little routines. The never-again-ness of that thought played through him and chimed with the sad inner harmony he had awoken to.

His loneliness now had a different quality to it. Before, it had been a panicked loneliness, desperately churning his mind to find something to cling to, just to take him away. He had sought comfort in distraction: Hungry Paul, the Roman book, and most of all, Shelley. He could see now how scared he had been. How utterly terrified that life itself was going to swallow him up. And yet he had turned and faced himself. He had sat late into the night with his book and in the end he had broken through. The fear had been nothing more than the deep love for his mother that he had not been ready to admit to himself, lest it drown him in grief.

He patted her pillow gently and made his way back downstairs through the house, which was really too big for one person anyway. Over the next few months he would have some choices to make, but there was no rush. He sat on the living room couch, his coffee beside him in his *New Scientist* mug, and opened *The Mill on the Floss* with every intention of reading it all weekend until he finished it, which is what he did.

Chapter 23: EASTER SUNDAY

Grace seemed to wake up on Easter Sunday with a dopey smile already on her face. Andrew had arranged a surprise date for them the night before, to mark their last Saturday together before they got married. Knowing that Grace liked classical music—it would have been truer to say that she liked only the good bits of the good composers—he had booked tickets to see André Rieu, thinking that he was paying for the best of the best. Grace burst out laughing when he told her, but quickly apologised and reassured him through giggling kisses that it was very sweet of him and that she was sorry for being a music snob, even if she had no intention of ever not being one. Andrew, who was not a music lover himself, felt a little wounded to have misjudged his nearly-wife's taste so badly, but nevertheless nudged Grace's elbow throughout the concert whenever he spotted her enjoying herself.

Andrew had also booked a late supper for after the concert, where they ate their second dinner of the day, having already shared yet another pizza on the couch earlier in the afternoon. They got a little tipsy and giddy at the meal and celebrated with a liqueur coffee afterwards, with Andrew pretending to play André Rieu's waltzes on the array of half-full glasses on the table.

Though they had kissed in the taxi home, by the time they got to bed they were both too tired for anything other than sleep. When Grace woke up the next morning, Andrew was snoring on his stomach in his usual position, his limbs at ninety degree angles, like the chalk drawing of a body at a crime scene.

She smiled to herself when she remembered Andrew haggling with the shop assistant in the late night newsagent to buy her an Easter egg that came with its own mug. The shop assistant wouldn't drop his price, but Andrew bought the egg anyhow, saying that was what André Rieu would have done. When Grace's body clock, with its usual inflexibility, prevented her from going back to sleep on that Easter morning, she resisted her habit of getting up early and alone, and instead spooned in behind Andrew, hoping to either wake him up or hold his warmth against her until he did.

Even though she was notoriously awkward about respecting tradition for the sake of it, Grace had conceded that she and Andrew ought to spend the eve of the wedding apart. It would be strange leaving him later on to head over to her parents' house, where she would stay the night, but then, she thought, maybe it's not such a bad thing to miss your husband a little bit on the day before you marry him.

Over at Parley View, Helen and Hungry Paul had already made an early start, as they wanted to visit the hospital to bring some Easter eggs to the nurses and patients before organising all the last minute bits and pieces at home ahead of Grace's visit. They arrived at the hospital a little late, having been delayed when Hungry Paul insisted on checking the best before dates on all the eggs his mother had bought, ignoring her protest that chocolate doesn't go off. As Helen stood chatting to the nurses, Hungry Paul entered the ward by himself. He could see that Barbara was on the phone to someone, presumably one of her emigrant children, and that the middle bed was empty. The curtain was pulled around Mrs Hawthorn's bed. Hungry Paul paused outside the curtain and listened for a bit until he could figure out what he would be intruding on if he were to pop his head around. He wanted to give Mrs Hawthorn the egg he had bought for her specially. It was a moment of self-doubt where he wished for a door knocker or doorbell, just to signal his intention and avoid the embarrassment of walking in on a medical examination.

'Hello,' he called unclearly, his voice being a little phlegmy having not spoken in a while.

'Hello,' he tried again after a few moments.

'Hello,' came a male voice. 'Who's that?'

Hungry Paul leaned his head inside the curtain to see a well-dressed man—about his own age—sitting in the chair beside Mrs Hawthorn, who was sleeping.

'Hello,' said Hungry Paul for a third time, 'we're just doing the rounds visiting patients to see if they want a chat. Are you a relative?'

'Yeah, she's my mum,' he said pointing to her with his thumb. 'She's asleep though—been snoozing since I got here about ten minutes ago. I'll give her five more minutes. No point staying here if she's not even awake. So I'd say you're okay for today. Thanks though,' he said returning to scrolling through his phone.

'I'll just leave this here then, will I?' asked Hungry Paul with the Easter egg.

'I'll take it. She won't eat it. I'll bring it home to the kids,' the man said, putting it on the floor.

Hungry Paul paused a moment. 'If you're under time pressure, I don't mind sitting with your mother for a little while. I mean, I'm here for the next hour one way or another.'

The man lifted his eyes from the phone and weighed it up briefly before accepting. 'Actually, that would be great. Doesn't look like she'll be awake soon and it's a bit of a trek to get over here, so it would be good to beat the traffic.'

'It's no trouble. Don't forget the Easter egg,' said Hungry Paul as the man got his bag and coat.

'Oh yeah, great. When she wakes up just tell her Daniel was here. Tell her that I waited as long as I could but that I had to go. I'll try and get back over next weekend if I can,' he said, slipping through the curtain. 'Don't feel you have to stay too long.'

Hungry Paul waited until he had left and then drew back the curtain, which let in a little more of the limited light that the north-facing ward attracted. He took his usual seat and waited beside Mrs Hawthorn, who was pale and had lost weight. He stayed there for the rest of the hour, with Mrs Hawthorn asleep the whole time.

Helen spent her time with Barbara, who had been busy on the phone all morning as her grandkids rang her to wish her a happy Easter and tell her how many eggs they had got. Barbara had finally got word that she was to leave on Tuesday.

'I got good and bad news, though I actually got the bad news first. Turns out I have diabetes, though they have to give me final confirmation tomorrow when the last set of tests comes back. Maybe I should eat that Easter egg before they confirm it. So that's the bad news, though it could have been worse, and it was nowhere near as bad as the news I thought I was going to get. The good news, or less bad news, is that they can deal with it using tablets so I won't have to inject myself or do any of that awful stuff. So, not too bad overall. When you get to this stage you're always bargaining, settling for things you would have been worried about previously. To tell the truth, it's my own fault. I got in trouble for not exercising and for eating the wrong things, although when I asked the doctor if it could be genetic he admitted that it was possible. He wasn't pleased when I threw that back at him—I could see that!'

Helen and Barbara filled their hour easily as they always did, with talk of the wedding and Barbara's updates on her family and the goings-on in the ward. Apparently the woman in the middle bed just disappeared one day while Barbara was doing tests. She was sent home, although they weren't told whether it was because she had recovered or whether it was to allow her to be looked after by her family, maybe even with palliative care for all Barbara knew. Ward neighbours had no rights in these things, she said.

Hungry Paul came over for a quick hello before they went home, so Barbara gave him a hug and a kiss to wish him well for Grace's wedding day, saying that he would be next and for Helen to keep an eye on him. It was the kind of comment that Hungry Paul didn't usually enjoy, but which he was getting better at dealing with.

The rest of the day was spent on the minor details. Peter and Hungry Paul did a dry run in the car to the church to judge how long the wedding journey would take, and erected the coloured direction signs along the route so that guests wouldn't get lost, even if the signs looked disappointingly small and illegible once they were in place. Helen got the house ready, as a parade of well-wishing neighbours called over to see Grace, who spent the evening being genial and walking around the house in flip flops, with tissues between her painted toes. There were still some small jobs to be done at the church, which had been off-limits all week because of the Holy Week embargo on wedding activity, but otherwise Grace's organisational nous meant that everything was attended to, checked and double-checked. Even the flowers arrived on time and were stored in the kitchen, where the radiator was left off so as not to wilt them; a minor panic about the lack of vases to hold them in was resolved with a quick knock on the doors of neighbours who were happy to help.

After a week of take-aways, restaurants and snacking, Grace was happy to relax on the couch with a simple home-cooked meal made by Peter: chicken with fluffy mash and marrowfat peas. It was the kind of food Grace loved but never made herself, she being of the cook book generation that tended to overcomplicate things. Inevitably, Hungry Paul made the suggestion of taking out the Scrabble board, in response to which Grace gave the air a tired punch and said 'bring it on!'

The game was cagey, with each of them trying to maximise their scores, giving the board a congested look with few two-letter possibilities. This led to long pauses between goes, which were naturally filled by conversation.

'We're going to miss all this buzz when it's all over,' said Helen, 'it's been nice to have something to look forward to.'

'I'm afraid that if you're looking at me,' said Hungry Paul, 'it will be a while before you get to wear your outfit again.'

'Maybe we should renew our vows, love?' suggested Peter.

'I'd rather amend them. There are a few new requirements I want to put in the small print,' said Helen, playing 'fa' and explaining it was 'fa' as in do-re-mi-fa-so-la-ti-do.

'You'd better not—they might revoke our marriage licence,' answered Peter.

'I've already revoked your marriage licence—too many penalty points,' said Helen, slapping Peter's hand as he tried to put down his word out of turn. 'Hold on, it's Grace next.'

'That's why I keep saying you need to do something for yourselves,' pushed Grace. 'Do a nice break away. Get out of your routine and do something you always wanted to do. Seriously, you just need to book something and make it happen.'

'I know, I know. I'll see how we're fixed after the wedding,' said Helen.

'And you should try and do something special too,' said Grace, turning her attention to Hungry Paul. 'Maybe go away with Leonard. You have your prize money now, so you could try and do a trip of your own—or maybe do a course, you know, train in something. I don't know, computer skills or learn to drive, or something like that.' Grace played ZEN which Hungry Paul knew wasn't allowable because it is a proper noun, but he didn't feel like challenging her when it was the eve of the wedding and she was already in the middle of hassling him.

'Maybe—we'll see. I've already got a lot on my plate with judo and the post office and the hospital visits.' Hungry Paul had not yet told his family about the National Mime Association job. 'And anyway, Leonard has woman trouble. He was supposed to be here tonight, but he said he wanted to take it easy and save himself for the long day tomorrow. I suspect he's still upset about Shelley.'

'Who's Shelley?' the other three asked in unison.

'His girlfriend, or I think ex-girlfriend. She has a kid, but I think she and Leonard are still broken up. Some sort of misunderstanding.'

'Really? Good man Leonard,' said Helen, 'At least he's out there trying. I thought he was going to be a bachelor for life, but there you go.'

'I suppose it's a lot of change at once, what with his poor mother and everything,' said Peter.

'Poor Leonard,' said Grace, 'Maybe he needed the plus one after all. I must remember to say it to him tomorrow. It can be hard being single at a wedding when you're going through a break-up. I remember doing it once and I ended up all drunk and weepy in the toilets.'

The other three said nothing at this slightly disturbing episode of oversharing from their perfect family member.

Peter laid down ISCHORD onto Grace's D and gave a triumphant yelp at using all seven letters, only to be corrected that there was no 'h' in 'discord' and besides, it wasn't his go.

The evening unwound once everyone's good intentions for an early night got the better of them. Peter and Helen headed out for a late evening walk together, during which they promised to discuss holiday plans. Just as Hungry Paul was getting set up to brush his teeth, Grace knocked and came in. As in most houses, their family bathroom was a busy concourse where privacy was but an aspiration. As Hungry Paul brushed away, Grace sat on the side of the bath, wearing what looked like a set of pyjamas from the second division, depicting Minnie Mouse eating a hot dog, with little hot dogs all over the trouser section.

'I'm sorry to be a nag about stuff by the way,' offered Grace.

'What do you mean?'

'You know, about getting your act together. I don't mean to be on your case.'

'It's okay. I ignore it.'

'Well, I was hoping you wouldn't do that either. I don't like to have to be the sergeant major in the family, telling people to shape up. I want to be the laid-back, popular one.'

Hungry Paul continued to brush with extraordinary thoroughness, leaving a silence that Grace found hard not to fill.

'What's going to happen, do you think?' she asked.

'Huh?'

'I mean, are you just going to stay here forever? Are Mam and Dad going to look after you for as long as they're around? What happens when they're older?'

Hungry Paul gave a swirl and a spit.

'I don't know.'

'Don't you worry about these things, or plan for them?'

'I know that things will take their course. I don't dwell on them.'

'I know you don't. Maybe that's why I worry about them so much. I'm doing all the family worrying.'

'Grace, it's the night before your wedding. Why bring this up now? You should just be looking forward to tomorrow, thinking about seeing Andrew, getting excited about your honeymoon, being married, your future, all that stuff. What's up? Why be so heavy, tonight of all nights?'

'This whole time I have been trying to feel enthusiastic about the wedding and about being married, but it feels like the hand-brake is on. I can't let myself enjoy it or be carefree, because I'm not carefree. I can't move on when I still feel so . . . so duty-bound about everything.'

'But why? You've always been so kind to everybody, nobody is expecting anything from you.'

'You say that, but what happens if Mam and Dad need help in the years ahead? What if something happened to one of them and the other fell to pieces? What are you going to be like when they're gone? I want to just be myself and plan my own life, but I feel this little vortex forming behind me that's going to suck me back in. Do you know what I mean?'

'I think so, even if I don't see it that way. I don't know what you want me to do or say.'

'I want you to move on. I want you to become independent, so you can be a positive force in all this. If you're on your own two feet, then the folks will feel liberated. They'll live their lives fully. And then, if things play out in a serious way in the future, you and I can be a team. But now, all I feel is that the whole thing will fall to me. No matter what life I build with Andrew, all the problems of Parley View will land at my doorstep saying "Here Grace—fix this." I can't be some sort of family superhero.'

'Who asked you to be that?'

'Who will handle all the heavy stuff otherwise?'

'What heavy stuff?'

'Don't be so evasive. You know what I'm talking about. The *future*.'

'Grace, I know that I disappoint you. I know it but I am okay with it. Whatever happens I will do my best. If you're here I will do my best, if you're not here I will do my best. There's no point planning for what you're trying to plan for. I know that, more than anything, you would like me to see the world your way, to wake up to your way of looking at things and to become the version of myself that you're most comfortable with. But then what? Are you going to keep checking in on me every few months to make sure I haven't drifted? How are you going to ensure that once I'm fixed I stay fixed? But what about you—what are you going to do?'

'Me? I'm the one who's been holding it together all these years! You've been floating about like bloody Winnie the Pooh all your life, spending a whole day looking for a fishing rod, or thinking about the shapes clouds make, while Mam and Dad and I deal with money, jobs, problems, y'know, that sort of thing.'

'Look. Whatever duty you have imposed on yourself towards me, I now absolve you from it.' Hungry Paul knighted Grace on each shoulder with the toothbrush and continued, 'I love you, but I don't need you to look after me. I haven't needed you for a very long time. I am not your responsibility. I am not anyone's responsibility. I am only telling you this now because I think you're ready to find out that you can't help me. I am just sorry it took me so long to realise I was holding you back, but not in the way you think. I have been holding you back by letting you hold onto this precious, fictional version of yourself. You're addicted to your own competence. I should have tried sooner to help you so that you could discover for yourself how impossible it is to help somebody.'

'Look, I don't mean to have a go at you, but what changes out of this? Mam and Dad still have to look after you.'

'This is my home. I live here. They are my family. I love them. I love *you* too, even with your hot dog pyjamas and all. This isn't a business relationship. It's not a transaction. I spend my days with them. I am here whenever Mam wants a little company. I help her with stuff and we chat about this and that. I sit with Dad when he's reading, and we watch TV together and talk about it afterwards. Nobody keeps count and nobody keeps score. We all think the world of you Grace, but you're simply not here. You ghost in with your busyness and then ghost off, leaving a to-do list behind you. But that's okay. I accept you the way you are. I don't have any expectations of you. But I do wish you were happier, for your sake, but you're not. You have this strange mix of a victim complex and a superiority complex. And yet, and *yet*, I *am* happy. So what do I say when you want me to substitute a bit of your unhappiness for what I have in my life?'

'So, what's your advice then? What do *you* think I should do? If you were the family superhero, what would you do?' asked Grace.

'We don't need a family superhero. You have created a world for yourself where you have this load-bearing filial and sisterly duty, but it's all over now, if it ever truly existed. The film is finished. You can just be Grace. Be whichever Grace you want. Disappoint us if you want. We'll love you anyway. Yes, our parents will grow old and yes they will get sick and yes they will die, but that will happen to us two as well. Where you're wrong is that you think that's a problem in the *future*. But it's not. The answer to that problem is to spend time with them *now*. Be in their lives so that when the worst happens—which we hope is many years away—there will have been ten, twenty, however many years of Scrabble, University Challenge, curries, walks, gardening and whatever else behind us. And then, when the time comes we'll know what to do. Not because we'll have it all figured it out but because we will have had the habit, the practice, of loving them and being with them, and the utter clarity that comes with that. Mam and Dad have enjoyed the wedding so much because they speak to you all the time and you're calling over, and you're including them. You being here has reminded them of how much they miss you when you're busy. They don't really want a holiday, they just want to know that you won't forget about them when it's all over. You need to go and be happy with Andrew, and unfetter yourself from this story you have about your role in the family. And then, when you come over—once a week, once a month, whenever you can, it doesn't matter—just hang out and be yourself. No versions of Grace any more. Not world-on-her-shoulders Grace; not why-can't-you-all-get-your-act-together Grace; no deferring-of-happiness Grace. Just come over, and who knows? Maybe I'll have moved on. Maybe I'll be a hotshot. Or maybe I won't. But let's not test each other. Let's just be happy. While there is still time.'

Hungry Paul gargled with mouthwash, and then leaned over and gave Grace a hug. 'C'mon. Teeth time,' he said tapping the handle of her brush on the side of the sink.

It was difficult for Grace to hear some of that. The competitive side of her wanted to argue back, to counterpunch, but she knew Hungry Paul well enough, and trusted him enough to know that he didn't care about winning an argument. All his life he had never wanted anything at her expense. And that's what was hard to hear. An attack would be fine. An attack was something she was durable enough to withstand and retaliate against. But kind truth, gentle truth, was harder.

As she lay in bed, the single bed from her teenage years, she could hear Hungry Paul's clumsy bedroom routine next door: drawers and wardrobe doors creaking open and closed, looking for something or other. Always, always onto the next thing. Downstairs she could hear her parents coming in from their walk in the evening cold, Helen offering Peter a cuppa, and Peter offering to warm up his wife's hands.

Chapter 24: WEDDING DAY

When Hungry Paul came downstairs the next morning—his body trained for early starts on Mondays—he found Grace was already sitting at the kitchen table in her dressing gown, drinking tea quietly and enjoying the gentle orange morning sky. She had just been out to fill the bird feeders, which reminded her of her own neglected feeders at home.

'Hey champ,' she said.

'Hi,' said Hungry Paul, kissing her on the forehead, 'Married yet?'

'No, not yet. I came down early in case Andrew had broken in and was waiting for me, but alas, all I found was a pot of leftover marrowfats. Did you sleep well?'

'Like a baby, not that babies are good sleepers, as any parent will tell you. How about you?'

'Slept like a tired log. I thought I'd be a bit wound up with wedding details, but once I started reading one of the paperbacks on the shelf in my old room my head started nodding, so I just had to give up in the end.'

'What book was it?' asked Hungry Paul.

'*That Night It Rained*—one of your old favourites.'

'That's a great book. Or should I say the first fifty pages are great. I have read them several times. I have also read the last page, so I can tell you how the crime is solved, if you're interested? I'm going to make some porridge—can I fix you something?'

'I'm okay thanks. I've had some muesli. Thanks for last night by the way. Our little chat, I mean.'

'Ah, yes. Well, you know me, I don't usually make speeches, but that was from behind the breast pocket of my pyjamas. I felt a bit talked-out afterwards actually. Just as well I'm not doing a speech today—are you doing one?'

'Just some thank yous. Nothing complicated.'

They enjoyed a nice relaxed breakfast, not talking too much, Grace drinking tea from a Crunchie Easter egg mug and Hungry Paul from one that professed 'I ♥ London.'

Before long Helen and Peter came down, full of babbling excitement and making breakfast with all the chatty chaos of a daytime cookery programme, family houses being so easily transformed from a monastery to a circus once the morning peace is broken and all the early energy of the day begins to gather. Helen turned on the radio and was fiddling around to try and find something other than news or white noise, not realising that she had accidentally bumped the FM switch to LW. Peter sat with his back to the wall and had a go at the unsolved crossword clues from the Sunday paper, which was a leisurely way to spend time on such a busy day, and something which did not go unnoticed by Helen. Hungry Paul took over responsibility for the radio, popped it back into FM, and before long they were listening to ABBA, a band nobody in the house ever put on by choice, but one which met with broad approval whenever they came on the radio by chance. It was nice for Grace to be in a busy house again.

After breakfast Peter answered the door to the wedding hair-dresser, who had arrived with two aluminium cases of make-up and hairdressing gear. Even at 8am, she was already dressed as if she were on her way to the divorcée discount drinks night. Not long afterwards, Grace's two bridesmaids arrived: Karen, whom she had known since college but didn't see that much these days; and Patty, a girl from her old job who used to be her drinking buddy, back at a time in their lives when that was a synonym for best friend. Peter would have to stay on at the house until the wedding car arrived four hours later, an absolute eternity for an introverted middle-aged man to spend with three hyper young women and their hairdresser. Helen, who had opted out of the limelight and didn't want to walk down the aisle herself, would bring Hungry Paul and Leonard to the church first thing to set out the flowers, tie bows to the aisle ends, and run the Hoover over the church carpet if necessary, as she reasoned that the usual cleaners wouldn't have been in over the bank holiday weekend. Once they had set up the church, the plan was to check into the hotel early where they would get dressed and ready for the church service.

Helen became a little tearful when it was time to go, knowing that the next time they saw each other Grace would be in her wedding dress and things would be very much under way. She waited outside Leonard's house and beeped with the engine running, as if picking him up for a high school date. Leonard came down the drive dragging his overnight case behind him in one hand and draping his suit bag over the opposite shoulder. He had spent a quiet and contemplative weekend at home by himself, where he had given the house a good clean and generally used his hands to keep his mind busy. On Saturday he had gone to the concert hall alone to see a performance of the Bach cello suites, his heart gently pulsing with the music as he indulged in a little aching over Shelley. Overall though, aside from a few little moments that he allowed himself, he didn't wallow or daydream too much.

Leonard decided to sit in the front with Helen, rather than in the back with Hungry Paul, who was enjoying a bit of quiet with the window down. As the shotgun seat also brings stereo privileges, he was given first choice of the cracked CD boxes jammed in the cubby between the front seats. Leonard, being both a gentleman and a consensus builder, ran his choices by his other two passengers and got ready consent, both Helen and Hungry Paul having surprisingly good taste for people who didn't talk about music much. In the end he chose an Everly Brothers *Best Of*, which was somewhat drowned out by the Fiat's plucky engine, as it struggled with motorway speeds. Leonard did feel a little self-conscious as Phil and Don played song after song about heartbreak, worried that Helen and Hungry Paul might think that he was in a pining mood, so he overcompensated with inane chatter to the effect that he really loved a good old wedding.

When they arrived at the church, which was miles outside their own parish and at the junction of a country crossroads, it was open but unoccupied. Inside, the air still held the sacramental smells of Easter: incense, candles and exhaled prayers. It was a small cruciform building with a vaulted wooden ceiling but otherwise free of any grand features. On Grace's instructions, they would only use the rows of seats in the central nave, leaving both transepts empty and available in case any locals dropped by for the mass, as she had been told locals sometimes did. Leonard briefly indulged his usual church habit of looking at the depiction of the Stations of the Cross; though not a believer, he admired the Passion as a piece of epic and timeless storytelling. The Stations in the church had flat, two-dimensional figures that had little in the way of real feeling. The eleventh station, in which Christ is nailed to the cross, had a cartoonish Roman in it, with an almost sadistic smile as he raised the mallet in his hand. Having spent many hours trying to capture Romans with sensitivity, the image jarred with Leonard. He knew that the legionary responsible would have had to drive the nail between the bones of the forearm near the wrist, while taking care not to severe any major arteries or veins. It would have been surgical violence, done without thuggery or glory. He wondered how that legionary became assigned to the job, which was surely a career backwater. Was it the same legionary who offered Christ vinegar and who was party to the drunken jeering? How does a man like that feel every morning, waking up sick with another day of brutality before him? Who would marry such a man? What would a man in that situation hope for from life?

Leonard was soon recalled from his daydream by Helen who asked him to help Hungry Paul lift the altar flowers in from the car. The flowers from Easter Sunday were still on display, so Helen put them to good effect around the church to cheer up the place on what was beginning to look like an overcast day. Leonard and Hungry Paul tied the bows to the aisle ends with all the inept enthusiasm of a schoolboy trying to teach himself to tie shoelaces. In the end Helen redid them herself, and asked the boys to do the cleaning-up instead, which turned into a two-man job with Leonard hoovering and Hungry Paul pointing out the bits he missed. It didn't take long to make the church look well, its simplicity being hard to improve upon. Before they left, Helen couldn't help pausing at the bottom of the aisle to enjoy the view that would meet Grace on her arrival, the butterflies from her own wedding day recreated from memory as she stood there.

They got to the hotel in plenty of time. It was an old country house with notions of castlehood; inside, it was a moneyed mix of old and new, and looked recently renovated. There was expensive modern art in the reception area, some of which looked a little formulaic for Leonard's tastes, and real books lining the walls, though no sign of classics like *The Mill on the Floss* or *That Night It Rained*.

As each other's plus ones, Hungry Paul had booked a room for himself and Leonard to share. They were brought there by an older concierge who made chit chat as best he could on the way, though Hungry Paul was unable to respond because of his internal panic over whether and how to tip a man who was old enough to be his father. Their room was bright and modern with a lovely view over the mountains and two complimentary bottles of water. Though it seemed churlish to nit-pick, Leonard couldn't help noticing that it appeared to have just one double bed, and a four-poster one at that.

'You're taking this plus one business quite seriously aren't you?' he asked Hungry Paul.

'I thought there would be two beds, not one.'

'What did you ask for when you were booking?'

'I just said we needed a room for me and my plus one. But, when she checked, I deliberately told her I wanted a *double* room, not *this*!'

'But this *is* a double room. A double room means a double bed!'

'I thought that was a twin room! I mean I did doubt myself but then I figured that you have conjoined twins, so a twin room must be when the two beds are conjoined so to speak, and if you have double of something you have two of it—I mean if you asked for a double scoop of ice cream you don't just get one giant scoop—so I thought there would be *double* the number of beds,' explained Hungry Paul.

'So what will we do? Will we see if there's another room?'

'We can try, but I know that Grace said that this hotel was booked out by wedding guests ages ago. The latecomers had to book the B&B down the road, so I think it's going to be difficult unless someone we know is willing to swap.'

'Okay, well that seems unlikely. Looks like we'll just have to share then. I hope your pyjamas have a full trouser leg—none of this boxer short business, with hairy legs making their way over to my side,' said Leonard.

'I'm a paisley man like yourself, Leonard. Full and respectable coverage, though I do like to stick a leg out for coolness.'

'Me too. Okay, so that's that. Left or right?'

'How about I take right as it's closer to the bathroom in case I need a sleepy wee during the night.'

The two men then did their best to get ready and dressed for the wedding, while sensitively avoiding any unnecessary embarrassment, although, inevitably, when you share a small hotel room you can't help but notice things like the surprisingly ostentatious colour of a clean pair of pants laid out on the bed.

For the third time that week Hungry Paul wore his new suit, to which he had added his purple Quality Street tie and another new shirt, this time with single cuffs. Leonard wore the suit he had bought for his mother's funeral, its sombre greyness transformed by his birch leaf green tie.

When the time came, they met with Helen at the hotel reception where she was chatting with Andrew's parents. Hungry Paul often marvelled at Helen's ability to set aside any occasion and engage in small talk. If she were taking the penalty in a cup final she would still find a moment to chat to the opposing goalkeeper about his plans for when he retired, or if she were transplanting a baboon's heart into a sick child on the operating table, she would comfortably enquire of the nurse whether her grandson still had braces. Her interest in people was genuine and inquiring, her view being that people often opened up more easily over the smaller things.

When they returned to the church, there were some young men from Andrew's extended family smoking outside, something Hungry Paul thought looked wrong at a wedding though he couldn't say why exactly. The sacristan was lingering and looking to speak to someone discreetly about his honorarium, and was eventually put in touch with the best man, who had been among the smokers. Inside, Leonard and Hungry Paul took up their positions at the foot of the aisle to guide people to the bride or groom side, and to hand out the homemade wedding missalettes, the typing and formatting of which had caused Grace to develop a maritime swearing habit. Most guests seemed to know instinctively which side to go to, even Grace and Andrew's shared friends, who revealed a subtle bias in electing for one side over the other. Leonard was happy to help out, especially as it spared him a socially awkward half hour idling in his seat alone, but also because it legitimised his status at the wedding—a 'friend of the brother of the bride' didn't otherwise sound like someone who ought to have made the cut at a wedding where numbers were known to be tight.

Things were a bit more complicated for Hungry Paul. His lack of assertiveness and lifelong social invisibility meant that people tended to walk by him before he had a chance to establish eye contact and offer to help. Also, he was not good with faces and worse with names, a failing that was not helped by the passage of time during which he had forgotten the existence of grown-up cousins who now looked very different to their childhood selves. They all seemed to know him though. His father's brother, Uncle Michael, came up and gave Hungry Paul a two-handed handshake and called over his two adult sons to say hello. As kids, they used to like sniffing the glue in Hungry Paul's art box whenever they visited. Uncle Michael's wife, Jane, had died a few years previously and he had gone off the rails a bit, doing sex tourism in the Far East, then becoming a seminarian, before settling back to a more normal retirement mix of volunteering for the church and doing evening courses.

Hungry Paul's Aunt Sarah—his mam's sister, who had made the cake at his parents' wedding—came over and gave him a warm hug and a kiss which landed on his ear. She had never married but had a long-time 'special friend' Colette, who came with her everywhere, including to the wedding. Sarah hadn't been asked to make the cake this time, and was expected to be hard to please when it was being handed out later on.

Hungry Paul also recognised a few of Grace's old college friends and friends from the local area: a mix of Taras, Susans, Lisas, Lindas and Louises, who were all a lot taller than he remembered because of their wedding heels, and who had between them a mixed taste in plus ones. One couple did catch his eye though: a dapper man in his eighties with a glorious, wave-like backcomb and his elderly wife whose hair was dyed dark brown, which made it look as though her face was emerging happily from a hedge. Neither of them was above five feet tall and they smiled the whole time. The man clapped Hungry Paul on the lower back and leaned in to speak, but then seemed to change his mind and instead offered his elbow to his wife and glided off to sit in the second row on the groom's side, smiling and waving to everybody.

The church had been filling up steadily, with a gentle simmering of conversation around the place. The women were complimenting each other's outfits; the more experienced of them knew to bring a coat or fake fur stole to an April wedding. The men did that usual male small talk thing, keeping it light and general. Friendliest of all were the plus ones who had no choice but to be amiable good listeners for the day. The sacristan was busy at the altar making sure all was as it should be, like a roadie for the headline act. The priest was speaking with Andrew's parents and with Helen, who had been feeling self-conscious sitting by herself. Up at the very front, Andrew was chatting away with his best man, and exuded his usual composure, every bit the consummate groom. He wore a beautifully-cut blue Italian suit, a burgundy tie and a crisp white shirt, with double cuffs and a set of pearl cuff links his father had worn at his own wedding. The only signs of his nerves were the quick little glances he made towards the frosted glass of the vestibule, where Grace would arrive whenever she was ready. Throughout it all, the organist, who was no slouch as a negotiator by all accounts, played background voluntaries, a mix of warm gelatinous chords and some playful cantering with the right hand, ignoring the church organ's demonic side.

It was the sudden scurrying of the outside smokers into the church that confirmed the arrival of the bridal party. The organist paused his playing and a general, giddy hush fell on the church as everyone stood up. Hungry Paul stood beside his mother at the front of the church as Helen got a tissue ready for herself. Leonard, a natural people-watcher, looked ahead at the priest who had an avuncular smile spread across his face, giving away his secret that the early romantic stages of the ceremony were the bits he liked best. Andrew stood calmly and happily, privately grateful to Grace for being punctual on the one day that it truly mattered to him.

The bridesmaids entered first, slightly shy under the paparazzo enthusiasm of the guests and their phones, and walked up the aisle one at a time to take their places at the front.

Then, with a nod from the photographer and with no small appreciation of dramatic tension, the organist struck the opening notes of Bach's *Harpsichord Concerto No.5 in F Minor*, otherwise known to Andrew as the song Grace had picked from *Hannah and Her Sisters*.

And there she was.

She stood for a moment, demure and delighted, wearing an expression intended to sing ta-da!

She wore a stunning tea-length ivory satin dress. But everyone's eyes were drawn to the flash of colour in her jade green shoes, a choice that was both unexpected and yet somehow quintessentially Grace. She walked up the aisle linking Peter's arm as he made every effort to go slowly, a beautiful pride welling inside of him. Andrew had watched Grace through every step and thanked Peter with the subtlest of smiles as he took Grace's two hands in his own.

'Well, here I am,' said Grace simply.

'You look so beautiful,' answered Andrew, simpler still.

All around the church, girlfriends were squeezing the hands of their plus ones, and wives were leaning into their husbands' shoulders. The priest, not wishing to break the moment but nonetheless duty-bound to get on with things, offered some welcoming words to Grace and Andrew and to the wider congregation. He introduced each part of the service by explaining its symbolic importance, which was an experienced way of tipping the participants off that it was their turn to approach the altar for their bit. His homily was a light-hearted meditation on love and family, emphasising the philosophical over the spiritual, churchmen being well used to glossing over the question of religious commitment in order to focus on a longer game, with baptisms, communions and confirmations all still to play for.

Throughout the previous few weeks Grace had consistently said that the religious service was the bit she was least looking forward to, as she felt fraudulent in her lack of faith, but now that it was under way she wanted it to go on forever. Even though she had slaved over the missalette, and so should have known the readings and prayers off by heart, she sat in rapt attention listening to them as fresh new words and sentiments, lived advice about abiding love and its many depths and difficulties. Though her recollection of mass as a child was one of countless long hours, the wedding service seemed to flash by, happiness bending her sense of time.

When the moment came to repeat their self-composed vows, the rings that they had sworn to wear for life slipped on easily. And so, among their family and friends, through an ancient ritual that never gets old, they became married.

When the service was over, they made their smiling way back down the aisle to Handel's 'Arrival of the Queen of Sheba', the organist worth every penny.

After photos, congratulatory hugs and choruses of good wishes, Grace and Andrew climbed into the back of their Regency Red Jaguar Mark 2, which Grace had chosen in homage to her TV hero, Inspector Endeavour Morse. Sitting there, on red leather seats and with limited leg-room, they held hands and waved out the window like a pair of royals.

'Well now,' said Grace. 'That was nice.'

Chapter 25: RECEPTION

At the hotel reception, Hungry Paul had to abandon Leonard to help with the family photos, having been assigned responsibility for rounding up stray relatives who had become bored and wandered off just when they were needed.

As Grace and Andrew were both a little older getting married, the crowd was that bit older too, and less prone to heavy drinking on an empty stomach during the pre-dinner hiatus in what would later become the residents' bar. Instead, there were a few yawns as the early start caught up with people; the male partners of pregnant guests went looking for seats; and couples who had come without their kids were checking in by text with babysitting grandparents.

Other than Hungry Paul and his immediate family, Leonard didn't know many people at the wedding. He wandered through the reception with his complimentary flute of champagne and picked up a few nibbles from a tray—an onion bhaji and a salmon something. The hotel pianist was playing tunes from the Great American Songbook, and all around suit jackets were hanging on the backs of chairs and women were slipping out of their heels for a few minutes. In the past, Leonard would have felt a little too conspicuous in a situation like this, as though his aloneness was the talking point of the whole room. He would have had that familiar sense of social retreat: the desire for invisibility among the crowd, his confidence having folded itself away. But now that he had found a little shelf of peace within himself, he could feel the happiness in the room and no longer felt excluded from it.

The hotel manager walked through the bar ringing a school bell, which was the cue for the starving masses to find their names on a mounted table plan near the main dining room. The guests took their seats, making introductions as best they could from opposite sides of the large round tables, while waiting for the bride and groom and, of course, the food. Leonard was to sit between Hungry Paul and someone called Gloria Grimes, Andrew's aunt, who had only made the invite list because Leonard had surrendered his plus one. Grace had seated her next to Leonard because she was a writer, but it soon became clear that she was also a talker.

'I always say that a wedding is the best way to meet new people,' she began, 'I mean the very best way. Where else do you get to meet people without an agenda? I mean, I write, as I think you may be aware, so I do a lot of these book launches and wine and canapé things, but everyone's always looking over your head or past you, worried about who they're missing. It's like they have this radar of who can do something for their careers and they're forever anxious about committing to a conversation because they are *so worried* about who they are *not* speaking to, and as I always say, the greatest courtesy you can pay someone is to give them your full attention. I mean, what kind of writers could they be if they are simply not interested in people—'

Leonard was trying to interject a question, but his timing was off.

'—of course I never thought I'd be a writer. A journalist maybe, as I was always good technically, but I have always doubted my imagination, but I suppose we never really know where our imagination comes from, perhaps it's not created at all, but just a manifestation of what's already inside us. But as I always say, I may not have the strongest ideas, but I know how to get the most out of what I have, and that's the greater part of the battle. I mean there used to be this writer I knew, poor man had pancreatic cancer—cheated on his wife, God rest her—but you should have seen how he transformed the house after she died. Such an eye! I mean, who knew?'

Leonard took his chance, 'So what type of boo—'

'He had a wonderful way of making you read in the accent he was writing in. Dutch, Welsh, Indian, I mean even if you can't do accents, and I certainly can't, it doesn't mean you can't *read* in an accent. Such a wonderful man. Left his money to the cats and dogs home—of course his son was furious, but he wrote accents *so* well. I mean, ask any professional writer and they will tell you how hard that is.'

She paused to butter some of the bread that was being passed around—Leonard was already on his second slice. He enjoyed her in a strange way. He realised that he kind of liked weird people. Maybe it was their intensity.

She started up again, having quartered her bread without eating any.

'The one thing I cannot stand, I mean I just cannot *bear,* is this whole business of people sticking to one thing and doing it over and over again. I mean, what's the point? It's just cutting short your whole career because you lack confidence. That's all it is! A lack of confidence. Call it what you will. This woman who used to be in my writing class—I mean, I was giving the class and she was a student—every story she did was about her childhood and she was always using phrases like: "There was an empty chair by the door." You know, *trying* to be depressing, because she thought it was more writerly, but I'm sure you've seen it yourself, some people get so lost in writing they forget to tell a story. It drives me mad!'

She waved her butter knife from side to side as if to dispel the spirit of bad writing.

'So, Grace tells me you're a writer, not that she needed to tell me, I mean, I can always tell—it's a way you have about you. Maybe I have read one of your books? Crime fiction isn't it?'

'No. Children's encyclopaedias,' answered Leonard.

Aunt Gloria went quiet.

'Oh. Very nice,' she said, having her first bite of the bread.

A waiter approached Leonard, having first lifted his name-plate to check that he had the right person.

'Excuse me sir, your sister is in reception for you.'

'My sister?'

'Yes, sir. In reception. Through the double doors, past the cloakroom.'

'Oh, I see. She's not actually my sister, she's my friend's sister,' said Leonard pointing to Hungry Paul's empty seat beside him.

'She did ask for you by name, sir. Just letting you know.'

'Grace probably has some minor emergency she needs help with—back in a mo,' he said to Aunt Gloria, who had already turned to her other side to talk to the dapper elderly man with the backcomb and his wife with the hedge-like hair.

Leonard walked towards the reception with the jaunty gait of someone in a polite hurry.

When he got there he saw Shelley standing by herself at one of the bookshelves, chewing on her thumbnail.

'Oh. Hi,' he said.

'Surprise,' said Shelley with half-embarrassed jazz hands.

'Well, this is unexpected. What brings you here?'

'I came to see you. I even drove, if you can believe that. I had to borrow my sister's car.'

'Oh. I see. I'm actually at a wedding at the moment.'

'I know *that*. You told me it was on here today. I asked them to call you out. Sorry, I had to tell them you're my brother. I thought they might not help if I said I was your ex-fire warden.'

'Indeed,' he said, nonplussed and looking around. 'Why don't we sit down over here?'

He led her over to a quieter spot near a log fire, where they sat facing each other on opposing couches, a low wooden table between them.

'Would you like some tea, coffee maybe?' he asked.

'No thanks.'

'So, how are things? It feels like ages since I've seen you.'

'I'm okay. Well not really. Y'know.'

'Yeah, I know. It's been a strange week.'

Shelley tried to use her fingers to peel off the bit of nail she had been half way through chewing.

'Shelley, I don't mean to be direct but . . . is everything okay?'

'Margaret called over today. From work. She brought over the egg you bought for Patrick and your book.'

'Oh, I see.'

She hesitated.

'Your book is beautiful, Leonard.'

He wasn't sure what to say.

'Thanks, Shelley.'

The conversation stalled. She looked at him directly.

'I just wanted to tell you that.'

'How come you came all this way? I'll see you in the office tomorrow, you know. I'm not disappearing or anything.'

'I left my job Leonard. I won't be in the office.'

'Not because of me, I hope.'

'No. Not because of you. It's *thanks* to you, but not because of you. I saw how much of yourself you put into your work, all your ideas, and how you have never lost touch with the passion you had as a kid. You're still so alive inside. You haven't become cynical or drowned in practicality. You've never lost your curiosity. I decided I'd ring work to take a few days' leave because I just felt so off, so sick of running around and trying to handle everything: Patrick, the job, money. I was overwhelmed, especially after things just seemed to slip away between us. My boss, who doesn't even work in the building and wouldn't notice if I took a month off, said he wasn't allowing leave until the two vacancies were filled, so I told him my side of things and, well, you can imagine. So, anyway, I left and now I need to figure out my next move.'

'You've had quite a week. Sorry about your job.'

227

'Please don't be. It was soul-crushing and stressful. I had just got used to the money and they gave me afternoons off, which will be impossible to get elsewhere, but I would have died in that job.'

'Shelley, I'm not sure what to say. I mean, I'd like to talk, but it's Grace's wedding today. I just wasn't expecting this.'

'I know, I know, it's over the top. You have a couple of missed calls and a text or two by the way. I just wanted to tell you that I really like your book and that Patrick really loves it.'

'I'm so glad. I wasn't sure I drew him right.'

'You were pretty close. In real life he has a beard, a glass eye, a wooden leg and a hump, but the rest of it wasn't too far off. The box about him having a big heart and a big imagination really touched me, you know.'

'I wanted it to be special for him. And you.'

'It really is, Leonard.'

There was an uncertain pause, silence showing its awkward side.

'I had better get back. It was nice to see you again, Shelley,' he said, making to get up.

'Don't punish me, Leonard,' said Shelley. 'Don't be withholding just because I hurt you.'

Leonard stalled for a moment, unsure of himself. He sat back down, this time beside Shelley on her couch.

'I'm not trying to withhold anything, Shelley. Or punish you. Why would I do that?'

'So what's going on between us then?'

'I don't know, Shelley. I don't know because I don't know. I'm not used to these conversations. I don't know the rules. They're too cryptic. I feel like there is some formulation of words you are willing me to say but I don't know what it is, and I'm worried that unless I say the right thing you'll walk away.'

Shelley looked at him intently. A seriousness hung in the air between them.

'You can't keep testing me, Shelley. I guarantee that I will fail each and every time. I can't be spontaneously profound. And do you know what? It doesn't matter. Or rather it shouldn't matter but it does, at least to you it does. Anyone can say something beautiful in the moment. Anyone can deliver the right line. But that's not real. That doesn't prove anything. What matters is what a person is really like. What matters is what a person is prepared to reveal to you in real time in the real world, when there is no soundtrack in the background and no games going on. I care for you very much, but I'm not scared to be by myself. I can't perform for you, Shelley. I have thought about Patrick a lot, though. I think about him as being me at his age. I can remember what that was like. I can remember it in my bones. It has never left me. I have no idea what I would have done had I met him that time. I had no plan and no clever answer that would have unlocked everything. But I know I would have been real with him. I wouldn't have played with his feelings. But I know how important he is to you. I don't necessarily understand it the way you do, but I *do* appreciate what he means to you. I have no wish to be a threat to that, but I also know that maybe I'm just too inexperienced or clueless about relationships to avoid doing or saying the wrong thing sometimes. You ask me these questions to make me work, to prove something to you, but I can't live like that. I can't be on edge, wondering when the next spot check is going to happen. When the next sphinx riddle is going to be posed. But I'll do my best to be kind. To listen to you. To learn about being with a girl I care about. I'm just not sure whether that's going to be enough for you.'

Leonard stopped, having realised that he had said more than he meant to. Once he began, he had just kept talking and talking, saying things that he had only understood as he said them. True things. The fruit of his grief.

Shelley, who had been twisting a loose thread around her

finger all through Leonard's improvised speech, took a breath and blinked back some tears before speaking softly.

'You know, the whole time I was driving here I kept running through the script of what I wanted to say. My plan, just so you know, had been to unload and explain a whole bunch of things about myself that it now turns out you probably already understand. I knew I was being impulsive in coming here, but I just needed to get past that limiting voice inside me that says "be careful" every time I have a chance at life. I think that I have constructed this idea of myself as Patrick's protector; but over the past week, if I am honest, I have come to realise that I have been using him as a reason to protect myself from the world. At the first sign of danger I retreat. Safety first, as they say.'

Leonard, who had lived much of his life that way, listened quietly.

'But after a while,' Shelley continued, 'you get to the stage where you realise that if you don't give your own life some air and sunlight, it becomes this sad little place inside you. And now I feel stuck in this scary new situation where I can't figure out the right balance between opening up to the world—and to you—and protecting myself and Patrick from what I know could happen. Does any of this make sense?'

Leonard nodded, though he left unsaid the reflection that even the Romans struggled to balance the twin urges of expanding out into the world and defending themselves.

Shelley reached over and took Leonard's hand, leaning her tearful cheek into his chest and leaving a mark on his birch-green tie. Leonard kissed the top of Shelley's hair and put his arm around her shoulder, gently stroking her ear with his thumb.

Inside, in the main dining room, Peter was getting to his feet, promising not to keep the hungry diners too long, as he began his speech.

Chapter 26: THE NEXT MORNING

The next morning, Leonard woke up happy. The previous evening, he and Shelley had found a new closeness after sitting together quietly long enough for Leonard's wedding dinner to go cold. They had left unanswered the question of where they stood with each other, other than having a proper make-up kiss and agreeing to meet for lunch later in the week. He had walked her out to her sister's car and kissed her through the gap above the window which would only wind down half way. She pulled away with a 'beep, beep' and a wave, driving like a cyclist and ignoring the car park's one-way system.

Sitting up in bed with a pillow at his back, Leonard rested a cup of hotel-room tea on his tummy and watched the muted morning brightness creep through a gap in the drapes. He had to draw his legs towards him slightly on account of Hungry Paul, who was sleeping across the bed in a position known in heraldry as 'bend sinister.' Hungry Paul had every reason to be tired after a full and energetic evening, where he had stayed off alcohol and instead drank Lucozade, something which he had only previously enjoyed as a childhood cold remedy with suspect healing properties. When drunk throughout the night and combined with the high spirits of a family wedding, however, it inspired him to come into his own as a wedding guest. Surely no man has ever put the Lindy Hop to better purpose, at one stage finding himself at the centre of a large circle from which he plucked countless female partners to Hop with, Gloria Grimes, the writer, being among those to go back for a second spin. Of his solo dance performances, it was hard to top the one-man show he put on during 'Kung Fu Fighting' when he broke out his judo moves, the tie around his forehead an improvised touch that he was later proud of. Once the music finished and most of the guests went to bed, Hungry Paul stayed up in the residents' bar—though having switched to hot chocolate at that stage—and played Top Trumps with Grace. It was the 'Mythical Beasts' set which Hungry Paul had been carrying in his breast pocket all day. Even though it was her wedding day and she had been so good to him over the years, he still trounced her, though it would have been hard to do otherwise since he had been dealt the Kraken, which was unbeatable on every category except speed. In fairness to Grace, she was somewhat distracted by Hungry Paul telling her the news about his job at the National Mime Association and his plans for Quiet Club, which Lambert had loved and was helping him organise. For once, she let her pride silence her scepticism, sisters sometimes having the good sense to know that practicality isn't everything.

Upstairs, in the bridal suite, Grace and Andrew had woken up to breakfast in bed, including a complimentary bottle of Prosecco from the hotel. Before going to sleep, Grace had ticked everything on the menu and hung it on the outer doorknob. They had the usual selection of juices, porridge, toast and a cooked breakfast, which even included the more modern additions like hash browns. She didn't remember ticking the box for kippers, but in any event, there they were—she toyed with the idea of putting them under the duvet on Andrew's side in case he tried to creep back to bed after his early morning wee.

The wedding day had been magical. Grace had enjoyed a cheerful serenity all day, her facial muscles now feeling the strain of the posed smiles, not to mention the hilarity of the evening reception. She had been a social and gregarious bride, table hopping to make sure she had conversations with every-one, and then dancing in her bare feet to 'Come On Eileen', her legs kicking a raucous can-can. At one stage, Andrew snuck her outside for a little walk and a covert slice of wedding cake. They did a turn around the castle by themselves, and she could see how happy he was. Already he was calling her his wife every chance he got and looking at her in a love-struck staring way whenever she was talking to him.

As he came in from the en suite, drying his hands and fiddling with his ring and the soap stuck underneath it, he leaned over and kissed Grace on the back of her neck.

'Have you enough to eat?' he asked.

'I got you your kippers by the way. If you loved me you'd eat them.'

Andrew did a barfing face.

'What was your favourite thing?' she asked. 'I mean about yesterday. And don't say "Your beautiful dress Grace, or your loving eyes." I mean what was really the best?'

He thought for a few seconds.

'Let me see, maybe the church? Or the first dance? Actually, do you know what it was?'

'Go on—surprise me.'

'My favourite bit was sitting in the Inspector Morse Jag just after we got married. Our first private moment as a married couple. Just the two of us. Happy. Starving, mind you, but yes, happy. How about you?'

Grace went quiet for a sec.

'I think it was my dad's speech. He just emptied himself into it without being mawkish. It had such emotional clarity. He has known me all my life and our relationship just seems to have got richer now that we're both older. It was a big moment for him, I know that. He really, *really*, wanted to capture it just right. He was so . . . what's the word I'm looking for? Tender. Yes, that's it, tender. I had never realised that it was possible to make someone feel so loved at the very moment you are letting them go. I'll never forget it.'

She lifted the bell covers off the plates and started into her first married breakfast, clearing the mushrooms onto Andrew's plate and taking his hash brown.

She swivelled around.

'How about let's eat this and then go back to bed? What do you think?' she asked.

Andrew clinked his apple juice with hers and poured honey on his pre-coital porridge.

Downstairs, Helen was sitting at the roll-top writing desk in her room, having a coffee and looking out over the foggy morning. Peter was still asleep after another snorey night, his hay fever made worse by the wheat beers he had been drinking. He had done well. She had known he was good at presentations at work, but had not heard him give a speech since their own wedding all those years ago. The way he opened up and spoke about their family and what it meant to him. The way he spoke about Helen. 'The one true love of my lifetime,' he had said. And he an economist of all things.

It had been a special day, those long phone calls with Grace over the previous few weeks paying off as all the meticulous details came together beautifully without seeming fussy. Helen would miss those calls. Grace would soon be off on her extended honeymoon and it wouldn't be cheap to call from Japan. After that, who knows? Grace getting married that little bit older meant that they wouldn't delay starting a family. 'The fun is in the trying,' her own father had said to her at that stage.

After Hungry Paul had explained to her the previous evening about his new job and the availability of an executive bedsit, Helen couldn't deny the nascent feeling that she was entering a new stage in her life, that some important decisions and choices would have to be confronted soon, but could wait for now. It was strange that after all the years of getting the kids to be independent, she would feel so daunted at having her life back.

But it was the nature of being a parent. The kids' lives are their own. From day one you are handing it back to them bit by bit, until they move on.

She looked across at Peter sleeping. The man she had spent her life on and whom she loved so much. It had been so long since they had had an unencumbered relationship. They had talked about it on and off: travel plans, date nights, maybe even downsizing and freeing up a few bob. She could barely admit to herself the minor panic in her abdomen at the thought of it being the two of them, and just the two of them, from here on in.

She finished her coffee and hopped back into bed. Her feet were a little cold and Peter stirred as she warmed them under his legs. He pulled her gently towards him, still fitting like two jigsaw pieces after all these years.

Chapter 27: DEAD ZOO SANDWICHES

Things were slow at work for Leonard. The work-from-home illustrators were busy with their kids during the mid-term break so there were no new drafts to go over. The boilerplate Roman book was in pre-production and wouldn't be ready for checking for another fortnight. He had been told that there were another couple of projects in the pipeline, but nothing definite had been assigned to him—a rumoured book about world religions had been mothballed as 'too topical.' His admin was up to date, and he had killed twenty minutes changing his desktop wallpaper and experimenting with the more esoteric settings on his computer. Things got so bad that he had wandered over to Helpdesk Greg voluntarily for a chat.

'Hi Greg. Busy?'

Helpdesk Greg was carving open a foot-long baguette on his desk and had a pot of all-in-one sandwich spread ready and waiting; it was basically the normal ingredients of a salad sandwich, blended to look like septic pus.

'Just putting the finishing touches to this masterpiece. My body is a temple, Leonard, and my stomach is its altar. Of course the way to a man's heart is through the stomach,' he said, raising his voice and directing it at Margaret, Shelley's erstwhile colleague, who was on a call to an unhappy customer. She threw a pen at him without even looking.

'What brings you to my confession booth, Leonard? I hear that love is no longer blossoming in your pants. Sorry to hear about that. Men like you and I just can't seem to catch a break.

Fussiness is the precursor to *loneliness*,' he said, again directing his voice at Margaret.

'Oh, well, things aren't so bad. Any news on the new colour cartridges coming in for the printers? I have a few things that I'm waiting to print out, to see how they look.'

'No need to print off internet porn Leonard. There are magazines for men like you who prefer printed amusement. Dirty books too.'

Greg widened his jaw in preparation for an attack on his baguette. Margaret wore a frozen expression of disgust as she watched. Leonard had to admit that he was kind of curious himself about whether Greg could eat the whole thing.

Helpdesk Greg didn't disappoint.

He shouted in triumph, raising a double thumbs-up while chewing the last chunks of bread in his open mouth, churning like a washing machine on its final cycle.

'Okay. Best be getting back,' said Leonard.

'The young challenger leaves,' said Greg, doing a nature programme voiceover, 'Defeated by the alpha male, who will celebrate a successful hunt with the rest of his harem.'

This time the flying stapler actually hurt.

When Leonard got back to his desk, there was an email from Mark Baxter, BEd:

From: himark@markbaxterbed.com

Hi Lenny,

Had a great meeting with the guys over at Factorial Publishing. Some seriously sharp people there— going to take the encyclopaedia business to the next level. Totally disruptive.

They loved your book. And I mean *loved* it. Only problem is, they say it's not for them. They say it's not really a fact book. More of a story book. I told them, I said 'No way! It's a totally disruptive fact book – absolute game changer!' They were cool with that but said they'd never get shelf space in the reference section for it, and they're not a fiction publisher, so it's kind of falling between stools I guess. They say they want to stick with regular reference books and try to be disruptive that way.

So, I'm sorry my friend. Thanks for coming to me with it. Anytime you want to bounce something off me, just treat me like a friendly old squash court.

Take it easy (but not too easy!).

You may wish to note the above.

Mark Baxter, BEd

Leonard sent him a quick response, thanking him for trying and wishing him well with his next project, and saying that he hoped they would get to work together again sometime soon. It goes without saying that he suggested that Mark Baxter, BEd, may wish to note the above.

Naturally, he was a little disappointed. He had put everything into that book, but he had also got a lot out of it. Although, if he was completely honest, once he had decided to write the book for Patrick, it no longer mattered to him if anyone else ever read it. Sometimes that happens, he thought, the motive only revealing itself after the fact.

A slow morning had finally crawled to lunchtime. Leonard grabbed his jacket and went to meet Shelley. She had picked the Natural History Museum as the venue for their lunch date, and Leonard liked to think there was a subtle note of compromise in her choice. She had even promised to treat him to a vegetarian lunch, although it struck him that it was a somewhat futile gesture given that they would be eating in what was effectively a room full of hunting trophies.

When he arrived there was a train of primary school kids filing out of the museum all wearing hi-vis bibs, a young teacher counting heads as they passed. Leonard climbed some old wooden stairs that creaked like a boat with each step, towards the mammal section where they had arranged to meet. He passed by the first few rows of glass cases, which housed stuffed wildlife royalty like lions, tigers, polar bears and chimps. In the middle clearing, under a humpback whale skeleton that had faced the wrong way for a hundred years, he saw Shelley sitting with a sketch pad in front of the bull hippo, and beside her, instantly recognisable from her description, sat Patrick.

'Hello folks!' said Leonard. 'Hope I'm not interrupting.'

'Hey, just in time. We're just finishing our pictures. Patrick, say hi to Leonard. Remember I told you we'd be meeting him today. He wanted to hear what you thought about the Roman book.'

Patrick looked up.

'Hi Leonard,' he said. 'I'm just finishing this, so just let me do this bit, around here, a little line here, just a few of these, there! Finito!'

He showed it to Leonard.

'Oh, I like this,' said Leonard, crouching down to cancel the height difference.

'It's like a regular hippo, only with lots of improvements,' said Patrick. 'Those are turbo boosters, so he can get away from predators. That's a crying lion saying "Oh, why am I so slow I can't even catch a slow clumsy hippo" and those things on the hippo's feet are wheels, which are hidden inside his feet but which come out whenever he's near train tracks, and then train tracks shoot out of his tusks to lay tracks wherever he goes, so he can still use his train wheels on dusty paths and regular roads.'

'And what's that spot there?' asked Leonard.

'Oh, that's the bullet hole where he was shot by the French.'

'Why the French?'

'Oh, they owned Africa a long time ago and there were lots of wars, but when I'm in charge of the world, there's going to be none of that. Any country that fights—zzzhhhttt!—off with their heads!' said Patrick, slicing his pencil across his throat.

'And how did they shoot the animals without breaking the glass display cases?'

Patrick flipped his head back and groaned.

'They didn't shoot them in here. They shot them in Africa and countries like that, and then put them in the cases. You should know that if you write books.'

'Here's your sandwich by the way,' said Shelley, smiling and pulling out a slightly squashed lump of bread wrapped in cling film and handing it to Leonard.

'Oh, thanks. Do you mind me asking what's in it?'

'Egg.'

'Egg?'

'Yes, egg,' said Shelley. 'I don't want you to run low on protein. Got to look after yourself.'

'Indeed. It's just that egg makes me gassy and, well, we can't open the windows in our office.'

'You'll figure something out. Patrick! Come here for a sambo.'

'Eh, I'm okay for sandwiches. Any treats? Or if I can't have a treat, can I get something in the gift shop, pleeeeeeeze?'

Patrick was swinging from Shelley's sleeve.

'We'll see,' she said, and then, looking at Leonard, 'We'll see.'

Chapter 28: QUIET CLUB

At the National Mime Association Hungry Paul and Lambert had arranged the room beautifully for the first Quiet Club. The seats were in a circle and there were Christmas lights across the foot of the stage, a nice idea suggested by Lambert, who was quite visual as it turned out. The living statues took their positions at intervals around the room: Marley's ghost at the door where people came in, a Windswept Man beside the reception desk, and various chimney sweeps and Mozarts mixed in with the seats. Hungry Paul had John Cage's 4'33 playing in the background, just to relax everybody.

Naturally Helen and Peter were there. Helen in particular was keen to see what the bedsit was like, though Hungry Paul explained that they had not yet fixed a date for Arno's girlfriend to move out, which he felt was a matter of some delicacy that would resolve itself in time.

Though Grace was on honeymoon, she said that she would still like to be involved; after all, she said, with its temples and shrines, Kyoto was perhaps the capital of silence. At the appointed time, she and Andrew would arrange to sit quietly in a nearby Zen temple, so that they could share the moment, though thousands of miles away.

Leonard was of course in attendance and had been happy to help out. It had been his idea to have tea and biscuits afterwards, taking it a step further by asking in the shop for the quietest biscuits they had, which were Jaffa Cakes obviously.

Shelley couldn't come, unfortunately. The Sunday night slot

clashed with the orientation lecture she was attending for the part-time BA in Fine Arts that she had signed up for, having been inspired by Leonard and encouraged by her father. Shelley's sister did her bit by writing out a reusable babysitting voucher for whenever she needed a bit of help. Patrick had also made his own voucher, entitling him to a later bedtime and a sugary cereal whenever he was being babysat. Shelley said she would love to come to next month's Quiet Club.

Helen had also mentioned it to Barbara, who had left hospital and was looking to try new things. Though she confessed that she'd never been quiet for a full hour in her life before, she thought it sounded healthy and peaceful, and that it could be a nice way to meet new people. She came early and brought her own diabetic biscuits.

Hungry Paul had been in to see Mrs Hawthorn earlier that week. She had been asleep for several days and was not getting better. He had stayed with her for over an hour, holding her hand and enjoying the silence for both of them.

At judo during the week, where Hungry Paul was still stiff from the wedding day Lindy Hop, he mentioned it to his sensei and to Lazlo. Not being chatty by nature, they were both taken with the idea and came along before their night shift as security guards at a warehouse. Hungry Paul was touched to see them on non-judo time, and felt that they were beginning to warm to him.

Lambert had asked at the supermarket whether he could put a poster on their noticeboard and got chatting to the same duty manager who had opened Hungry Paul's tin of Roses. He had no problem with them using the noticeboard and even said that if they ever needed help fundraising he could provide them with a Saturday afternoon bag-packing slot. Lambert thanked him sincerely and invited him along, but it wasn't his thing: he was like a shark, he said, had to keep moving.

There were even a few new faces who showed up: a woman in exercise gear holding a rolled-up yoga mat, two Italian students, and a man in dungarees who would only say that he was an old friend of Arno's, touching the side of his nose as he said this.

When the time came, Hungry Paul placed a potted sunflower on a stool in the middle of the circle. A hush, had it been needed, would surely have fallen on the assembled group.

'Okay everybody,' he began, 'Thank you for coming to the first Sunday Night Quiet Club. When I take my seat, we will begin sitting for an hour. There are no special instructions, except that we should do our best to be as quiet as this flower.'

Each of the participants had their own experience during that hour, which goes to show the infinite variety in life: even when doing nothing, people do it differently. Sensei and Lazlo sat stock still and concentrated on the silence, their mental discipline from the martial arts being too deeply rooted to do otherwise. By contrast, Barbara was utterly distracted, looking around the room for someone to share eye contact with, hoping to convey her sense of novelty about the whole situation. Lambert, who had done so much to arrange the evening, sat and marvelled at the intimacy of sharing silence so deliberately with others. The living statues excelled themselves; having to share a small indoor space brought out their competitive side, as they tried to match each other's imperturbability. Arno's friend adopted an ostentatious meditation pose, intended to signal an affinity with the attractive yoga lady, while the Italian students sat quietly, wondering whether they were in the right place at all.

It didn't take long for Peter to start dozing off, while Helen used the time to take stock of the changes in her family and the new life that was slowly opening up before her. Across the other side of the world, Grace sat cross-legged at a Zen temple, Andrew struggling in the early morning heat beside her. Leonard, for whom silence was as comfortable as bed, sat and enjoyed the time, his universe once again expanding.

In the middle of it all sat Hungry Paul, with who-knows-what going through his mind.

To think that so much has been written and said about flowers over the centuries, and yet it took someone as special as Hungry Paul to notice how quiet they are.

ACKNOWLEDGEMENTS

I owe everything to my wife Sinéad. This book would never have been written without your love and support.

Thanks to my two wonderful sons, Thomas and Jacob. This book was written at a table surrounded by your encyclopaedias and board games, and with your enthusiasm all around me.

I will be forever grateful to Kevin and Hetha Duffy and everyone at Bluemoose Books for the life-changing decision to publish *Leonard and Hungry Paul*, and for all your hard work, creativity and passion.

Special thanks to my editor Lin Webb for all the care, attention and insight you brought to the editing of this book. I am a better reader and a better writer as a result.

Thank you to Fiachra McCarthy for the beautiful cover design.

Thanks to Michael Stevens for inspiring me to try writing a book, and for encouraging me while I was doing it.

Thank you to Anna Carey for your generous advice.

Thanks to Conor and Gillian Rapple for being early and supportive readers.

Thank you to all the staff at Baldoyle library in Dublin for being so helpful and for providing me with a lifetime's supply of interesting books.

My sincere thanks to all those who listened to me talk about writing and who said nice things when I needed it: you know who you are and I am forever grateful.

To all my family, friends, and colleagues: you are all amazing, but you don't feature in the book, so relax.

Thanks to Honest Ulsterman, The Bohemyth, Brilliant Flash Fiction and Flash Fiction Magazine for publishing my early stories, and to all those who read them.

RÓNÁN HESSION is an Irish writer, musician, and social worker based in Dublin. As Mumblin' Deaf Ro, he has released three albums of songs, and his most recent album, *Dictionary Crimes*, was nominated for the Choice Music Prize for album of the year. *Leonard and Hungry Paul* is his first book.